CRIME,
PUNISHMENT
AND
RESURRECTION

Also by Michael Collins

CRIME, PUNISHMENT AND RESURRECTION

DAN FORTUNE THRILLERS BY

MICHAEL COLLINS

DONALD I. FINE, INC.
New York

Library of Congress Catalogue Card Number: 91-58667

Library of Congress Cataloging-in-Publication Data

Collins, Michael, 1924–
Crime, punishment and resurrection : Dan fortune thrillers / Michael Collins.
p.   cm.
ISBN 1-55611-295-5
1. Fortune, Dan (Fictitious character)—Fiction. 2. Detective and mystery stories, American. I. Title.
PS3562.Y44C75   1992
813'.54—dc20   91-58667
CIP

Manufactured in the United States of America

10 9 8 7 6 5 4 3 2 1

Designed by Irving Perkins Associates

Some of these stories have appeared in *New Black Mask, A Matter of Crime, Alfred Hitchcock's Mystery Magazine, Ellery Queen's Mystery Magazine, The Thieftaker Journals,* and *An Eye for Justice,* Mysterious Press, Robert J. Randisi, Ed.

"The Big Rock-Candy Mountains," and the novella, "Resurrection," appear here for the first time.

To Philip Shelton, friend and colleague.
Thanks, big detective.

Contents

Introduction

When Michael Collins first approached me and asked if I'd write the introduction to this collection of short fiction, I agreed without hesitation, though with a soupçon of apprehension. I've known Michael Collins since 1969 and while I've long been an admirer of both the man and his novels, I'd never actually read a Dan Fortune short story.

My own experience with the short story has taught me an inordinate respect for the hazards of the process. Crafting a mystery short story is like painting on the lid of a pillbox using a brush with one hair. Compared to the generous framing of the novel, the canvas is small and the requirements of space, when added to the already stringent requirements of the mystery, give the writer precious little room in which to navigate. Character must be suggested in the lightest of brush strokes, setting implied in a simple line or two. The tone of the story needs to be established quickly and the structure—its inherent beginning, middle, and end—must be organized with efficiency and finesse. Since Michael Collins has always wryly referred to himself as "long-winded," I must confess I was uneasy at his ability to tailor his expansive talent to the strictures of the form.

On reading the manuscript, I realized I needn't have worried.

Michael Collins approaches the short story from every possible angle, writing with irony, playfulness, or a touch of cynicism, but always with restraint. Sometimes the tale turns on the discovery of the killer's motive, sometimes the revelation of the nature of the murder weapon, or the hidden relation of the criminal to his unsuspecting victim. As in "real life," there are occasions when Dan Fortune knows perfectly well "whodunit" and the thrust of the story is his attempt to prove his case.

Whatever the focus of a particular tale, Michael Collins's touch is deft and his use of language is economical. His characters range from the rustic to the rich, from the innocent to the corrupt. Throughout the collection, the writer's style is crisp and his voice authoritative. Underlying the whole is the social and political sensibility that has become the hallmark of his work. Collins writes with the journalist's spare prose and the novelist's eye for detail. Early in every story, he takes command of the reader's interest, and from that moment on —to use his own phrase—"he lays it out short and neat."

SUE GRAFTON
January 1992
Santa Barbara, California

CRIME, PUNISHMENT AND RESURRECTION

Crime and Punishment

Back around the time of The Revolution, I told James Crawford, there was so much counterfeiting they made the punishment hanging, drawing and quartering, boiling alive, gouging the eyes out, or any slow, horrible death they could think of, and printed the punishment in detail on the money. The counterfeiters went right on printing the phony money, punishments and all.

"It didn't stop them. They had to have money to live."

"It stopped the ones who were executed," Crawford said.

But this story doesn't start with James Crawford, it starts with the Tracy Detective Agency, an international outfit with offices coast to coast and in fifty cities overseas. Mr. Donald Meredith heads the New York office. He's a big, classy man with thick gray hair going white at the temples, and a smooth pink face that gets shaved daily in his office. His muscles are hidden under a thousand dollars of gray banker's flannel, and he hasn't broken a strike, caught a bank robber, or faced a killer in twenty years.

"Sit down, Fortune."

"Hiring extra guards yourself now, Meredith?"

He's *Mister* Meredith these days, but he'd turned me down once when I'd tried to join Tracy because he didn't employ one-armed men as detectives. Besides, he'd called me.

15

"You want an easy job or not?"

"What kind of job?"

"A killing, small and simple." He tented his hands, stared me down. "We don't usually take private cases anymore, pretty much all corporate and government work. But Dr. Walter Payne Crawford was a client, his son is an executive in a corporation where we're on retainer."

He laid it out short and neat. Dr. Walter Payne Crawford had been shot three times in the back of the head two weeks ago in his Oyster Bay house. Nothing had been stolen. The house was in a guarded development, no strangers had been seen anywhere in the neighborhood. Crawford had been alone in the house, no one heard the shots. The Crawfords were important people, but the police and Tracy had come up with nothing except the footprint of a workboot and a small cut on his neck. No witnesses, no suspects in or out of the family, and no motive.

"How come he was alone in the house?"

"It was the day his wife visits her mother, his son plays poker, the help takes the day off."

I must have stared. "That's a lot of coincidence. It had to have been planned."

"We don't think so. It was his own gun."

"His own gun?"

"Gun's missing, but the desk drawer where he kept it was open. He had a firing range and the police found slugs that matched. No prints. I can't waste men on a wild-goose chase after some passing psycho high on angel dust. I told the son it was a police job, but he says we owe him. It's a touchy situation, I have to give him a man."

"How much?"

"Three hundred a day and expenses. Work a couple of weeks, then back us up and drop it."

"That's not half what you're getting."

"Five hundred then. We've got to recoup the overhead."

"Seven-fifty. I don't care about your overhead."

It wasn't their full fee, but I had to leave him enough to explain to the board it was worth it.

The house in Oyster Bay was big, white, and sprawling. James Crawford looked at my missing arm, my duffel coat and beret, and wasn't impressed. That was probably why Meredith had picked me.

"My father was murdered in cold blood. I want the animal who did it caught."

"Why did your father have a gun?"

"We all have the right to defend our home."

"A lot of good it did him."

"He had to have been taken by surprise, or the killer would be the one who was dead."

I dug into the family and Crawford's medical practice and associates. Checked taxis, buses, the trains for any suspicious strangers. Talked to the neighbors, the cops, his friends.

"No enemies we can find," Lieutenant Watts of the Oyster Bay Police said. "No outside business activities except investments. We can't trace the workboot to anyone he knew. No one knows how he got that cut on his neck."

"How'd the killer get the gun?"

He shrugged. "Crawford kept it in his desk."

His wife and son were the only immediate family, both lived in the house, both had ironclad alibis. Mrs. Crawford was still in tears, too distraught to even count her money yet.

"We were married thirty-two years, Mr. Fortune. Walter never looked at another woman."

Neighbors and associates agreed.

"If they didn't love each other, they sure loved the same things—money and comfort."

And added, "Honest, hardworking, dull, that was Walter."

His fellow doctors at the hospital had a mixed picture, depending on who they were themselves. The more dedicated physicians saw one man, the rich golfers saw another.

"He still had the first buck he made, and every other one he could get," an emergency room doctor told me.

"The best plastic surgeon on the East Coast, and a hell of a guy."

"Accepted no Medicare or welfare patients, never put in an hour of community or free-clinic time."

"Generous to a fault, a good sport."

"Liked by his rich friends, didn't have any poor friends."

After a week of this, I came up as empty as the police or Tracy. It was time to agree with Meredith and bow out.

"He killed my father," James Crawford said. "I want him caught and executed. I want to stop others from killing men as fine as my father."

That was when I told him about the Revolutionary era counterfeiters and deterrence, and he said:

"It deters the one who is executed."

"We're not going to deter this one," I said. "And I don't believe it was any passing psychotic. It had to be planned, but there're no leads, no motive and no witnesses. It's not going to be solved except by chance or time, and that's a police job."

"I'll double what I pay Tracy. I want you to keep going."

"Two thousand a day?"

"I want to see justice done."

Occam's Razor says the simplest explanation of anything is the right one. Fortune's Law says that when everything is ruled out, what's left has to be the answer.

About all that was left was hobbies. I talked again to everyone at the yacht club and the country club, at the medical

associations and in the neighborhood. Everywhere and anywhere. At two thousand a day, I was in no hurry, but slow or
fast the answer was the same. The doctor had had no hobbies
except making and investing money.

So I sat down in the study where Dr. Walter Payne Crawford had died and went through each drawer until I knew
every one of his investments. Call it the sensation of a possibility. A notion. Crawford had been heavily invested in New
York City real estate. Three of the buildings had addresses on
the Lower East Side. I took the train back into the city.

The first two buildings were in the shadows where the El
had darkened the streets when I was a boy. The El had gone,
but the darkness remained. There were no front doors, only
black holes like the mouths of tunnels. The lightless corridors were as dim and silent as ancient cliff dwellings. In the
vestibules broken mailboxes hung open. Pools of urine covered half the grimy tile floors. Inside, the floors were gouged
and splintered to bare wood. The walls were disfigured with
leaks and filth and violent graffiti. The apartment doors had
no paint, and the hall toilets had no doors. The stairs were
broken and the banisters gone. The stench was overpowering.

Standard slumlord operation. Buy up buildings in such bad
condition it's better for the former owner to sell at a loss than
fix them up, then run them down even further. Never spend a
cent on them, overcharge the tenants who are poor, intimi-
dated, can't speak English, or all three. Lawyers are cheaper
than repairs, so bribe the inspectors, fight condemnation, pile
up the profits.

The third was just up the block. Or it had been. I stood in
front of what was left. Fire had destroyed the entire building
from the ground floor up, gutted the top two floors leaving
only jagged outside walls against the sky. A year ago, maybe
two. The damaged buildings on either side had been cleaned
up and more or less repaired.

When everything is ruled out, what's left has to be the answer.

A tenement fire doesn't rate much news coverage unless someone is killed, not a lot even then.

It took me most of the day in the 42nd Street library before I found it. The building had burned a year and a half ago, a cold winter day when the firemen had trouble with their hoses. The *Times* called it a slumlord building, gave the name of the owner: Dr. Walter Payne Crawford of Oyster Bay. The cause of the fire was the gas line of an illegal heater chewed through by rats while the tenants slept. The building's central heating system had been broken for five years. One woman died.

The *Post* coverage was about the same, but with a lot more gaudy prose. The woman had been pregnant, and a heroine.

Newsday had a wire-service photo and a caption. The photo showed two black children crying on a dirty, snow-covered street beside a fallen black woman. The caption read: *Two small boys cry beside Pearlie Jordan who collapsed outside her Lower East Side apartment Monday after leading her mother, brothers, and two nephews to safety from the burning building. The 26-year-old pregnant woman died later in a New York hospital.*

Detective Alex Callow nodded in the precinct squad room.

"I remember. They gave the woman a posthumous medal for saving the people she did, brought charges against the landlord. He got off with fines, orders to clean up his buildings."

"She was married?"

Callow shook his head. "Lived with her mother, two kid brothers, a couple of nephews. There was a boyfriend. Raised hell in the hospital."

"You have his name?"

"Hell no. It wasn't a police case."

"What hospital did she die in?"

"Bellevue, where else."

At Bellevue, the death of one black woman in a tenement fire a year and a half ago wasn't something easily remembered. But this one was a heroine, had been in all the papers.

"Sure," the nursing supervisor said. "She arrived in a coma, never came out of it. Smoke inhalation, burns, shock. Those run-down tenements torch like Roman candles."

"Do you remember her boyfriend?"

"I wasn't on that night."

She sent me to the Medical Records librarian. The record on Pearlie Jordan showed her mother as next of kin, no mention of a boyfriend, but had the names of the nurses on duty that night. Two had left the hospital, but two were still there and even on duty. They both remembered the boyfriend.

"He took it real hard," one said.

"Sat with her the whole time," the second said, "but she never regained consciousness."

"Even after she died we couldn't get him away."

"He tried to go with the body to the morgue."

" 'It's my son, too,' he said. 'I got to stay with my son.' "

"Four months pregnant. A real shame."

I said, "Do you remember his name? Where he lived?"

They didn't. No one in the whole hospital knew his name. I went back to Medical Records. The body had been released to the mother, but the only address they had was the tenement that had burned. And the mortuary that buried her.

At the mortuary the records said Pearlie Jordan had been sent back to her native town in North Carolina for burial. The mortuary had been paid in cash, no record of who paid it.

"But we sent the papers after burial to her mother."

"To a burned-out tenement?"

"No, she had a new address by then. I think we have it here somewhere."

It was another tenement not six blocks from the one that had burned. In better condition, almost livable, the dark living room clean in the light of the single lamp.

"Pearlie had some insurance," the mother said, "we got us a better place."

She was a white-haired old woman fifteen years younger than she looked, thin as a rail and stooped as if she'd spent her life in the fields of her native North Carolina. She hadn't, the stoop only the weight of her struggle to survive.

"I'm looking for Pearlie's boyfriend. The father of the child."

"What you want with Noah?"

"That's his name? Noah? Noah what?"

"You don't know his name?" The suspicion instant. Who was I to be looking for a man whose name I didn't know? "Cop?"

"Private detective. Dan Fortune."

"So?"

"The landlord who owned the building that burned was killed three weeks ago out in Oyster Bay."

"You want I should cry?"

"Executed," I said. "Like a murderer."

"That supposed to mean something to me?"

"I think so," I said.

A few times in your life there is a moment when you know you've made a mistake. A bad mistake. I knew it now.

The faint sound was behind me in the dark apartment. It had never occurred to me he might be living with the mother.

"See if he got any guns, Momma. Any tape recorders."

The knife blade behind me caught the light of the single lamp, the point drew blood from my neck.

I said, "Is the knife how you got Dr. Crawford to sit in that chair so you could shoot him?"

The old woman was shaky and scared, but she knew how to search. She shook her head to the man behind me.

"Nothing, Noah. You maybe oughta not—"

"Anyone in the hall? On the street?"

"I'm alone," I said.

The old woman went away.

"Noah what?" I said.

The woman returned. "I don't see no one, Noah."

The knife dug deeper into my neck. "How'd you get here?"

"No one out there can figure a motive. I found he owned the tenements, came up with you."

He was silent for some time.

"What do they have?"

"A footprint."

"That's okay."

"Look, Noah—"

"What else?"

"Nothing," I said, "but they will have. They'll find the gun. They'll—"

"They won't find the gun."

The old woman said, "Noah works in a foundry."

I said, "Someone will remember seeing you. Out there you had to stand out too much. Someone's going to remember you when they ask."

The knife went away. He walked past and stood facing me in the light of the single lamp.

"No, they won't."

He was Caucasian. Or close enough. A white man of medium height, ordinary face, nondescript. In a plain blue suit and hat like a thousand commuters. An everyman. He sat down, the knife still in his hand. "He murdered Pearlie, and they fined him. He murdered her and my son, got slapped on the wrist, bought more buildings."

"You learned when the house was empty? Knew he had a gun?"

"They just guard at the gates. His kind always have guns. Someone had to make him pay, stop him killing more people."

"You can't stop killing with killing."

"The state executes murderers. If they can, I can."

"They'll find you, Noah."

"He had to pay for Pearlie and my son. I've never been in any trouble. I'll never do anything again. You can't prove I did anything. You made some guesses. You found me, but you've got no proof. There's no way they can prove anything, and if they try I'll get off. Tell the police, go ahead. If they want to arrest me I'll get my time in court, tell the whole story. Maybe that'd be better. Show all the other animals like him what's gonna happen to them when they murder people. Maybe it'll stop all the slumlords."

"It won't," I said. "Go in yourself, Noah. Tell them."

"You tell them. They won't even arrest me. Go on, get out of here."

I didn't argue with him. I got out of there.

In the silent Oyster Bay house John Crawford listened impassive. When I'd finished he spoke without moving.

"Is that murderer under arrest?"

"I don't know."

"You don't know? He murdered my father in cold blood, and you don't know if he's been arrested?"

"Your father made a fortune buying substandard buildings, renting them to the poor five to a room, letting them run down into garbage dumps. Just take the rent and run. Sewers an animal shouldn't live in. One place burned to the ground. A pregnant woman died."

"My father made an investment. An accident happened."

"To Noah he executed a murderer."

"He's insane!"

"He believes in capital punishment."

"You can't just kill anyone you want to!"

"No," I said, "you can't. Not in a civilized world. So I went to the police. I told them what I've told you. But he'll deny it. There aren't any witnesses. He isn't the kind of man anyone would particularly remember. He's not worried about the footprint. The gun is probably melted down in a batch of iron. I don't think the D.A.'ll even bring an indictment."

"He killed my father! He has to be punished!"

"Get a gun and do it yourself. Then one of his friends can execute you. Keep it up until someone is caught and the state can finish the job."

He sat there, the hate in his eyes. "You don't expect to be paid, do you?"

"I did my job. I'll send you my bill. The rest is up to you and the state. Call it justice."

I took a cab back to the station, the train into the city. In the morning, Callow at the East Side precinct said they'd arrested Noah and charged him, but the D.A. wasn't optimistic. I called the best lawyer I knew who owed me a favor.

The Tracy Agency put every available man on finding evidence against Noah. After a couple of months they had to give up. My volunteer lawyer put on the pressure, and the D.A. dropped the charges for lack of evidence.

Down on the Lower East Side, Pearlie Jordan's insurance

money ran out. Her mother, brothers, two nephews, and Noah were evicted for nonpayment, disappeared from the city.

James Crawford took over his father's business. The publicity brought the city down on him, his lawyers are in court every day fighting complaints, citations, condemnation proceedings. It doesn't worry Crawford. Win, lose or draw, the tenements will make him a nice profit before he loses them or they fall down.

No One Likes To Be Played for a Sucker

It can be a mistake to be too smart. Deviousness takes real practice, judgment of human nature as fine as a hair, and something else—call it ice. The ice a person has inside.

Old Tercio Osso came to me with his suspicions on a Thursday morning. That alone showed his uneasiness. Old Tercio hadn't been out of his Carmine Street office in the morning for twenty years—not even for a relative's funeral.

"Business don't come and find you," Tercio pronounced regularly.

Osso & Vitanza, Jewelry, Religious Supplies and Real Estate, and if you wanted to do business with Tercio, or pay your rent, you went to his office in the morning. In the afternoon Tercio presided in his corner at the Mazzini Political Club—a little cards, a little *bocci* out back.

Lean old Cology Vitanza, Tercio's partner of thirty years, reversed the procedure, and at night they both held down the office—thieves struck at night on Carmine Street, and there was safety in numbers.

It was Cology Vitanza that old Tercio came to me about.

"We got troubles, Mr. Fortune. I think Cology he makes plans."

The old man sat like a solemn frog on my one extra chair. He wore his usual ancient black suit, white shirt, and black tie with its shiny knot so small it looked as if it had been tied under pressure. The shabbiness of my one-room office did not bother Tercio. On Carmine Street, no matter how much cash a businessman has in various banks, he knows the value of a shabby front: it gives the poor confidence that a man is like them.

"What kind of plans?"

Tercio shrugged. "Business it's not good. We make some big mistakes. The stock market, buildings not worth so much as we pay, inventory that don't sell."

"I didn't know you made mistakes, Mr. Osso."

"So?" Tercio said. "Maybe I'm old. Vitanza he's old. We lose the touch, the neighborhood it's change. The new people they don't buy what we got. Maybe we been playin' too much *bocci*, sit around tellin' too many stories from the old days."

"All right," I said. "What plans do you figure Vitanza is making?"

Tercio folded his plump hands in his broad lap. "For six year Cology he got no wife. He got ten kids what got lotsa kids of their own. We both gettin' old. We got insurance, big. We talk about what we do next year and after and we don't think the same, so? Then I see Cology talking to people."

"What kind of insurance have you got?"

"On the inventory, on both of us, for the partners."

I sat back in the gray light from my one window that opens on the airshaft. "You're saying you think Vitanza is making plans to collect on the insurance?"

"I see him talk to Sid Nelson yesterday. Three days ago he drinks coffee alone with Don Primo."

Don Primo Veronese was a lawyer, a member of the Mazzini Club, and, by strong rumor, a fence for small hoods. Sid Nelson was a hood, not small but not big—sort of in between. A thief, a killer, and a careful operator.

"You and Vitanza talk to a lot of people."

"Sure, I talk to Don Primo myself," Tercio agreed. "I don't talk to no Sid Nelson. I don't say we should make a special inventory. I don't take big money from the bank, put in envelope, carry in my pocket. I don't go to Mass five times in one week."

"What do you want me to do, Mr. Osso?"

A slow shrug. "In winter the wolf comes to the streets of the city. The old lion he got to learn new tricks or starve. Maybe I'm crazy, okay. Only you watch Cology. You be a detective."

"That's my work," I said. "All right, a hundred in advance."

"A horse works on hay," Tercio said, and counted out two nice crisp fifties. "You tell me nine o'clock every night."

After old Tercio had gone, I rubbed at the stump of my missing arm, then phoned Lieutenant Marx at the precinct. I told him Tercio's story.

"What do you want me to do?" Marx said.

"I don't know," I said. "Tell me that Tercio Osso is a smart old man."

"Tercio is a smart old man," Marx said. "All I can do is stand by, Dan. At least until you get something that can be called reasonable suspicion."

"I know," I said.

"You can check out most of it," Marx pointed out.

That's what I did. I checked out old Osso's story.

It checked. Other people had seen Cology Vitanza talking to Don Primo Veronese, and, especially, to Sid Nelson. The firm of Osso & Vitanza was in trouble—cash tied up, notes overdue, interest not paid, a few bad deals the other Carmine

Street financiers were grinning about, and the jewelry stock not moving at all.

Vitanza had been going to Mass almost every day. He had withdrawn $5,000 in cash. (A teller I knew, and ten bucks, got me that information.) I had to take Tercio Osso's word about the special inventory of the unmoving stock, but I was sure it would turn out to be true.

I began tailing Cology Vitanza. It wasn't a hard tail. The tall old man was easy to follow and a man of routine. He never took me out of the ten-square-block area of Little Italy. I reported to Osso every night at nine o'clock by telephone.

On Friday I spotted Vitanza talking again to Sid Nelson. The hoodlum seemed interested in what Vitanza had to say.

I ate a lot of spaghetti and drank a lot of wine for two days. I saw one bad movie, and visited the homes of twenty old men. That is, Vitanza visited and I lurked outside in the cold getting more bored every minute. I wore out my knees kneeling at the back of a dim church.

But I was there in the Capri Tavern at six o'clock Saturday night when Vitanza stopped to talk to a seedy-looking character in a rear booth. A white envelope passed from Vitanza to the seedy type. I waited until the new man downed his glass of wine and ambled out. Then I switched to tailing him.

I followed the seedy man through Little Italy and across to the East Side. He looked around a lot, and did all kinds of twists and turns, as if he figured he might be followed. That made it hard work, but I kept up with him. He finally headed for the Bowery.

A block south of Houston he suddenly ducked into a wino joint. I sprinted and went in, but he was out the back way and gone. I went around through the alleys and streets of the Bowery for another hour trying to pick up his trail, but I had no luck.

I went back to Carmine Street to find Cology Vitanza. He wasn't at the Mazzini Club, and neither was Osso. I tried their other haunts and didn't find them. The lights were on behind the curtained windows of the shop and office on Carmine Street, but I couldn't go in without tipping my hand, so I took up a stakeout.

Nothing happened for half an hour. Then some people tried to get into the store, but the front door was locked. That wasn't right for a Saturday night. It was almost nine o'clock by then. I made my call to Osso from a booth where I could watch the front door of the store. There was no answer, so I called Lieutenant Marx.

"I don't like how it sounds," Marx said. "Too bad you lost that Bowery character. I've done some checking on their insurance. They've got $50,000 on the inventory, $25,000 life on each payable to the other, and $50,000 surviving-partner insurance with option to buy out the heirs.

"A nice haul," I said. "What do we do?"

"Sid Nelson hasn't moved. I put a man on him for you."

"The Commissioner wouldn't like that."

"The Commissioner won't know," Marx said, and then was silent a few seconds. "We've got no cause to bust in yet."

"And if nothing's wrong we tip off Vitanza."

"But they shouldn't be locked up on Saturday night," Marx said, "The patrolman on the beat ought to be suspicious."

"I guess he ought to," I said.

"I'll be right over," Marx said.

Marx arrived with two of his squad inside three minutes. He'd picked up the beat patrolman on the way. I joined them at the door to the store. We couldn't see anything through the curtains.

"Pound the door and give a call," Marx instructed the beat patrolman.

The patrolman pounded and called out. Nothing happened. Marx chewed his lip and looked at me. Then, as if from far off, we heard a voice. It was from somewhere inside the store, and it was calling for help.

31

"I guess we go in," Marx said.

He kicked in the glass of the door and reached inside for the lock.

❧

At first we saw nothing wrong in the jewelry store. Then Marx pointed to the showcases where the expensive jewelry was kept. They were unlocked and empty.

In the office in the back a rear window was open. A man lay on the floor in a pool of not-quite-dry blood. A .38 caliber automatic was on the floor about five feet from the body, toward the right wall of the office. There was a solid door in the right wall, and behind it someone was knocking and calling, "What's happen out there? Hey, who's out there?"

Marx and I looked at each other as one of his men bent over the body on the floor. It was not Tercio Osso, it was Cology Vitanza. Marx's second man swung the door of the safe open. It had been closed but not locked. It was empty.

Marx went to the solid door. "Who's in there?"

"Osso! He knock me out, lock me in. What's happen?"

Marx studied the door. There was no key in the lock. I went and searched the dead man. I shook my head at Marx— no key. One of Marx's men pointed to the floor.

"There."

The key was on the floor not far from the gun. I picked it up. It was one of those common old house keys, rough and rusted, and there would be no prints. Marx took the key and opened the door.

Tercio Osso blinked at us. "Mr. Fortune, lieutenant. Where's Cology, he—"

Osso stepped out into the office and saw his dead partner. He just stood and stared. Nothing happened to his face. I watched him. If anything had shown on his face I would have been surprised. Everyone knew he was a tough old man.

"So," he said, nodding, "he kill Cology. It figure. The crazy old man. Crazy."

"You want to tell us what happened?" Marx said.

"Sure, sure," the old man said. He walked to his desk and sat down heavily. I saw a trickle of blood over his left ear. He looked at Vitanza's body. "He come in maybe hour, two hours ago. What time is it?"

"Nine-twenty," Marx said.

"That long?" Osso said. "So two hours since. Seven-thirty, maybe. One guy. He comes in the front. I go out to see. He got a mask and a gun. He push me back to office, me and Cology. He makes us go lock the front door, clean out the cases and then the safe. He work fast. He shove me in storeroom, knock me out."

The old man touched his head, winced. "I wake up, I don't know what time. I listen. Nothing, no noise. I listen long time, I don't want him to come back for me. Nothing happen. I hear phone ring. So I start yelling. Then I hear you bust in."

Osso looked around. "He got it all, huh? Out the window. Only he don't keep the deal, no. Cology is crazy man. A guy like that don't keep no deals."

There was a long silence in the office. Sirens were growing in the cold night air outside as the police began to arrive at Marx's summons. Marx was chewing his lip and looking at me. I looked at Osso.

"You're telling us you figure Vitanza hired a guy to rob the store for the insurance, and then the guy killed him? Why?"

Osso shrugged. "Who know? Maybe the guy don't want to split with Cology. Maybe the guy figures the jewels is worth more than a cut of the insurance. They fight, Cology's dead. How do I know, I'm locked inside the storeroom."

The assistant medical examiner arrived, the fingerprint team, and two men from Safe and Loft. I went into the storeroom. It was small and windowless. There was no other door. The walls were white and clean, and the room was piled with lumber, cans, tools, and assorted junk. I found a small stain of blood on the floor near the door. The walls seemed solid.

When I went back out, Marx's men had finished marking the locations of the body, the gun, and the key. The M.E. stood up and motioned to his men to bring their basket.

"Shot twice in the back," the M.E. said. "Two hours ago, maybe more, maybe a little less. Rigor is just starting. He's a skinny old man. Died pretty quick, I'd say. The slugs are still in him—.38 caliber looks about right."

"The gun's been fired twice," one of Marx's men said, "not long ago."

"Prints all over the place, all kinds," the fingerprint man said. "It won't be easy to lift them clean."

Marx growled. "Prints won't help. What about you Safe and Loft guys?"

A Safe and Loft man said, "Rear window opened from inside. Some marks on the sill could have been a man climbing out. The yard is all concrete, no traces, but we found this."

The Safe and Loft man held up a child's rubber Halloween mask. Marx looked at it sourly.

"They all use that trick now. The movies and TV tell them how to do everything," Marx said, and came over to me. He lit a cigarette. "Well, Dan?"

"Everything fits," I said. "Just about what I was supposed to figure that Vitanza was planning—except for his killing."

"Neat," Marx said.

"Too neat," I said. "Let's talk to Osso."

While his men and the experts went on working, Marx took Osso into the storeroom. I went with them. The old man watched us with cold black eyes.

"This is just what you expected when you went to Fortune," Marx said to the old man.

"I got a hunch," Osso said.

"What does Cology figure on getting out of it, Tercio?" I said. "The insurance on the stock, no more. Maybe he figures on keeping most of the jewels, too, okay. But figure what you get out of it. You get the whole works—stock insurance, life insurance on Cology, partnership insurance, option to buy it all."

"So?" Osso said, watched me.

"So if Cology was going to set up a risky deal like this it ought to be you who's dead, not him. The thief should have killed you and knocked Cology out. Then there's a big pie to split with Cology."

"You think I set this up?"

I nodded. "It smells, Tercio. We're supposed to figure that Vitanza hired a punk to fake a holdup, but not kill you when there was more riding on you than on the stock? Then the hired hood kills Cology for some reason and leaves his gun here on the floor? Leaves his mask out in the yard to prove he was here? Leaves the key on the floor so we know you were locked in?"

Osso shrugged. "You figure I set it up, take me down and book me. I call my lawyer. You find the guy I hire. You do that. I tell the truth. I hire no one, you won't find no one. I'm inside the storeroom, so how I kill Cology?"

Marx said, "It's too neat, Osso. You practically told Fortune how it was going to happen."

"So book me. I get my lawyer. You find the man I hire." And the old man smiled. "Or maybe you figure I kill from inside locked room?"

Marx snapped, "Take the old man down, book him on suspicion. Go over the place with a vacuum cleaner. Send anything you find to Technical Services."

They took Osso. Marx followed and I left with him.

The police had gone, except for a patrolman posted at the broken door in front, when I jimmied the back window and went in. I dropped into the dark office and flicked on my flashlight. I focused the beam on the marks that showed where the gun, the key, and the body had been.

I heard the steps too late. The lights went on, and I turned from pure reflex. I never carry a gun, and if I'd had a gun I couldn't have pulled it with my flash still in my lone hand. I was glad I didn't have a gun. I might have shot by reflex, and it was Lieutenant Marx in the doorway. That's the trouble with a gun, you tend to depend on it if you have one.

I said, "You, too, lieutenant?"

"What's your idea?" Marx said.

"The old man's too confident," I said. "He damn near begged you to book him on suspicion of having hired a man to fake the robbery and kill Vitanza."

"Yeah," Marx said, "he did. You think he didn't hire any-one?"

I nodded. I didn't like it, but unless Cology Vitanza had set it up after all, which I didn't believe, there had to be another answer. Marx didn't like it either.

"You know what that gives us," Marx said.

"I know," I said, "but Tercio's too smart to hire a killing and have a monkey on his back the rest of his life. No, he'd do it himself."

"You got more than a hunch, Dan?"

"The gun," I said. "It's the flaw in the setup. It sticks out. A thief who kills takes his gun away with him. Osso would know that."

"So?"

"So the gun being in the office has to be the clue to the answer," I said. "It was here because Osso couldn't do any-thing else with it. The jewels are gone, the mask was out in the yard, the front door was locked on the inside out in the shop. If Osso had had a choice he'd have taken the gun away and the key too. He didn't. Why?"

Marx rubbed his jaw. "So if he did it, it reads like this: he took the ice and stashed it. He planted the mask and left the rear window open. He killed Vitanza, and then he got into that storeroom and somehow locked himself in with the key outside and a long way from the door."

"Yes and no," I said. "If he killed Vitanza *before* he got into that room, he could have disposed of the gun to make it look more like an outside killer. He didn't. So he must have killed Vitanza from *inside* the locked storeroom.

"And then got the gun and key out?"

"That's it," I said.

Marx nodded. "Let's find it."

We went to work. The locked room is an exercise in illusion—a magician's trick. Otherwise it's impossible, and the impossible can't be done, period. Since it *had* been done, it must be a trick, a matter of distracting attention, and once you know what you're really looking for, the answer is never hard.

When we had dismissed the distraction—the hired-robber-and-killer theory—the rest was just a matter of logic. I sighted along the line from the body to the seemingly solid wall. The line pointed directly to a light fixture set in the wall. Sighting the other way, the line led to Vitanza's desk and telephone.

"Vitanza came in," I said. "Osso was already inside the locked room. Vitanza went to his desk. He probably always did that, and Osso could count on it. Or maybe he saw that the jewels were gone and went to his desk to telephone the police. Osso probably knew he would be sure to do that, too. They'd been partners thirty years."

"And Osso had to shoot him in the back," Marx said. "The desk faces the other way."

"Let's look at that light fixture," I said.

It was one of those small modern wall lamps with a wide circular metal base. It had been attached to the wall recently and was not painted over. The wall behind it sounded hollow, but we could not move the lamp.

"It doesn't come off, Dan," Marx said.

"Not from this side," I said.

We went into the storeroom. I measured off from the door to exactly where the light fixture was attached on the other side of the wall. We studied the wall. The whole wall had been recently painted. The cans of quick-drying paint were among the litter in the storeroom. On the floor there were a few crumbs of dried plaster.

"Quick-drying plaster," I said to Marx.

Marx found a hammer and chisel in the storeroom. There were flecks of plaster on the chisel. He opened a hole directly behind the light fixture. It opened easily. The back of the light fixture was clearly visible about two inches in, between vertical two-by-fours. The fixture had a metal eye on the back. It was held in place by a metal bar that passed through the eye and was angled to catch the two-by-fours.

"That's it," I said. "Simple and clever."

Marx had two hands. He reached in with his left, turned the metal bar, and held the fixture. He pushed the fixture out and to the left and aimed his pistol through the hole with his right hand. He had a clear shot at the desk five feet away—in direct line with where the body of Cology Vitanza had fallen.

I said, "He had this hole open on this side. He heard Vitanza come in and head for the desk. He pushed out the fixture. It didn't matter if Vitanza heard or not—Osso was ready, didn't care if he hit Vitanza front or back. He shot Vitanza, tossed the gun and key through the hole, pulled the fixture back and refastened it, plastered up the hole, and painted the wall. He knew no one would break in until after I called at nine o'clock. He hid here and waited."

I shook my head in admiration for the old man. "If we believe that Vitanza had set it up, fine, we'd be looking for a nonexistent thief and killer. If we think Osso hired a man, fine, too. We're still looking for a nonexistent thief and killer, and in a few weeks Osso cleans up this storeroom, and the new plaster sets so it can't be told from the old plaster. Maybe he fixes the light fixture so it's permanent in the wall. All the evidence is gone, and he's in the clear."

"Only now the lab boys should be able to prove some of the plaster is newer," Marx said, "the fixture moves out, and the evidence is in this room. We've got the old bastard."

Marx called in Captain Gazzo of Homicide. Gazzo took it to Chief of Detectives McGuire who got a judge to order the office and storeroom sealed. The D.A. would want the jury to see the office and storeroom just as they were when Vitanza was killed.

I gave my statement, Marx made his report, and Gazzo faced the old man with it. Osso was a tough old bird.

"I want my lawyer," Osso said.

He got his lawyer, they booked the old man, and I went home to bed. I felt good. I don't get many locked rooms to play with, so I was pleased with myself.

Until morning.

?◆

"It's not the gun," Captain Gazzo said.

I was in Gazzo's office. So was Marx. Gazzo held the .38 automatic that had been on the office floor—the gun that had been the tipoff, the weak link, the key to it all.

"This gun didn't kill Vitanza," Gazzo said. "Ballistics just reported. Vitanza was killed with a .38, yes, but not this one."

I said nothing. Neither did Marx.

"A locked room," Gazzo said sarcastically. "Great work, boys. Clever, very clever."

I said it at the start: it can be a mistake to be too smart. A locked-room murder is an illusionist's trick, a matter of the misdirection of attention. And the one who had been too smart was me.

"All he threw out was the key," I said. "That was all he had to throw out all along. The rest was to distract us."

There had never been any reason why Osso had to kill from inside the storeroom, only that he lock himself in from the inside and get the key out. The whole locked room had been a trick to distract us. A gun on the floor by a dead man. The right caliber gun fired recently and the right number of times. Who would dream it was the wrong gun?

"Only the key now?" Gazzo said. "First he's brought in on suspicion of hiring a man to fake a robbery and kill his partner. Next he's booked for having killed his partner from inside a locked room with a trick scheme. Now he killed his partner outside the room, switched guns, locked himself in, and tossed the key out. What next?"

"He killed Vitanza," Marx said. "I'm sure he did."

"I'm sure too," Gazzo agreed, "but what jury will believe us now with the speech his lawyer'll make about dumb cops and police persecution? You guys like fairy tales? How do you like the one about the boy who cried wolf? The D.A. is bawling on his desk thinking about facing a jury against Osso now."

"We'll find out what he did," Marx said. "We'll find the right gun and the jewels."

"Sure we will," Gazzo said. "Some day."

"And I bet it won't do us any good," I said.

It didn't. Three days after the killing the superintendent of a cheap rooming house on the Lower East Side reported that a tenant hadn't come out of his room for three days. The police broke in and found the man dead. It was the seedy character I had followed and lost.

He had been shot in the shoulder. The bullet was still in the wound. But that was not what had killed him. He had died from drinking whiskey with lye in it. The bottle was in the room. The police found some of the missing jewels in the room, but not all. They also found a .38 caliber automatic that had been fired twice.

"It's the gun that killed Vitanza," ballistics reported.

"Only the bum's prints on the gun," fingerprinting said.

"It's certain he died four or five hours *after* Vitanza died," the M.E. said. "The bad whiskey killed him. He might have been unconscious most of the time, but after three days we'll never prove it. He lost blood from that shoulder wound."

Ballistics then added the final touch. "The bullet in the bum's shoulder came from the gun you found on the floor of Osso & Vitanza's office. The gun was registered to Cology Vitanza himself."

With my statement and report on what I had observed Cology Vitanza do, on the actions Osso had reported and I had checked out, the evidence logically added up to only one story: the seedy character had been hired by Cology Vitanza to rob the jewelry store. For some reason there had been a fight while Osso was unconscious in the locked room. (Osso stated he had plastered the hole in the storeroom the day before. With the evidence against the bum, his story was better than Marx's and mine.)

Vitanza had wounded the bum, and the bum had killed Vitanza. Then the wounded bum had run for his room with the loot, but hid some of it on the way. In his room, weak from his wound, he had drunk the bad whiskey, passed out, and died. It was just the way a wounded bum would die.

I had a different story. The day after they dropped all charges against Tercio Osso I went to his office. He didn't try to evade me.

"I owe you a couple days and expenses," Osso said.

"You hired me in the first place just to make me and Marx suspicious," I said. "You figured I'd talk to the police and you knew we'd suspect a trick. You wanted us to accuse you right away of hiring someone to kill Vitanza."

Osso said nothing.

"You arranged all those suspicious acts of Vitanza's. It wouldn't have been hard. You were partners, old friends, and he'd do anything you asked him to do if you said it was business. You asked him to talk to Sid Nelson about something innocent, to take out $5,000 in cash for you, to meet the bum with a note, even to go to a lot of Masses."

The old man was like a fat black frog in the chair.

"You played us like trout. It was too easy and not smart for you to have hired a killer. We were sure to look for more. That's when you handed us the locked room and the gun on the floor."

Osso smiled.

"That gun would have made any cop wonder, and you expected us to figure out the locked-room trick. You wanted us to charge you with it, and you wanted time. You needed at least a few hours to be sure the bum was dead, and the locked room would keep us nice and busy for at least a few hours."

The old man began to light a thin black cigar.

"You killed Vitanza while I was tailing the bum. You took the jewels, locked up, went out the back window. You went to the bum's room and filled him with the bad whiskey, then shot him with Vitanza's gun. A wound that would bleed but not kill.

"Then you planted the gun that had killed Vitanza in the bum's room with some of the jewels. You knew no one would look for the bum for days. You went back to the office and laid out Vitanza. You put the gun that had shot the bum on the office floor. You locked yourself in the storeroom from the inside and tossed out the key through the light fixture hole in the wall.

"Then you sat back and led me and Marx into being too smart for our own good. You got the time you needed. You kept us away from the bum until it was too late. You've got what you were after, and you're safe." I stopped and looked at the old man. "One thing I want to know, Osso. Why did you pick me?"

Old Tercio Osso blew smoke and looked solemn. He shrugged. He took the black stogie from his mouth and studied it. Then he laughed aloud.

"You got one arm," Osso said, grinned at me. "You're easy to spot. I got to know where you are all the time to make it work, see? I got to make it easy for that bum to spot you and lead you a chase before he loses you. And I got to make it easy for the man watching you all the time."

"You had a man watching me?"

"Sure, what else? Good man, a relative, never talk." Osso studied his cigar some more. "You got good friends on the cops, and you're a real smart man, see? I mean, I know you figure out that locked room."

And Osso laughed again. He was very pleased with his shenanigans. I said nothing, just stared at him. He studied me.

"I got to do it, see?" Osso said at last. "I'm in trouble. Vitanza he don't agree with me no more. He was gonna ruin me if I don't stop him. So I stop him. And I fix it so you smart guys outsmart yourselves."

I stood up. "That's okay, Osso. You see, you made the same mistake Marx and I made."

"So?" he said, his black eyes narrowing.

"That's right. You forgot other people can be as smart as you. You fixed it good so that no one can prove in court what you did. But you made it too good. Everyone knows you did it. You made it too complicated, Osso. You're the only one who could have worked it all. What I figured out, and just told you, I also told Vitanza's ten kids, and the members of the Mazzini Club. They're smart, too."

"I kill you too!" Osso croaked.

"You couldn't get away with it twice, not with everyone knowing what you did. You're too smart to try. Bad odds, and you always play the odds."

I left him chewing his lip, his shrewd mind working fast. Who knows, he's a smart man, and maybe he'll still get away with it. But I doubt it. As I said, other men are smart, too, and Vitanza's kids and the Mazzini Club boys believed the story I had figured out.

I read the newspapers carefully now. I'm waiting for a small item about an old man named Tercio Osso being hit by a truck, or found in the river drowned by accident, or maybe the victim of an unfortunate food poisoning in a restaurant that just happens to be run by a member of the Mazzini Club.

Nothing fancy or complicated this time, just a simple, everyday accident. Of course, everyone will know what really happened, but no one will ever prove it. Whoever gets Tercio Osso won't even have to be particularly careful. A reasonably believable accident will do the trick.

After all, we're all human and have a sense of justice, and no one likes to be played for a sucker.

Black in the Snow

No more than a black spot in the unbroken snow.

The February afternoon sun reflected from the windows of the silent suburban house, and I looked at the small black dog dead in the white expanse of the front yard of the Ralston house. On the distant parkway the traffic throbbed in its endless stream, but on the snow, and in the white frame house with the green shutters, nothing moved.

"It ought to be an easy one, Fortune," the lawyer had said. "George Ralston never hurt a fly. A solid man, an executive. Married twenty years. No children, they lived well. Middle-class people with their own home, bank accounts, the works."

"What does Ralston say happened?"

"He hasn't any idea. Too broken up and under sedation to think about it," the lawyer said. "But it has to be robbery, some nut on the loose. They have a lot of burglaries out in Manhasset, Anna Ralston and the dog must have surprised him and he killed them."

"How?"

"Knife." The lawyer shuddered and shook his head. "The dog had its throat cut, Anna Ralston was stabbed twice. In the stomach and under the ribs. Blood all over the pantry. George Ralston doesn't kill that way, he's got a wall of guns."

"They find the weapon?"

The lawyer nodded. "It was next to the woman. A butcher knife from the kitchen."

"Their kitchen? It was their knife?"

"That's what I mean. Anna Ralston walked in, some junkie burglar panicked. Blood all over and none on George Ralston."

"Any prints?"

"Smudges. You know prints on a wood knife."

"Why are they holding him?"

"Nothing was stolen," the lawyer said. "The house wasn't broken into, no tracks in the snow. Some neighbor heard the Ralstons in a screaming fight the night before, and George's alibi isn't airtight. He was in Great Neck that afternoon, but could have gotten home an hour or two before he did."

"What's Ralston's story?"

"He stopped in a couple of bars, no one saw him. When he got home he found her dead in the pantry. He doesn't remember much after that except he called the police."

Lawyers see what they want to see, believe what they have to believe, tell an investigator just enough so he can find what they want him to find.

"Why the dog, counselor? Why kill the dog?"

"Maybe it attacked the killer."

"What kind of dog?"

Even he had the grace to look away. "Pomeranian."

"Some thief."

Lawyers don't give up easily. Without hard evidence, one theory is as good as another.

"Look," the lawyer said, "the wife always had a dog. Four in the twenty years they were married. Small dogs, maybe because she was small herself, Ralston says. He's a big guy, burly, used to work in the factory where he's vice-president now. He says she was always with the dog. She carried them around with her everywhere. So when she surprised the thief she had the dog. It got in the way or he had to stop it bark-ing.''

And then threw the dead dog out into the snow? Why? The lawyer would have had an answer, but I didn't. I stood in the evening winter light and looked at the silent suburban house and the small black dog dead in the snow without footprints or any other tracks leading to it.

There were drops of blood in the center of the pale carpeting in the hallway to the front door, and then no more until the narrow pantry behind the kitchen. The large, formal living room was immaculate with green brocade period furniture, the dining room furnished in light, delicate woods from what could have been the same antique period. The silver on the sideboard was rubbed to a soft glow and probably used every day.

I stood in the doorway between the dining room and kitchen and imagined the Ralstons eating dinner every night in the spotless formal room with its perpetually polished silver. Two middle-aged people alone at the long table. He, from what the lawyer said, a big, burly man who liked shirtsleeves, she a small, slender woman still pretty and birdlike, the small black dog at her feet if not in her lap. It was a picture violence had no place in. Boredom, maybe, but not violence.

The windowless pantry across the kitchen held a different picture. Blood black on the walls, the floor, even the ceiling. The random slashing of a psychotic, or terrified amateur, or drug-crazed thief? I let my eyes take it in, squatted down to study the floor. The blanket and basket of the dog's bed were soaked with blood, and the floor around it was literally coated. The killings must have happened there, and without much struggle, the spattered blood thin on the walls and ceiling. Savage, yes, but not the pattern of a random, senseless slashing.

The kitchen with its flowered curtains was polished but not immaculate: a dirty cup and saucer in the sink; a plate with a soggy crust; the coffee maker still with stale coffee; one chair moved from the kitchen table to the wall telephone. I looked again at the well-used dining room with everything in its proper place, at the living room barely dusty even after a week of being untouched, and then went upstairs.

There were two bedrooms, a small sewing-and-plant room with a half-greenhouse wall, and a den-office.

The faint sound came from below.

A key turning softly in the front door.

Footsteps of someone trying to be soundless. Inside the den-office I stood back behind the door. Who had a key besides me, George Ralston, and the police?

Then she was in the room. A woman with dark hair, slim and more than attractive, but with the hands of someone over forty.

"George?"

I stepped out. "You often meet George here?"

"Jesus!" She jumped a foot and turned scared. "Who . . . who are you?"

"Did Mrs. Ralston know about you and George?"

Her eyes were brown and confused. "You're the police? Have you found anything? I mean, the man—"

"Private detective," I said. "I've found something now. You want to tell me about you and George?"

The brown eyes blinked. "George and me?" She shook her head. "No, I'm his sister. You thought George—?"

Guns hung all over the den walls: modern military rifles and pistols, even a light machine gun, as the lawyer had said. But he had forgotten to mention, or hadn't known, that they were all inoperative. No matter how violent George Ralston got, they were no more than clubs.

"Private detective?" the sister said.

"His lawyer hired me."

"Then they think George could have—!"

"What do you think, Miss Ralston?"

"Mrs. Deming," she said. "Sarah. I think they're insane."

"Someone killed her and the dog."

The desk was piled with books, pamphlets, letters. There was a TV set, a small refrigerator to save trips downstairs for beer, and a convertible couch that had been used and left open. Someone had slept in the den sometime before the killings, and no one had made the bed.

"George drinks," Sarah Deming said. "Anna wouldn't let him sleep with her when he was drunk."

"Which came first?" I said.

"What?"

"Which came first, not sleeping together or his drinking?"

She flushed. "I wouldn't know. Perhaps a little of both."

Between the guns on the wall above the desk were photographs of men in heavy shoes and work clothes inside a factory. Only one face was in all the photos: a big, heavyset young man with a wide grin and his arms around his buddies.

"George is proud of having worked with his hands," Sarah Deming said. "Down on the factory floor with the real workers. He's never really gotten used to being an executive, goes out with his old work friends when he drinks."

"He drinks a lot?"

She shrugged. "Enough, Mr.—?"

"Dan Fortune. Were they having any trouble, Mrs. Deming?"

"Make it Sarah, okay? Deming and I busted a long time ago." She smiled for the first time. It was a nice smile that faded almost at once. "No trouble I know except his drinking.

That bothered her a lot. She even had a plan to get him to stop."

"She talked to you about it?"

"To all of us. The Wednesday afternoon coffee club just the day before she . . . died. She started talking about George."

They sit in the green brocade living room. Five ladies around the coffee table eating small cakes, talking.

"I'm not sure when he changed," Anna Ralston says. "He always drank, mostly beer with his friends. I never liked it, but he didn't drink when we were together, so it wasn't that important. But now he's drinking all the time."

Anna holds the small dog in her lap, a black puff of fur. A nervous ball of fur, its eyes fixed on Miss Guilfoyle as she speaks. Anna strokes the tiny dog, soothes, reassures. The dog turns its foxlike face up to her, its small blue tongue out.

"I don't know why men have to drink," Miss Guilfoyle says. She sells a little real estate, inherited a house from her brother, almost married a man named Donald once and has never forgotten. "Not that Donald drank. That wasn't our problem."

Grace Hill says, "My Fred says George can be very insulting when he's had too much, especially in the executive lounge."

"I'm sorry, Grace. You see, it's even affecting his work now. Something has to be done."

"He's forty-six," Sarah says. "Maybe it's change-of-life."

Barbara Oliveri giggles, "Men do get moody around fifty."

Anna says, "It's a wife's job to help her husband, my mother always told me, be a jump ahead of him."

"You've got some plan for old George," Sarah says.

Anna nods. "It came to me this morning when I was combing Mitzi."

She smiles down at the dog curled into her lap. The small dog lays back its ears and closes its eyes, oblivious now that

its mistress is talking, going to sleep while its body contin-
ues to twitch in the nervousness of all small animals.

Anna smiles at her friends. "I've decided to buy George a
dog of his own. I suddenly realized how unfair I've been.
He's wanted a big dog ever since he had to give that collie
away before we were married. Don't you think it's a fine
idea?"

"It would certainly give him something to do besides
drink," Miss Guilfoyle says.

Grace Hill isn't sure. "Two dogs are a lot of trouble."

"Especially a big dog," Barbara Oliveri says.

"Have you told him?" Sarah asks.

"I'm going to tell him tonight," Anna says, satisfied. "I
think it's a wonderful idea. Mitzi means so much to me."

I said, "Did she get him the dog?"

"No," Sarah Deming said.

We had moved on to the front bedroom. It was a large, light
bedroom that faced the front lawn with its evening sun glare
off the snow. Outside, the small smudge of black still lay
motionless in the expanse of white. Inside, a queen-sized bed
had only one side slept in. It was unmade too.

"Did she make the beds first or last?" I asked.

"In the morning," Sarah Deming said. "Always. She
cleaned like a temple every day, beds first."

The bedroom had a feminine, girlish aura: pastel pinks and
yellows; ruffles and skirts on the chairs and vanity; dried cor-
sages, old programs, high-school pennants; yellowed photos
on the walls. In the photos a girl in longish Fifties dresses,
and an older couple in dark, reserved clothes, mingled with
small oriental people in Japanese kimonos and polyglot Western garb.

"Anna and her parents," Sarah Deming said. "Missionaries
in Japan all through the war and after. Anna was born over
there."

"Where are they now?"

"Dead. Her father died soon after they came back in the late Fifties, her mother only five years ago. I met her a few times when she came to visit, didn't like her much. A real sour type full of pronouncements and wise sayings. A chip on her shoulder about something, probably the wicked world."

"Where did they go after Japan?"

"Nowhere. There was some trouble, they retired as missionaries when they got back. Anna didn't like to talk about it."

Nothing on the second floor showed evidence of an intruder as far as I could tell, and we went downstairs. Nothing in the whole house indicated an intruder. We stood in the kitchen.

"Was your brother messing around, Sarah? Another woman?"

"So they do think George killed her!"

"They don't know who killed her. Or why."

She shook her head, angry. "He just drank. Most people don't go to the effort of breaking out when they're comfortable, do they? Anna's mother said it: 'Give a man a home, take care of him, that's all he really needs.' Anna was good at that."

"Then he had a reason to break out?"

"He had a reason to drink." She shook her head. "He wasn't happy, hadn't been for years, but he wasn't the type to go to another woman."

"What about her? His drinking bothered her a lot."

"Anna? God, no! She had her house, her duties, and her dogs. She always had her dogs. Mitzi was the fourth since they were married. She got the first one while George was still on the factory floor and they had a small apartment in Queens."

"Any enemies? Maybe from the past? In Japan? Something to do with her parents? With their work?"

She shook her head. "I wouldn't know about that." She looked at me. "I just know George didn't kill her."

I wished I knew as much. Lawyers don't hire a detective to prove their client guilty. I wanted to talk to the neighbors, but it was dinner time in the suburbs, the men coming home. No one would want to talk now, and I needed a beer.

"Buy you a drink?"

Sarah Deming smiled. "Why not. As long as you're on our side. You are on our side?"

"I'll do my best."

ॐ

The Tavern was on the water overlooking Manhasset Bay. We both had Amstel Lights. She hadn't even asked about my missing arm.

"Why didn't she buy the dog for George?"

"He didn't want it." She poured the last of her beer. "You always knew George was home because her dogs started barking. That evening Mitzi barked even before we heard the garage door open. He always came in and sat in his big armchair, his suit coat off, his feet up on another chair. Anna hated that, but she never said anything because her mother told her you had to put up with things men did, make allowances. That was one of the mother's favorite sayings. Anna didn't always follow it with George, but that night she was eager to tell him her big idea."

"Two dogs are too much trouble, Anna."

"You always wanted your own dog, George. A nice big one. You can fence the back yard, even build a doghouse."

"The yard for my dog, eh?"

"A house is no place for a big dog. Certainly not a male."

George begins to laugh. "We could mate him to Mitzi. God, can you see the pups? Mitzi and a Great Dane?"

Sarah laughs too. Anna doesn't laugh. The small dog raises

53

its head on Anna's lap, its eyes watchful, alert. Anna holds the dog with both hands.

George shrugs. "I don't need a dog, Anna."

"You've always said you'd like a big dog."

"I don't need another damned dog!" George is up, walks to the liquor cabinet, pours a whisky. "Anyone else?"

"I'll have a beer," Sarah says.

Anna says nothing, the dog only watches, its lips skinned back from small, pointed teeth as it senses George Ralston's anger. George brings beer in a glass from the kitchen for Sarah, sits down again in his chair and stares moodily at his whisky.

"A real dog'd be nice. One you can tell what it is. With those little ones of yours I forget which was which. Never could tell one of the damned things from another."

"That's ridiculous!" Anna snaps. "Mitzi's a Pom. Mrs. Ching was a Peke and so was Dodo. Suzy Q was a King Charles."

"Remember the collie I had when we met? Admiral? We mated him once, got half the litter. I think Ed Riley had one. Dead now, of course. I saw Ed the other day down on the plant floor."

"I don't see how you could possibly confuse a Pom with a Peke or a King Charles."

"Sometimes I wish I'd stayed in the plant. Work hard all week, booze and whore on the weekend."

"I don't allow words like that, George!"

He drinks. "It's just a word, Anna."

"Sometimes I wish I'd never married you!"

He stands, drains his glass. "So do I."

"Go and drink." Her voice is shrill. "Go and get drunk!"

The small dog barks, teeth bared in Anna's lap, its high, yapping bark as shrill as her voice.

"Why not? Falling down drunk."

The dog goes on barking until the back door slams shut.

Then it stops, looks alertly up at its mistress for approval. Anna strokes it.

Sarah Deming swirled her second Amstel. "The dog stopped the moment George was gone, and Anna got up and started to wash the glasses, straighten up, and get ready for the Girls Club meeting she was having later. As if nothing had happened."

"Or as if it had happened a lot of times before."

She drank. "I suppose."

"What did you do?"

"Helped Anna, then went home."

"Where's home?"

"A few blocks from here. Deming at least left me a house."

"I'll escort you home after some dinner."

She smiled. "Not tonight, Dan. I'm . . . I'm still upset. You can't think George . . . ? Not George."

"No," I said, "not George."

I paid for the drinks, watched her drive off, then headed for the parkway into the city.

Next morning I lay in bed in my loft and thought. Then I got dressed, put a long scarf under my duffel against the wind that blew the old snow river to river, went out and had some breakfast at the diner on Eighth Avenue, and called on my client.

"No evidence of a burglar around the house." I took the chair that faced his desk. "I don't think there was an intruder."

"You talk to the neighbors? Any other burglaries around?"

A lawyer's job is get his client off. Innocent or guilty.

"The cops'll have done that."

"The cops aren't talking to me," the lawyer said, "but they

must have something. They released George Ralston this morning."

"They make an arrest?"

"Not that I heard. I'm paying you to find out what the cops have and maybe more, not make guesses."

I went up to the main library and checked old newspapers for the late Fifties, the publications of missionary societies. Then I drove my rental car out to the Nassau County Medical Center in East Meadow. The pathologist on duty read my credentials and the papers from the lawyer.

"What do you want to know about Anna Ralston?"

"Time of death first."

He opened a file. "Between four and five P.M. the afternoon she was found."

"Did she have scratches on her hands? Maybe her face? Rips in her clothes besides the knife wounds?"

He looked up at me. "You know something the police don't?"

"Then there are scratches?"

"Deep ones on both hands, even her face. Rips in the top of her dress that probably weren't the knife."

"Thanks."

If they'd released George Ralston the case probably hadn't gone to Mineola Homicide yet, so I drove to the Sixth Precinct in Manhasset. Frank Domenici was on the case, we'd worked together maybe three years ago.

"You don't buy the burglar theory?" I asked.

"Nothing to back it up yet."

"But you let George Ralston go."

"Only as far as home. He's got a so-so alibi, psychiatrist says he's really broken up, and we can't figure a motive."

"Not enough to hold him, but he's still your best bet?"

"Until somebody hands us the crazy burglar, or a stoned vagrant with red hands."

"Tell me about the screaming fight made you hold Ralston in the first place."

Domenici shrugged. "The next-door neighbor couldn't sleep the night before the killing, went out for a walk in the snow with his dog. He was right out front when he saw the light go on in the bedroom. He noticed because it was after two A.M., and he'd never known Anna Ralston to be up past eleven tops."

"Which bedroom?"

"The front," Domenici said. "The neighbor hears Ralston laugh, drunk and slurring which wasn't unusual, say she gave him an idea. The neighbor hears her say, 'Go to bed, George.' "

"She made him sleep in his office when he was drunk."

"What else is new?" Domenici said. "Only he won't go to bed, says something about old Mitzi earning her keep. She tells him to look at the time. The neighbor can see his shadow weaving around while he talks about money, and she's starting to yell."

"What about the dog?"

"It's up there, the neighbor hears it growling and yapping. Ralston's voice turns nasty, says something about 'upside down,' and the wife flips out. She's yelling 'animal,' and 'pig,' and the dog's barking like crazy, and Ralston's staggering around and laughing loud and nasty, and the wife screams not to touch her and get out, and finally Ralston leaves after yelling about tomorrow, and damned bitch, and like that."

"The neighbor didn't hear what about tomorrow?"

Domenici shook his head. "It's all silent after that, the neighbor goes on walking his dog. When he comes back the light's still on in the bedroom, he can hear her sort of singing real soft but can't hear the words. He goes home to bed, but he wakes up again around dawn and the light's still on. He doesn't hear anything more until Ralston starts bumping things in the kitchen and finally goes to work. He swears the light looked still on in the bedroom, but he didn't hear the wife moving around the way she usually did before he had to leave himself. He got back late, we were already there, Anna Ralston was dead."

"Can I make a phone call?"

"Is it about the case?"

"Yeah. You have Ralston's office number?"

He gave it to me. I dialed, told Ralston's secretary, Miss Kerry, who I was and what I wanted. I heard the protectiveness in her voice. She wanted to help Ralston's lawyer, but she didn't want to say anything that might make Ralston look bad.

"He left about three that afternoon, was going to a kennel in Great Neck. That's all I know, Mr. Fortune."

"When did Anna Ralston call?"

There was a silence. "About four. How did you know she called?"

"What did she want, Miss Kerry?"

"To talk to Mr. Ralston. It wasn't unusual,"

"I'm sure it wasn't. What did you tell her?"

"That he'd already left."

"What did she say?"

"She asked where he'd gone."

"Did you tell her?"

"Yes."

"What did she say then?"

"She thanked me and hung up."

I thanked her, hung up, and stood up. Domenici watched me.

"Let's go talk to George Ralston," I said.

"Am I going to like what we talk about?"

"I don't know," I said.

George Ralston sat in the immaculate green antique living room that wasn't so immaculate now, dust already on the brocade.

"There wasn't any burglar, Mr. Ralston," I said. "No dope addict, no psycho or punk vagrant."

"Yes," Ralston said. "He came in and killed Anna."

I said, "You want me to tell what happened the night before, and when you got home that day, or do you want to tell us?"

I had his attention, but he said nothing.

"A neighbor heard the fight," I said. "Not all the words, but I think I can fill in most of them. When I get it wrong, you correct me. You'd argued about her getting you a big dog, a yard dog, a male dog, and you went out and got pretty plastered and staggered home late. She was asleep, but you turned on the light, woke her up. You had this idea of your own."

Anna Ralston looks up at George's red face grinning down at her. He's drunk. Mitzi growls on the bed beside her. She only slowly becomes aware of what he is saying.

". . . got a great idea. Yessir. Know what gave me the idea? You did, with your big male dog."

"Go to bed, George."

"I'm in this bar, told this guy about you having all these damned little bitches and wanting to get me a big one and he said there was more money in little dogs than big ones. He says everyone wants small dog pups for apartments and that's when it hit me. Real pedigree pups're worth plenty. About time that Mitzi earned her damned keep."

"You're drunk! Look at the time."

George sits heavily on the bed. Anna shrinks, holds the covers to her chin.

George grins. "Mate her with a real good stud and the pups'll be worth a hell of a lot of money."

Anna is pale. "Mitzi's much too small. Go to bed now."

"Supposed to be small. Smaller they are, more the pups're

worth. Use a small stud. Feisty little stud shove it to her good." George laughs. "Guy says the bitches get so scared they try 'n hide with the damn little hard stud after 'em."

Anna's voice a rage of anger. "Go to bed, George!"

Mitzi, curled against her mistress on the bed, growls. Anna holds the covers tight, her voice angry, almost violent with a trembling violence that alarms the dog, its neck fur bristling. Its lips skin back over sharp teeth. George still laughs.

"After they get it you got to hold them upside down so the stuff doesn't run out. Can you see it? Old Mitzi fucked good and upside down?"

Then Anna is shouting, screaming in the pink and lace late-night bedroom. The small dog barks, snarling and barking and shrinking against its mistress. Anna drops the covers, holds the dog against her. "You leave my baby alone! You animal! No one is going to hurt my little Mitzi. Get away. Animal! Pig! Don't you touch my baby! Never! Animal!"

George gets to his feet, sways. "Tomorrow. Some damn good out of her."

Anna is trembling and shaking. She holds the dog, croons, "My poor Mitzi. Poor helpless little girl. He won't touch you, no. My little girl."

George glares at the small woman in the thin nightgown, and the small black dog held against her. "Damned little bitch."

He blinks at them, turns and staggers out and down the hall to fall onto the already opened sofa bed in his office-den. The house becomes silent except for the low snarls of the frightened dog and the thin, soothing voice of Anna as she croons to the little dog. The light does not go out.

Anna Ralston sits in the neat bed barely disturbed by her small body and holds the dog until it stops shivering and goes to sleep against her. She still doesn't turn out the light, sits the rest of the night holding the dog and watching the

*half-open door of her bedroom and the unseen office-den
along the hall where the faint snores of George Ralston go on
and on. Until the sky outside lightens into a morning gray.
Until the alarm she had set in George's den last night to
wake him for work goes off. Until George staggers up, swearing and groaning, bumps downstairs, crashes around the
kitchen, goes out and drives off. Until the sun is up and long
after.*

*She sits in the bed holding the dog until the morning is
half gone. Then she turns off the light, dresses, goes down
and feeds the small dog. After that she sits by the kitchen
telephone and waits. She does not make the beds, dust, run
the vacuum, clean George's breakfast dishes from the
kitchen, put her polished house in order. She waits by the
telephone. Because George will call to apologize. She knows
he will call. But he doesn't, and at four P.M. she calls his
office. She talks to his secretary. She hangs up. She calls
Mitzi to her.*

"Come here, little girl. Come to mother, little girl."

Then she takes the butcher knife from the drawer.

"You didn't call," I said to George Ralston where he sat in
the antique brocade chair. "You always called after a fight to
apologize, say you were sorry. This time you didn't. You went
to a kennel in Great Neck."

Ralston looked at his thick, heavy hands. "I was still mad. I
went to the kennel, but only to ask about a dog for me. Then I
changed my mind, didn't want a damned dog, stopped in
some bars.

"She'd grown up in Japan. Her father was accused of chas-
ing girls. It was hushed up, but they were forced to leave
Japan. Her mother probably never let him forget it. Or Anna.
She took the knife and the dog into the pantry. She cut the
dog's throat. It struggled and clawed and bit, there were
scratches all over her hands, her face. Then she used the knife
for herself."

George Ralston's voice was flat and empty. "They were in the pantry. On the floor as if they were asleep. She was still holding the knife in her. I used her dress and pulled the knife out. I picked up the dog. It was stiff, not much blood. I suppose I carried it all the way to the front door. I don't remember that part. I threw it out into the snow. I remember that. I threw that goddamned little bitch of a dog that had killed my wife out into the goddamned snow!"

Domenici and I waited, but Ralston said nothing more. Just sat there and stared at his hands and at nothing.

"You didn't want anyone to know she'd killed herself," I said. "Maybe you didn't want to believe it yourself."

Ralston still looked only at his hands. "She never wanted me, not from the start. I don't know why she married me."

"Because she was supposed to marry," I said. "She had to get married to someone. Her mother would have told her that."

He looked up at us. "The last few years there was nothing. I stank, I was coarse, I drank too much, I was an animal." An expression almost of surprise. "Married twenty years, I never saw her naked."

Domenici asked him to go to the precinct to make a statement. I rode with them to my rented car, called Sarah Deming and asked her to dinner. Over coffee I told her. She cried. We went home to her place. Neither of us wanted to be alone.

Who?

Mrs. Patrick Connors was a tall woman with soft brown eyes and a thin face battered by thirty years of the wrong men.

"My son Boyd died yesterday, Mr. Fortune," she said in my office. "I want to know who killed him. I have money."

She held her handbag in both hands as if she expected I might grab it. She worked in the ticket booth of an all-night movie on 42nd Street, and a lost dollar bill was a very real tragedy for her. Boyd had been her only child.

"He was a pretty good boy," I said, which was a lie, but she was his mother. "How did it happen?"

"He was a wild boy with bad friends," Mrs. Connors said. "But he was my son, and he was still very young. What happened, I don't know. That's why I'm here."

"I mean, how was he killed?"

"I don't know, but he was. It was murder, Mr. Fortune."

That was when my missing arm began to tingle. It does that when I sense something wrong.

"What do the police say, Mrs. Connors?"

"The medical examiner says that Boyd died of a heart attack. The police won't even investigate. But I know it was murder."

My arm had been right, it usually is. There was a lot wrong.

Medical examiners in New York don't make many mistakes, but how do you tell that to a distraught mother?

"Mrs. Connors," I said, "we've got the best medical examiners in the country here. They had to do an autopsy. They didn't guess."

"Boyd was twenty years old, Mr. Fortune. He lifted weights, had never been sick a day in his life. A healthy young boy."

It wasn't going to be easy. "There was a fourteen-year-old girl in San Francisco who died last year of hardening of the arteries, Mrs. Connors. The autopsy proved it. It happens, I'm sorry."

"A week ago," Mrs. Connors said, "Boyd enlisted in the air force. He asked to be flight crew. They examined him for two days. He was in perfect shape, they accepted him for flight training. He was to leave in a month."

Could I tell her that doctors make mistakes? Which doctors? The air force doctors, or the medical examiner's doctors? Could I refuse even to look?

"I'll see what I can find," I said. "But the M.E. and the police know their work, Mrs. Connors."

"I knew my son," she said, opening her purse. "This time they're wrong."

It took most of the afternoon before I cornered Sergeant Hamm in the precinct squad room. He swore at crazy old ladies, at his work load, and at me, but he took me over to see the M.E. who had worked on Boyd Connors.

"Boyd Connors died of a heart attack," the M.E. said. "I'm sorry for the mother, but the autopsy proved it."

"At twenty? Any history of previous heart attacks? Any congenital weakness, hidden disease?"

"No. There sometimes isn't any, and more people die

young of heart attacks than most other people know. It was his first, and his last, coronary."

"He passed an air force physical for flight training a week ago," I said.

"A week ago?" The M.E. frowned. "Well, that makes it even more unusual, yes, but unusual or not, he died of a coronary attack, period. And in case you're wondering, I've certified more heart attack deaths than most doctors do common colds. All right?"

As we walked to Sergeant Hamm's car outside the morgue, Hamm said, "If you still have any crazy ideas about it being murder, like the mother says, I'll tell you that Boyd Connors was alone in his own room when he died. No way into that room except through the living room, no fire escape, and only Mrs. Connors herself in the living room. Okay, Dan?"

"Yeah," I said. "Swell."

Hamm grinned. "Don't take the old woman for too much cash, Danny. Just humor her a little."

The Connorses' apartment was a fifth-floor walkup. It was cheap and worn, but it was neat—a home. A pot of tea stood on the table as Mrs. Connors let me in. She poured me a cup. There was no one else there, Mr. Patrick Connors having gone to distant parts long ago.

I sat, drank my tea. "Tell me just what happened. When Boyd died."

"Last night he came home about eight o'clock," Mrs. Connors said. "He looked angry, went into his room. Maybe five minutes later I heard him cry out, a choked kind of cry. I heard him fall. I ran in, found him on the floor near his bureau. I called the police."

"He was alone in his room?"

"Yes, but they killed him somehow. His friends."

65

"What friends?"

"A street gang—the Night Angels. Thieves and bums!"

"Where did he work, Mrs. Connors?"

"He didn't have a job. Just the air force, soon."

"All right." I finished my tea. "Where's his room?"

It was a small room at the rear, with a narrow bed, a closet full of gaudy clothes, a set of barbells, and the usual litter of brushes, cologne, hair tonic and after-shave on the bureau. There was no outside way into the room, and no way to reach it without passing through the living room. No signs of violence, nothing that looked to me like a possible weapon.

All that my searching and crawling got me was an empty box and wrapping paper from some drugstore in the wastebasket, and an empty men's cologne bottle under the bureau. Three matchbooks were under the same bureau, a tube of toothpaste was under the bed, and some dirty underwear littered the floor. Boyd Connors hadn't been neat.

I went back out to Mrs. Connors. "Where had Boyd been last night?"

"How do I know?" she said bitterly. "With that gang, probably. In some bars. Maybe with his girlfriend, Anna Kazco. Maybe they had a fight, that's why he was angry."

"When did Boyd decide to join the air force?"

"About two weeks ago. I was surprised."

"All right," I said. "Where does this Anna Kazco live?"

She told me.

At the address Mrs. Connors had given me, an older woman opened the door. A bleached blonde, she eyed me until I told her what I wanted. Then she looked unhappy, but she let me in.

"I'm Grace Kazco," the blonde said, "Anna's mother. I'm sorry about Boyd Connors. I wanted better than him for my daughter, but I didn't know he was sick. Poor Anna feels terrible about it."

"How do you feel about it?"

Her eyes flashed at me. "Sorry, like I said, but I'm not all busted up. Boyd Connors wasn't going to amount to a hill of beans. Now maybe Anna can—"

The girl came from an inner room. "What can Anna do?"

She was small and dark, a delicate girl whose eyes were puffed with crying.

"You can pay attention to Roger, that's what you can do," the mother snapped. "He'll make something of himself."

"There wasn't anything wrong with Boyd."

"Except he was all talk and dream and do nothing. A street-corner big shot. Roger works instead of dreaming."

"Who's this Roger?" I asked.

"Roger Tatum," the mother said. "A solid, hard-working boy who likes Anna. He won't run off to any air force."

"After last night," Anna said, "maybe he won't be running here again, either."

"What happened last night?" I said.

Anna sat down. "Boyd had a date with me, but Roger had dropped around first. He was here when Boyd came. They got mad at each other, Mother told Boyd to leave. She always sides with Roger. I was Boyd's date, Roger had no right to break in, but Mother got me so mad I told them both to get out. I was wrong. It made Boyd angry. Maybe that made the heart attack happen. Maybe I—"

"Stop that!" the mother said. "It wasn't your fault."

Under the bleached hair and the dictatorial manner, she was another slum mother trying to do the best for her daughter.

"Did they get out when you told them?" I asked.

Anna nodded. "They left together. That was the last time I ever saw poor Boyd."

"What time was that?"

"About seven o'clock, I think."

"Where do I find this Roger Tatum? What does he do for a living?"

"He lives over on Greenwich Avenue, number 110," Anna told me. "He works for Johnson's Pharmacy on Fifth Avenue. Cleans up, delivers, like that."

"It's only a temporary job," the mother said. "Roger has good offers he's considering."

The name of Johnson's Pharmacy struck a chord in my mind. Where had I heard the name? Or seen it?

Roger Tatum let me into his room. He was a small, thin youth who wore rimless glasses and had nice manners. The kind of boy mothers like—polite, nose to the grindstone. His single room was bare except for books everywhere.

"I heard about Boyd," Tatum said. "Awful thing."

"You didn't like him too much, though, did you?"

"I had nothing against him. We just liked the same girl."

"Which one of you did Anna like?"

"Ask her," Tatum said quietly.

"Not that it matters now, does it?" I said. "Boyd Connors is dead, Anna's mother likes you, an inside track all the way."

"I hope so," he said, watching me.

"What happened after you left the Kazco apartment with Boyd? You left together? Did you fight, maybe?"

"Nothing happened. We argued some on the sidewalk. He went off, I finished my deliveries. I'm not supposed to stop anywhere when I deliver, and I was late, so I had to hurry. When I finished delivering, I went back to the shop, then I came home. I was here all night after that."

"No fight on the street? Maybe knocked Boyd Connors down? He could have been hurt more than you knew."

"Me knock down Boyd? He was twice my size."

"You were here alone the rest of the night?"

"Yes. You think I did something to Boyd?"

"I don't know what you did."

I left him standing there in his bare room with his plans for the future. Did he have a motive for murder? Not really. People don't murder over an eighteen-year-old girl that often. Besides, Boyd Connors had died of a heart attack.

I gave out the word around the bars and flops on the East Side that I'd like to talk to the Night Angels—twenty dollars in it, and no trouble. Maybe I'd reach them, maybe I wouldn't. There was nothing to do that I could think of, so I stopped for a few Irish whiskeys, and went home to bed.

About noon the next day, a small, thin, acne-scarred boy with cold eyes and a hungry face came into my office. He wore the leather jacket and shabby jeans uniform, and the hunger in his face was the perpetual hunger of the lost street kid for a lot more than food. He looked seventeen, had the cool manner of twenty-seven with experience. His name was Carlo.

"Twenty bucks you talked," Carlo said.

I gave him twenty dollars. He didn't sit down.

"Boyd Connors's mother says Boyd was murdered," I said. "What do you say?"

"What's it to you?"

"I'm working for Mrs. Connors. The police say heart attack."

"We heard," Carlo said. He relaxed a hair. "Boyd was a fucking bull. It don' figure. Only what angle the fuzz got? We don' make it."

"Was Boyd with you that night?"

"Early 'n late. He goes to see his girl. They had a battle, Boyd come around the candy store awhile."

"What time?"

"Maybe seven-thirty. He don' stay long. Goes home."

"Because he didn't feel good?"

"He feel okay far as we knows," Carlo said.

I saw the struggle on his face. His whole life, the experience learned over years when every day taught more than a month taught most kids, had conditioned him never to volunteer an answer without a direct question. But he had something to say, and as hard as he searched his mind for a trap, he couldn't find one. He decided to talk to me.

"Boyd, he got a package," Carlo finally said, tore it out of his thin mouth. "He took it on home.

"Stolen?"

"He says no. He says he found it. He had a big laugh on it. Says he found it on the sidewalk, 'n the guy lost it could rot in trouble."

That was when I remembered where I had seen the name of Johnson's Pharmacy.

"A package when he came home?" Mrs. Connors said. "Well, I'm not sure, Mr. Fortune. He could have had."

I went through the living room into Boyd Connors's bedroom. The wrapping paper was still in the wastebasket. Mrs. Connors was neglecting her housework with the grief over Boyd. A Johnson's Pharmacy label was on the wrapping paper, and a handwritten address: 3 East 11th Street. The small, empty box told me nothing.

I checked all the cologne, after-shave and hair-tonic bottles —the box was about the size for them. They were all at least half full and old. I thought of the empty bottle under the bed, and got it. A routine men's cologne—empty. It had no top. I searched harder, found the top all the way across the room in a corner, as if it had been thrown. It was a quick-twist top, one sharp turn and it came off. I saw a faint stain on the rug as if something had been spilled, but a cologne is mostly alcohol, dries fast.

I touched the bottle gingerly, studied it. There was something odd about it. Not to look at, no, more an impression, the *feel* of it. It felt different, heavier than the other bottles, and the cap seemed to be more solid. Only a shade of difference, something I'd never have thought about if I hadn't been looking for answers.

I could even be wrong. When you're ready to find something suspicious, your mind can play tricks. It can find what it wants to find.

I decided to talk to Roger Tatum again.

He was working over a book, writing notes, when I arrived.

"Not working at the store today? Fired, maybe?"

"I don't go to work until one P.M.," he said. "Why would I be fired?"

"You lost a package you were supposed to deliver last night, didn't you?"

He stared at me. "Yes, but how did you know? And you think Mr. Johnson would fire me for that? It wasn't worth ten dollars, Mr. Johnson didn't even make me pay. Just sent me back this morning with another bottle."

"Bottle of what?"

"Some men's cologne."

"When did you miss the package, notice that it was gone?"

"When I got to the address. I guess I just dropped it on the street somewhere."

"You dropped it," I said. "Did anything happen between the drugstore and Anna Kazco's place? Did you stop anywhere? Have an accident and drop the packages?"

"No. I went straight to Anna's place. I had all the packages when I left, I counted them."

71

"So you know you lost the package after you left Anna Kazco's apartment."

"Yes, I'm sure."

❧

My next stop was the Johnson Pharmacy on Fifth Avenue. Mr. Yvor Johnson was a tall, pale man. He blinked at me from behind his glasses and counter.

"The package Roger lost? I don't understand what your interest in it is, Mr. Fortune. A simple bottle of cologne."

"Who was it going to?"

"Mr. Chalmers Padgett, a regular customer. He always buys his sundries here."

"Who is he? What does he do?"

"Mr. Padgett? Well, I believe he's the president of a large chemical company."

"Who ordered the cologne?"

"Mr. Padgett himself. He called earlier that day."

"Who picked the cologne? Wrapped it?"

"I did myself. Just before Roger took it out."

I showed him the empty bottle and the cap. He took them, looked at them. He looked at me.

"It looks like the bottle. A standard item. We sell hundreds of such bottles."

"Is it the same bottle? You're sure? Feel it."

Johnson frowned, studied the bottle and the cap. He bent close over them, hefted the bottle, inspected the cap, hit the bottle lightly on his counter. He looked puzzled.

"That's strange. I'd almost say this bottle is a special glass, very strong. The cap, too. They seem the same, I'd not have noticed anything if you hadn't insisted, but now they do seem stronger."

"After you packed the cologne for Mr. Padgett, how long before Roger Tatum took out his deliveries?"

"Perhaps fifteen minutes."

"Was anyone else in the store?"

"I think there were a few customers."

"Did you and Roger ever leave the packages he was to deliver unwatched?"

"No, they are on the shelf back here until Roger takes them, and—" He stopped, blinked at me again. "Wait, yes. Roger took some trash out in back, and the man asked me if he could look at a vaporizer. I keep the bulky stock, like vaporizers, in the back. I went to get it. I was gone perhaps three minutes."

"The man? What man?"

"A big man, florid-faced. In a gray overcoat and gray hat. He didn't buy the vaporizer, I had to put it back. I was quite annoyed, I recall."

"Roger took the packages out right after that?"

"Yes, he did."

I stopped in the public library. Mr. Chalmers Padgett was president of P-S Chemical Corp. Not as large a company as Yvor Johnson had suggested, and Dun & Bradstreet didn't list exactly what the company produced.

Chalmers Padgett met me in his rich office down near Wall Street. He was a calm, pale man in a custom-made suit.

"Yes, Mr. Fortune, I ordered my usual cologne from Johnson a few days ago. Why?"

"Could anyone have known you ordered it?"

"I don't know, perhaps. I believe I called from the office here."

"Are you married?"

"I'm a widower. I live alone, if that's what you mean."

"What would you normally do when you got a new bottle of cologne?"

"Do?" He stared at me a moment as if wondering if I was a little crazy, or maybe a lot crazy, but when I continued to wait for an answer he thought for a time. "Well, I'd put it into my bathroom cabinet, I suppose, use it when my old bottle was empty. I—" Chalmers Padgett stopped, then smiled at me. "That's very odd. I mean, that you would ask that. As a matter of fact I have something of a reflex habit—I smell things. Wines, new cheeses, tobacco. I expect I'd have smelled the cologne almost at once. But you couldn't have known that. How did you—?"

"Who could have known that? About your habit?"

"Almost anyone who knows me. It's rather a joke."

"What does your company make, Mr. Padgett?"

His pale face closed up. "I'm sorry, much of our work is secret, for the government."

"Maybe Rauwolfia serpentina? Something like it?"

I had done some more research at the library. Chalmers Padgett looked at me now with alarm and a lot of suspicion.

I said, "Do you have a heart condition, Mr. Padgett? A serious condition? Could you die of a heart attack—easily?"

He was silent a moment. "Have you been investigating me, Mr. Fortune?"

"In a way," I said. "You *do* have a heart condition?"

"Yes. No danger if I'm careful, keep calm, but—"

"But if you died of a heart attack, no one would be surprised? No one would question it?"

Chalmers Padgett studied me. "One of our subsidiaries, very secret, does make some Rauwolfia serpentina, Mr. Fortune. For government use."

"Who would want you dead, Mr. Padgett?"

A half-hour later, Mr. Chalmers Padgett, Sergeant Hamm, and I stopped for the drugstore owner, Mr. Yvor Johnson.

Padgett rode in the back seat of the car with Sergeant Hamm and me.

"Rauwolfia serpentina," I said. "Did you ask the M.E.?"

"I asked," Sergeant Hamm said. "Related to some common tranquilizers. Developed as a nerve gas for warfare before we supposedly gave up that line of study. Spray it on the skin, breathe it, a man's dead in seconds. Depresses the central nervous system, stops the heart cold. Yeah, the M.E. told me about it. Says he never saw a case of its use, but he'd heard of cases. Seems it works almost instantly, and the autopsy will show nothing but a plain heart attack. A spy weapon, government assassins. No cop in New York ever heard of a case. Who can get any of it?"

"P-S Chemical has a subsidiary that makes some. A very secret subsidiary, right, Mr. Chalmers?"

Padgett nodded, watched the city pass outside the car windows. He was paler than ever.

I said, "Under pressure in a bottle, it spurts in the face of anyone who opens it to sniff. Dead of a heart attack. The bottle drops from the victim's hand, the pressure empties the bottle. No trace—unless you test the bottle very carefully, expertly."

"In my case," Chalmers Padgett said, "who would have tested the bottle at all? I die of a heart attack, there would be no thought of murder. Expected. I ordered the cologne, the bottle belonged in my apartment. No one would even have noticed the bottle."

We stopped at a Park Avenue apartment house and I went up to the tenth floor. The man who stood up in the elegant, sunken living room when the houseman led us into the apartment was big and florid-faced. Something happened to his arrogant eyes when he saw Chalmers Padgett.

"Yes," Mr. Johnson said, "that's the man who asked me to show him the vaporizer, who was alone in the store with the packages."

75

Chalmers Padgett said, "For some years we've disagreed on how to run our company. He won't sell his share to me, and he hasn't the cash to buy my share. He lives high. If I died, he would have the company, and a large survivor's insurance. He's the only one who would gain by my death. My partner, Samuel Seaver."

I said, "Executive vice-president of P-S Chemical. One of the few people who could get Rauwolfia serpentina."

The big man, Samuel Seaver, seemed to sway where he stood and stared only at Chalmers Padgett. His eyes showed fear, yes, but confusion too, and incredulity, utter disbelief.

He had planned a perfect murder. Chalmers Padgett's death would have been all but undetectable, no question of murder. No one would have noticed Seaver's lethal bottle, it *belonged* in Padgett's room. But Roger Tatum had dropped the package, Boyd Connors had taken it home and opened the bottle. Boyd Connors had no heart condition. Boyd Connors's mother did not believe the heart attack. The bottle had *not* belonged in Boyd Connors's room.

Sergeant Hamm began to recite, "Samuel Seaver, you're under arrest for the murder of Boyd Connors. It's my duty to advise you that—"

"Who?" the big man, Samuel Seaver, said. "Murder of who?"

The Motive

You never know what's going to solve a case, what you'll have to do, who's going to help you. Later, Lieutenant D'Amato admitted the cops would never have known the old man's motive without me and Alice Connors, but after a week I wouldn't have given myself much chance of doing any better than the police.

At the end of that first week I drank a cold Beck's in Alice Connors's Queens apartment and waited for her to come out of the bedroom. She'd appeared in my loft on a Monday night with Marian Dunn, sent by Jim Flood of Your Family Friend Loan Company in Queens. Alice worked at Family Friend, and I'd done skip-tracing for Flood. Marian Dunn had stared at my empty sleeve. Alice hadn't. I'd liked her right then.

"The police asked us over and over about Bruce and Mr. Dunn and the old man," she'd explained. "I just don't remember Bruce ever saying the name, or talking about any old man." There were tears in her eyes. "Why did he kill Bruce?"

Not a pretty girl, but you didn't notice that. You noticed the dark eyes, her vulnerability. Twenty-five, olive-skinned, shy, the nose too large. Well-groomed. Black hair in a wild cut that said there was a passion inside her she wanted to let out but that had been stopped by something or someone.

"The police don't know why they were murdered?" I said.

"That's what they say," Marian Dunn said. She was a big woman, soft and uncertain. The kind who whispers nervously to the children as she urges them along behind an irate husband. "My son says some lawyer'll get that old man off, say he's crazy or something." She shook her head in despair. "I've got four kids at home, Mr. Fortune, not much insurance. We never took a dime off nobody, except Paul's dad a couple of times. Now he's gone. Forty-two. Alice and Bruce was going to get married. Bruce was twenty-six. You find out why that old man killed our men."

I got what little they knew about the murders, took their retainer, went down after they'd gone and put it in the bank. All but forty bucks I blew on dinner and Beck's at Bogie's. With a nice glow and money in the bank I got a good night's sleep, rode the subway to Queens next morning.

Sam D'Amato was C.O. of the precinct detective squad. I'd worked with him a few times over the years, he knew me. He also knew Marian Dunn and Alice Connors.

"We'd like to know the motive too," he said. "We'd like to know almost anything."

"I thought you had the killer."

"The killer, yes. The motive, no." D'Amato glowered at his wall. "Looks like he never even met them before that night."

My missing arm began to ache. "How about the details?"

He tossed me a thin manila folder. The two victims had been working late at Steiner Nissan on Northern Boulevard. Paul Dunn was Service Manager, Bruce Henry a front-end man. Joseph Marsak walked into the salesroom and asked for Dunn and Henry by name. The salesmen sent Marsak back to the service desk in the garage, heard Marsak ask if they were Paul Dunn and Bruce Henry. Someone laughed, shots exploded, no time for an argument.

The old man walked out the side garage door. No one tried to stop him, no one could give a real description. The police were stymied. Then they found the gun in a yard a block away. A 9-mm Luger they traced in half a day. It had been issued to Joseph Marsak by the army forty-three years ago, never turned in. They found Marsak's address in the phone book. The witnesses all identified him.

"He said, yes, he shot them," D'Amato said, "and, yes, he'd come with us, and that was and is all he'd say or has said."

Marsak lived alone on Social Security and savings in a room in an apartment off Roosevelt Avenue. He'd been a history professor in California, retired to New York. He'd lived alone in California too. His naturalization said he had been born in Russia in 1906, he'd served in the U.S. Army in World War Two.

"Witnesses, ballistics, and a confession. Isn't that enough to put him away?"

"Sure," D'Amato said, "but where? Without a motive his lawyer grins all the way. Senility, insanity. Creedmoor tops, maybe as low as probation and psychiatric treatment."

"Can I talk to him?"

D'Amato made a call, and we drove into Manhattan in his squad car, parked at the Tombs, and went up to a modern interrogation room of the renovated jail. Marsak's lawyer was waiting for us, a tough-looking type in an expensive blue pin-stripe suit. The old man had someone on his side. I tried a direct approach.

"What business were you and Paul Dunn in, Mr. Marsak?"

The old man's head turned slowly to look at me like a tank turret traversing toward a target. His eyes were all but colorless.

"Must I speak to this man?"

He had never been tall, but he had probably been solid. Now he was skinny, almost emaciated. His neck emerged from his shirt without touching the collar, his face was pale, and his thin hair and full mustache were white. His hands were pallid and bony. They hung limp, without strength or

79

even interest. As if the years had washed more out of him than color.

"You don't have to talk to anyone," his lawyer said.

"No one murders without a reason," I said to the old man.

"He doesn't remember why he did it," the lawyer said. "He had no idea what he was doing."

"They were bad men," the old man said.

"Bad?" I said. "How?"

The old man said nothing. He had an accent. Slavic, yet something else too. A different accent mixed with the Slavic.

"Where else did you live besides Russia?" I asked.

"I have lived many places."

"Why do you carry a gun, Mr. Marsak?"

"I do not carry a gun."

"You had a gun that night."

"I have a gun since the war."

"And you took it to the Nissan agency to shoot Paul Dunn and Bruce Henry. No accident, not a matter of chance."

"I kill the enemy," the old man said.

The lawyer rubbed his hands happily. "Crazy as a loon."

I said, "Paul Dunn and Bruce Henry were your enemies?"

"They are the enemy."

The lawyer was almost dancing, but I didn't think the old man was crazy. He spoke in a firm, calm voice. Literally, the words sounded paranoid at least, but I didn't think Marsak was being literal. He was telling the truth, but not the facts.

Outside, the lawyer laughed. "Not even an indictment."

D'Amato didn't contradict him as he left, still grinning.

"Who's paying the lawyer?"

"Marsak's old army buddies."

It was late afternoon when I came out of the Tombs, headed uptown for my loft/office. Four potential clients had left messages on my answering machine. None panned out. I went to Bogie's for some beers and thought about why an eighty-year-old man would kill two total strangers.

In the morning I rode the subway out to Queens and the loan company. *Tired of bank red tape? No house to mortgage? Own a car? Come to your Family Friend and walk out with cash.* Alice Connors was going to lunch.

"Bruce took me to lunch twice a week," she said. "That's the kind of man he was. Now—" She wiped at her eyes.

"Want to talk at lunch?"

In the Peking Restaurant I had *moo shu* pork. She ordered *kung pao* chicken.

"How long had you known Henry?"

"You make him sound like a stranger." She sipped tea. "He was the nicest man I ever met. He took me into New York. We had fun. Before I met Bruce I lived with my folks. I got my apartment so we could be together. Now I'm alone in it."

That was when I heard the shadow in her voice. Something held back inside her besides the passion. Something she didn't want to tell me, maybe didn't want to tell herself.

"Why couldn't you be together where Bruce lived?"

"His mother was old and sick, so he lived with her."

"Was?"

She nodded. "His mother died four months ago. That's when Bruce asked me to marry him. It was going to be in August."

She broke then. I let her cry. I guessed that Bruce Henry had been the first man to pay any attention to her beyond trying to get her into bed on the first, and probably last, date.

"How long have you worked at the loan company?"

"Six years, nearly seven."

Her first job after high school, and she still had it. Ninety percent of young girls from Queens work in offices in Manhattan. More money and more men. Local jobs went to older women who'd tried Manhattan and given up. An unconfident girl, lonely now, and a little lost.

"How long *had* you known him, Alice?" I asked.

"Two years. Two wonderful years."

81

There was defiance in her voice and eyes. Something about those two years had not been wonderful.

When I took her back to her office I watched her run in. Seven years and she still rushed back to work scared. Not the kind of woman who married the kind of man who got murdered. Either she was a different woman than she seemed, or Bruce Henry had been a different man than she said.

I took her for drinks after work all the next week while I got nowhere on the killings. Tonight we'd gone to dinner. Now I waited for her to get comfortable. When she came out of the bedroom she wore a purple robe zipped up to her throat. "You've never told me how you lost your arm," she said.

She sat on the small couch of the neat little living room and tried to smile at me. She was being bold, her bare foot out from under the robe. Her eyes were up and watching me, and I saw her nakedness in them, her awareness of her naked body under the robe.

"I was seventeen," I told her. "We were looting a ship. I fell into a hold, crushed the arm. Except for that I'd have joined the gangs and be dead by now. Instead I got away, saw the real world. When I came back to Chelsea I wanted to do more than be a big wheel in the world as it was."

I was talking too much. It was the bare foot beneath the hem of the robe, her dark eyes trying to be bold. As if she had to answer some question about me, or about herself.

"After Henry's mother died, where did he live?"

"He got an apartment near where he worked. He'd become a full mechanic for Mr. Dunn. He could afford his own place."

She was evading what I was asking.

"Why didn't he move in here, Alice?"

"We weren't married yet."

She looked at the floor and I saw that shadow inside her. "You never slept with him, did you?"

She sat there, her toes protruding from under the long robe. I waited. She would tell me in her own time. I drank my beer and thought about her and Bruce Henry and Paul Dunn and his nervous wife and all I hadn't found in a week of hard footwork.

❧

I'd started at Steiner Nissan. It was the usual showroom where salesmen hovered like gigolos meeting the tourist train in Venice. The garage for shining up trade-ins and fixing lemons was in back. The sales manager talked about Joseph Marsak.

"He wasn't any customer. We all compared notes."

"Were Dunn and Henry working on anything unusual?"

"Routine all the way. The cops checked every work ticket the last three years. *Nada.*"

"Could they have been operating a sideline?"

The manager licked his lips, his eyes bright. "You mean maybe crooked? Illegal? Dope or something?"

"Maybe moonlighting. Working on stolen cars?"

He shook his head. "Paul hated anything illegal or immoral except one thing, right?" He gave me the fraternal wink.

Was jealousy a motive for an eighty-year-old man who lived alone? I know at least two octogenarians who married women half their age, and they aren't sleeping in twin beds.

"Is there anywhere the two victims hung out?"

"Over in Ryan's every lunch hour and after work."

"What about weekends?"

The manager shook his head again. "Paul moved out to Little Neck, I don't know anything about what the hell Bruce did."

Across the street, Ryan's was a neighborhood saloon with a

kitchen, an old shuffleboard along the right wall, and booths
in the rear. At eleven-thirty only a few morning regulars were
in—the kind who would be there for closing at a far-off two
A.M., had learned to pace themselves. The bartenders were
glad to see me. I had a Beck's, asked about Dunn and Henry.

"Ain't safe nowhere today," one barman said. "If Arabs
don't hijack a ocean ship, some old nut walks up and plugs
you right on the goddamn job."

Neither of them knew Joseph Marsak, neither had noticed
Dunn or Henry meet anyone, buy or sell anything.

"Paul got in plenty of arguments," one said. "He didn't
take shit from no one, liked the women, but that's all."

"What did his wife think of his interest in women?"

"Wouldn't of worried Paul. He used to say a man brought
in the dough, did what the hell he wanted."

"Bruce too?"

The bartender snorted. "Talked big, but never saw him
make a move. Tagged along after Paul."

"Either of them have any particular woman in here?"

The bartender hemmed and hawed, but finally admitted
that Paul Dunn and Grace Callas had been chummy. He gave
me an address in Jackson Heights. I got a taxi.

It turned out to be the top half of a semidetached on a
shaded block of maples and oaks. There was no answer to my
rings and knocks.

I went to meet Alice Connors and take her to lunch.

After lunch I walked to the apartment house where Joseph
Marsak lived, climbed to his second-floor rear apartment.
There were voices inside. I knocked and a square little man
opened the door. He said he was Joseph Marsak's landlord.

"My wife died, I got too many rooms and no one to talk to
so I sublet. Marsak been here five years. So he's moody, who
ain't got trouble, right?"

"Moody about what?" I said.

"Who knows? Maybe something out in California, maybe a

long time ago. He's too damned quiet. Sometimes I think he ain't home, I go into his room and there he is sittin' in the dark."

Marsak had no visitors the whole five years, didn't even have a telephone in his room, went out to a movie, to eat, to the library and maybe the cleaners. Laundromat once a week like everyone else. Only everyone doesn't take a gun and calmly shoot down two men who seemed to be total strangers.

"You want to see his room like the cops done?"

The single room was bare and spartan, except for a large modern stereo. Shelves were filled with records, tapes and compact disks, the bookcase was crammed with books in many languages. Above the bookcase were framed photographs of a family on a picnic; in a boat on some lake with mountains and pines; on the streets of an old city with stone buildings and cobblestones; in front of a country house with white walls and dark beams and a thatched roof. Two adults, two girls, and a boy. The woman was in her mid-twenties, dark-haired. The man was short, stocky and mature. The photos were old. The man could have been a young Joseph Marsak.

When I left, the landlord was hunched in front of his television set talking to it. "Watch that guy!"

I left him with his video friends, checked with D'Amato who had nothing, tried Grace Callas again with no luck, and gave up for the day. In my office I had a call from a lawyer with a client, wasted the next morning in the lawyer's office waiting for the client who never showed. I got back to Queens that afternoon. Rock music played inside Grace Callas's apartment. I knocked. A curtain moved.

"Don't you cops get tired? I said I don't know nothing about Paul's damn business." The music went up louder.

I shouted, "I'm a private detective hired by Dunn's wife."

The music stopped. The door flung open.

"Don't go trying to hang anything on me! I didn't know he was married."

"Sure you did," I smiled, "but that's your business. All I'm interested in is why the old man killed him."

She looked me over. A big woman. Paul Dunn had liked big women. Grace Callas was as tall as Mrs. Dunn, but there the resemblance ended. Callas was angular and athletic. The kind who would stride out, head high and hair in the wind.

"Want a manhattan?"

She'd been lying on the couch, all the curtains and shades drawn, drinking manhattans and listening to the stereo.

"Too early for me," I said.

"I work nights. I hate to drink alone."

"Why do it then?"

"I do a lot of things I hate. At least the drinking alone gets better the more you drink."

"You have a beer?"

"Does the Mayor like his picture taken?"

She brought a can of Coors, lay down on the couch again, sipped her manhattan. I sat in an armchair with my beer.

"Did Paul Dunn like to drink in the afternoon?"

"He liked to screw in the afternoon." She drank. "No, that ain't right. He liked to walk out of Ryan's to screw in the afternoon. He liked to leave his buddies to go and screw in the afternoon. He liked to haul me to his car to go and screw in the afternoon."

"If he was like that, why pick him?"

"You seen the other guys in Ryan's?"

"Why do it at all?"

"Why do I get up in the morning?"

"I don't know. Why?"

"I don't know either."

She went to make another manhattan. I drank my beer. When she returned I asked her about Joseph Marsak, but she'd never heard of him. Paul Dunn didn't come there to talk, and if he did it was all about his service empire at Nissan. She didn't know of any sidelines, but wouldn't have put anything past Dunn.

"He was starting to be a pain," she said. "I was just to show his buddies what a big man he was. Time I had a new guy." She nodded to my beer.

"No more for me." I didn't want to take Paul Dunn's place.

"Suit yourself." She looked at my empty sleeve. "It might've been fun."

I left her thinking about all the fun we might have had, and found Alice Connors again. She knew nothing about Grace Callas, Bruce Henry had never mentioned her. She was shocked to think of Paul Dunn like that, begged me not to tell Marian Dunn.

Now, a few days later on a hot Queens night, Alice Connors sat in her living room, looked down at her bare toes visible under the hem of the purple robe as she talked about Bruce Henry.

"He wanted us to wait until we were married. He was like that. His mother was real narrow, hated any girl he took out."

"So you never . . . ?"

"No." She reddened, smoothed the purple robe over her lap. "At first I . . . I was scared. I fixed it so we never had a real chance. Then I wanted to, got this place. My father was mad, but I didn't care. Then Bruce said we should wait. He had too much respect for me to do anything before we were married."

Men like that could be on the increase again with the sexual backlash, but the Bruce Henry who drank at Ryan's didn't sound like he respected women any more than Paul Dunn.

"He said he wanted our marriage to be the most important

moment in our lives." She looked up at me. "I didn't want to wait. He said I was only saying that because I thought he needed sex but he didn't. He got that apartment and would never let me go there. Then he started taking me home early, saying goodnight downstairs, showing up late for dates, even breaking them sometimes. Was there another girl, Dan? Is that why he was killed?"

"Paul Dunn had a woman, but . . ."

She wasn't listening to me. Her dark eyes were large and wide and fixed toward me. "What's wrong with me, Dan?"

"There's nothing wrong with you."

She sat and stared at me in the living room above the quiet Queens street in the warm night. Then she stood and walked toward the bedroom, her bare feet showing under the robe at each step. She looked back, the need in her eyes. I followed her. There was nothing wrong with either of us once she dropped the robe in the dark bedroom.

Afterwards she went to sleep curled close to me as if she needed a mother more than a lover. I didn't go to sleep. It was too early for my sleep clock, and I didn't need a mother. I lit a cigarette, thought about the rest of my long week.

The day after I had gone to Marsak's apartment and talked to Grace Callas, I had to testify in an old case, didn't get the LIRR out to Little Neck until afternoon. Marian Dunn lived in a big, shabby frame house. A teenage girl answered the door, stared at my missing arm.

"Yuk, I hate cripples."

I leaned down close to her face. "Honey, tell your mother Dan Fortune's here or I'll spank you with my stump."

There are those who think the maimed, the sick, and the poor aren't really human, not people the way they are. Most of us have it civilized out of us before we're the age of Paul Dunn's teenager. Kids tell you a lot about their parents.

"Mr. Fortune?" Marian Dunn dried her large hands on an apron. "Did you find out why . . . why . . . ?" Her hands fluttered helplessly without a husband.

"Not yet, Mrs. Dunn. Can we talk about your husband?"

Her face collapsed, she sat down on a chair in the entrance hall. "Paul was a good man, Mr. Fortune. Made good money, never missed work, didn't drink too much or gamble. Nice to the girls, always taking the boys fishing, bowling. He worked ten, twelve hours a day, six days a week. Service manager before he was forty. Brought us out here after the blacks started moving into the old neighborhood. A good husband, Mr. Fortune. Now—"

"Did you know about Grace Callas, Mrs. Dunn?"

She sat for a time, then stood and walked into a large run-down living room. The girl who hated cripples sat watching TV with a stocky youth in Marine green and a younger boy. Marian Dunn spoke low to the Marine.

"Okay, out," the Marine ordered. "Me 'n Ma got business."

The kids looked at me with directionless anger. Marian Dunn smiled at the Marine, grateful for his taking charge. She sat on the seedy couch. The Marine stood.

"They know why that old man killed my dad?" the young Marine said. "I get him he hangs by his bare balls."

"Don't swear, Paulie," Mrs. Dunn said. "Your dad never—"

"I'm getting a different picture of his dad, Mrs. Dunn. A man who did what he wanted when he wanted."

"A real man, my dad," the Marine grinned.

Marian Dunn reddened. She knew all about Paul Dunn's women. She would probably say that made him a real man too.

"That old kike gunned him without no warning," the Marine said.

89

"What about Bruce Henry?" I asked Marian Dunn. "Did he have a woman on the side too?"

"I don't know," she said. It didn't surprise her that Henry, about to marry Alice Connors, might have had other women. I was getting a clearer picture of life with Paul Dunn. "He was a good husband, Mr. Fortune, he—"

"I know," I said. "Hardly drank at all, didn't gamble, paid the bills. Nice to the girls, a pal to the boys. But he was late to dinner a lot, took long lunch hours in Ryan's."

The voice came from the open archway, low and angry. It was an older girl I hadn't seen before.

"Tell him the truth, Ma. Tell him Grace Callas wasn't the only one. Tell him about Joey."

Marian Dunn said, "Your father never lied, Agnes. Some men got to be that way."

"He drove Joey from the house. His own son."

"Joey's a fucking fag," the Marine, Paul Jr., said.

"Joey's a gentle boy who hated everything Dad stood for the same as I do." The girl crouched in front of her mother. "Ma, he's gone. You should thank that old man. We all should."

The Marine moved as if to hit the girl. I caught his wrist. Under the uniform he was still a boy, and I've got a lot more strength in my one arm than most people expect. The Marine was pale, unable to break free without using both hands and that wouldn't be manly.

"Mr. Fortune, stop!" Marian Dunn said.

I let the boy go.

"Paul was a good husband, Mr. Fortune. The children are too young to know, and other people are all fools and atheists."

I got the next LIRR train back to Woodside, but Alice Connors had her dance class, so I made a date for dinner the next day and walked to the apartment house where Joseph Marsak lived.

"So?" the landlord said. "The cops was here again too. You still got no answers?"

"I haven't even got questions," I said. "You said he was a man with trouble. Money? A woman? Old? New?"

The square little man thought. "The kind of trouble you got it so long it's part of you like your skin."

"But he acted like everyone else?"

"Just an old man lives alone."

"Was there anything about him not like everyone else?"

The landlord shrugged. "That crazy modern music he listened to, I guess. Maybe that girl downstairs."

"Girl downstairs?"

"A nutty kid plays her guitar too loud, got a whole rock band down there. Her and two other girls in the garden apartment. Sit out in the yard in those bikinis they should be naked it wouldn't be no different. Marsak'd sit in his window and watch her down in the yard and talk to her."

I described Paul Dunn and Bruce Henry, asked if he'd seen them with the girls. He hadn't.

"What's the name of the girl downstairs?"

"Janice Stevens."

I went down to the apartment below. Janice Stevens wasn't home, but a roommate was.

"Jan? Murder? God, come on in." She talked all along the hall. "I'm Madge. You got the wrong person. Jan wouldn't hurt a fly. She's the kind that takes in stray kittens, you know?" In a small kitchen she worked over a pie, put on a layer of walnuts. "You like walnut pie? I die over it. Who got murdered?"

I told her who had been murdered, described Dunn and Henry.

"Never heard of them. No one like that ever around Jan."

"How about Joseph Marsak? Have you heard of him?"

She stopped laying walnuts on the pie. "You mean the old guy upstairs? What's he got to do with anything?"

"He killed Paul Dunn and Bruce Henry."

"That old guy? You're crazy! Why would he kill anyone?"

"That's what we don't know, Madge," I said. "What's his relationship with Jan Stevens?"

"Well . . ." She frowned even more, suddenly wary for her friend. "The old guy sits in his window and watches Jan practice guitar in the yard and they talk. Sometimes he shows up when we do a gig, watches us, buys us drinks on breaks. He just likes Jan, I guess. I mean, he even likes our music, you know?"

I got nothing more. It was time then for my dinner date with Alice Connors. A date I hoped would be more than dinner.

It turned out to be a lot more than dinner, and, when she woke up again around 2:00 A.M., maybe more than I could handle for long. At my age she was a little frightening. This time she didn't go to sleep afterward. We talked.

"Did Bruce ever mention a Janice Stevens?"

"No. Was that the other girl he had?"

"Maybe."

"I hate him! For her and for all the time I wasted!"

She was more than ready to go on making up for the lost time, but I had the case on my mind and she had to work tomorrow, so we both eventually went to sleep.

I was still thinking about Janice Stevens when I woke at seven. I slipped out of bed, dressed, and went out for some breakfast. Over three cups of coffee, I thought about what else had changed in Bruce Henry's life in the last four months —he'd been promoted to full mechanic for Paul Dunn, a man who liked to impress barflies by shacking up in the afternoon. Could Marsak, and Dunn or Henry or both, all have been after Janice Stevens?

I walked to the saloon across from Steiner Nissan, Ryan's. The bartenders had never heard of Janice Stevens, had never seen Dunn or Henry with a young girl. At Steiner Nissan I got a different answer.

"Sure," the sales manager said, "she worked here a couple of months. Switchboard girl. Big boss let her go two weeks ago. Made too many mistakes, always playin' that damn big portable tape deck."

"She worked with Paul Dunn and Bruce Henry?"

"Hell no, the kid was strictly front office."

I headed for the old apartment house off Roosevelt Avenue. Janice Stevens had worked in the same place as Dunn and Henry, had lived in the same place as Joseph Marsak.

A tall girl with intelligent eyes opened the door of the apartment below Joseph Marsak's this time. She stood with a hand on her hip. It was a nice hip in black tights, white Cossack style shirt, and low white boots. I told her who I was.

"Want to talk about Joseph Marsak?"

She walked into a living room jammed with electric guitars, amplifiers, an electronic keyboard, a drum set, microphones, and a four-track tape recorder. Wires curled in a maze on the floor. There were two open suitcases and some empty stereo boxes.

"Going somewhere?"

She shrugged. "It's go home or starve."

"Why'd you get fired?"

"How the hell should I know!" Her dark eyes raged at me. "I was good at that job. They never even warned me!"

"Anything to do with Paul Dunn or Bruce Henry?"

"I didn't even know them."

"But you know Joseph Marsak."

Her face became sad. "I don't know why he shot them. I couldn't believe it. He's such a nice old man."

"How well do you know him, Janice?"

She gave me a cold, disgusted stare I guessed she used often on eager young men. A stare of contempt that sent them slinking away. I don't slink that easily.

"Don't try to tell me it didn't cross your mind."

She sat down. "All right, I wondered at first. He was so damned nice, so interested in all of us. Then he seemed to fix on me. He'd sit up there at his window and watch us practice. He came to our gigs, bought us drinks. But he never made a pass, and I know from passes, believe me."

"You never went out with him? Nothing ever happened?"

"Never and nothing."

"And you didn't do anything with Paul Dunn or Bruce Henry? They didn't make passes, try to make dates?"

"They never talked to me, for God's sake! I barely knew who Dunn was, and I didn't know what Henry looked like!"

"What happened the day you were fired?"

She shrugged. "I finished work on Friday night. The boss told me not to come in Monday, I was through."

"What did you do?"

"Went out and got drunk. What would you do?"

"Was Marsak around when you got drunk?"

"Not that I know."

"He killed two men who worked where you did. There was no reason for him to kill them. Then why did he?"

"How should I know? What do I know about him or them?"

I left her looking glumly at her instruments, cabbed to the Woodside LIRR station and rode out to Little Neck. Marian Dunn was at home alone, had never heard of Janice Stevens. Paul Dunn had hated rock music. I rode the empty noontime train back to Grace Callas. She wasn't alone, let me know I'd missed my chance, knew nothing of Janice Stevens, and the two men were waiting below her stairs. In coats and hats. One of them had a gun, the other got my lone arm and hustled me behind a garage.

"We want you to leave Joe Marsak alone."

CRIME, PUNISHMENT AND RESURRECTION

"Let the police and the lawyers take care of it, Fortune."

They knew what they were doing, but they breathed too hard, and their moves were stiff, out of practice. Their speech was too good for hoods, and I saw gray hair under the hats.

I said, "You're the old soldiers who hired his lawyer."

"He was a damned hero, let him alone. You hear?"

"Let the lawyer work, Fortune. We won't kill you, but we'll put you in the hospital."

They left, a car drove away. I went to talk to D'Amato. He was out. It was five when he got back, looking as tired as I felt. I told him about Janice Stevens and the old soldiers.

"No girl like that shows up around Henry or Dunn. An old man sits in a window and ogles a young girl. Where's a motive?"

"Unless he did more than ogle, and she's lying about Dunn or Henry," I said. "What about the old soldiers?"

"He was a hero. OSS behind the lines with Soviet partisans. They say they don't know why he shot those two, but it had to be a war flashback. The lawyer loves them as witnesses."

I left. Last night had been nice, Alice Connors expected me back, but it had been a short night and a long day, so I took the subway home. I'd call Alice, tell her I got too involved, make it up to her tomorrow. I should have known better.

She'd waited a long time to break out, was waiting on the stairs in front of my door. We went inside. She had her clothes off before I locked the door.

A lot later I told her about talking to Janice Stevens and Marian Dunn and Lieutenant D'Amato. Suddenly she started to cry, her whole body shaking with a kind of grief.

"What happened to him, Dan? He was so gentle, so attentive. Then his mother died, he got that apartment and he was horrible!"

"Horrible?"

She nodded, hiding her tears by leaning close to me. "I didn't want to tell you. You'd laugh at me, think I was just another neurotic female." Her face was against my good shoulder. "One night a month ago he got real drunk and started acting like waiting was all my idea, he was tired of my little girl crap. He scared me so I said no. He threw me on the floor and I thought he was going to rape me but he was so drunk he couldn't do anything. I got into the bedroom, locked the door, and heard him staggering around half the night. In the morning he was gone and didn't call for three days." In the dark of my loft with the early morning sounds of Eighth Avenue outside I sensed the start of a picture of what had happened to Bruce Henry. "He called me less and less. He'd say he'd call, but he didn't. Almost like he wanted to see me, but after that night when he tried to rape me he couldn't."

She pressed tight against me. I said, "His mother died and he got an apartment. He went to work under Paul Dunn, started hanging around with Dunn, drinking with Dunn." I had half an answer, but where was the other half? "Alice, did Bruce talk about a switchboard girl who got fired at Steiner Nissan?"

"No." In the dark beside me she moved closer. "Mr. Dunn was trying to fire a man who wouldn't take orders, but nothing about a girl. Bruce was going to get the man's job, but someone warned the man and ruined it. Mr. Dunn was furious, was going to get even with whoever told."

Joseph Marsak had murdered two men he didn't know. The enemy. Not "enemies," but "the enemy." And in my mind I saw the photographs on the wall of Joseph Marsak's room.

He was a big, grizzled black with the years of working on greasy engines ground into his large hands. His name was Walter Davis, and he sat in Ryan's with his back to the bar.

"Yeah, they was out to get me. I knows too much 'bout cars I gonna let Dunn tell me how I gotta work."

"Could he have gotten you fired?"

"He was working on it. I was drinking too much. He could get younger guys as good. I was bad for morale. All that shit."

"But you were warned and didn't get fired."

He grinned. "I'm at Steiner twenty years longer'n Dunn. I tol' the boss I wasn't doin' nothin' 'cept not let Dunn push me around, wasn't drinkin' no more'n ever, was the best mechanic in town an' Honda wanted me he didn't. That always gets 'em."

"Janice Stevens warned you."

"Nice kid, likes things clean an' fair. She heard Dunn and Henry talkin' on the phone 'bout me. She heard Dunn tell Henry he'd get my job. They laughed about it, so she told me."

"And got fired for it."

"I talked to the big boss all that next Monday. He said it wasn't my business, Dunn and Henry had nothin' to do with it. She just wasn't no good at the job, listened to music all day."

"What do you think?"

"They got her for sure. The boss threw her to them to make up for keepin' me. Can't prove it, really lose my job I try."

"Yeah," I said.

Janice Stevens was at her apartment with her two roommates. They were finishing her packing, none of them looked happy.

"Tell me the real story of the night you got fired."

She turned away. "My dad's coming in ten minutes. The new roommate's coming. I don't feel like talking, okay?"

"Not okay. You left too much out. You know why Marsak killed those two men."

The blonde, Madge, said, "Hey, you're crazy."

"Leave her alone," the other roommate said.

I said, "Start with that Friday night, with what Marsak heard when he sat up in the window."

After a time, Janice Stevens started to talk in a low voice. "The big boss gave me my check, told me not to come back on Monday." Then she was crying. "I needed that job. I was only there two months, I'd spent all the money on the apartment and paying the agency fee and making payments on my guitar. If I lost that job I'd have to go home. I begged him not to fire me. I asked him what I'd done wrong? He said I wasn't fast enough, I didn't have enough experience, all that bullshit and none of it meant anything but I was fired and he wouldn't even tell me why!"

She raged and cried, paced the living room, smashed one hand into the other. She was going through that night again, the pain and the defeat. Her first job, her first apartment, her first break from parents who told her she couldn't survive on her own. She had done it in spite of them. Had come to New York, gotten a job, joined a band, had an apartment. Then, in an instant it was gone. The loss of her dreams, the loss of everything.

She wiped at her tears. "I just sat there in the office on the floor. I couldn't stop crying. I wanted to smash the boss, smash everything, but all I could do was sit on the floor and cry. Then I heard them."

The doorbell rang. A roommate opened the door. A girl came in, and behind her a graying man in a suit. The new roomer and Janice Stevens's father. Janice didn't look at either of them.

"They were just outside the office in the garage. Dunn and Henry. They were laughing. Laughing and smirking. Laughing at me! They saw me crying and they just laughed and laughed and I got up and ran out and ran all the way here. I knew why I was fired. They'd lied to the boss, told some story, gotten me fired, and then they'd laughed at me."

She started to cry again. The roommates looked at her in silence. The new roomer looked like she wanted to cry too. The father looked uncomfortable.

"You came home," I said, "went out in the backyard to cry and tell your roommates exactly the way you've just told me. All about why you were fired and how they laughed at you when you cried. And Joseph Marsak sat up in his window and heard it all."

She wiped her face. "I don't know why he did it, but I knew he'd tried to help me, and I didn't want anyone to hurt him."

She was the kind who took in stray cats, pulled thorns from the feet of battered dogs. She'd tried to help a black mechanic and had her world destroyed for it, and when she knew what Joseph Marsak had done she had tried to protect him by saying nothing.

"We better talk to the police," I said.

"I hated them," she said. "I liked the old man. I was glad they were dead, and I didn't want him hurt."

"I know," I said.

"I wanted to kill them myself, crush them, blow them away! Blow all the mean, laughing goons away!"

"It's in all of us," I said, "but we fight it. That's what civilization is supposed to be."

Her father said, "I'll drive you to the police."

At the precinct, D'Amato listened to her story with a dazed look on his face. He looked at me.

"Marsak shot them because they got a girl fired? A girl he barely knew? I mean, a girl young enough to be his granddaughter who lived downstairs and was lively? Christ, he is nuts."

"Not because they got her fired," I said. "Because they laughed. Because they watched her suffer and laughed."

D'Amato was silent.

"You remember the accent he has, the accent that isn't

Russian? It's probably German. You remember he said he lived in many places in Europe? How those soldiers told us he worked behind the Nazi lines in World War Two?"

D'Amato said, "Paul Dunn was just born then. Henry's *father* was a kid."

"You remember the pictures on his wall? The family before the war? How he's lived alone ever since the war?"

D'Amato drove us down to the Tombs, took me and Janice Stevens into the interrogation room. They brought Marsak in a few minutes later. When he saw Janice Stevens he stopped, then he sat down. He looked at me.

"You are a good detective."

D'Amato said, "Can we see your arm, Mr. Marsak?"

He shrugged. "There is only a small scar. They removed the tattoo in the OSS, it would have been too obvious."

I said, "Your family?"

"My wife and son. My two daughters. I escaped, they did not. I watched the Nazis laugh while my wife died, while my son died, while my two daughters died. They killed them and they laughed. Those two laughed at the pain of Janice, at her suffering. I have heard those laughs all my life. I took my pistol and went there. They laughed at me too. I shot them."

D'Amato was pale. "You didn't even know them. Dunn had a wife, a family. Henry was going to get married."

"I know them," the old man said. "Family men, dog lovers, beer drinkers, but they are who make Auschwitz possible. They build Auschwitz, they staff it, they permit it. Leaders cannot exist without followers. They are the enemy."

"They could be changed, Mr. Marsak," D'Amato said.

"I saw their eyes. I know those eyes. They do not change. I am an old man, I do not matter. They must be stopped."

I got up and walked out. I lit a cigarette and was smoking when D'Amato and Janice Stevens joined me. D'Amato was still pale. Janice went to her father.

"I'll be back, Mr. Fortune. They won't beat me."

She would be. D'Amato watched them go.

"The D.A.'ll faint," he said. "The Mayor'll run screaming. It'll make that subway vigilante mess look like a cakewalk."

He was stalling before he went to tell the D.A. he would have to prosecute an eighty-year-old man who had lost his whole family in the Holocaust, risked his life against the Nazis, and killed two men he didn't know because they had laughed at the pain of a girl. I only had to report to my clients, but I needed some beers before I went out to Little Neck.

The Marine opened the Dunns' door. "Get lost."

"A chip off the old block. Call your mother."

He turned red, but he was still a boy, uncertain. He'd grow up, and then he'd be certain.

"The cops called," he said sullenly. "She's in church."

He slammed the door in my face. The church was three blocks away. Marian Dunn was kneeling at a small shrine with a hundred burning candles. She'd been crying again.

"That old man killed my Paul for nothing. He wasn't the best husband, he wasn't even such a good man, but he was my lawful husband, and a woman should love her husband."

She started to pray for Paul Dunn, and Bruce Henry, and Joseph Marsak, and her daughter, and even for me. She prayed for forgiveness for thinking bad thoughts about her lawful husband.

I rode back to Woodside. Alice Connors wasn't home. I went to my loft. She was there waiting for me. She cried a little for Bruce Henry, but mostly for Joseph Marsak, and then we made love in the late afternoon. Later we talked.

"What will happen to him, Dan?"

"A lot of loud talk about law and justice. Then declare it delayed psychotic trauma and put him in a mental hospital. It's probably the right answer, even the truth."

We had a good month. Then she got a better job in Manhattan, met a younger man with two arms and flew off to the Bahamas. She would always be grateful for what I'd done. She was just starting in life, and, thanks to me, she knew she was going to be okay. She even kissed me goodbye.

The Woman Who Ruined John Ireland

"Someone tried to shoot me," Isabelle Kucera said. "Isn't it wonderful?"

Isabelle is a file clerk in a midtown office where everyone sits in front of a CRT screen all day and feeds a computer. She works nine to five and half a day on Saturday. This was a Saturday, we were in my one-room loft overlooking Eighth Avenue, and she had come to hire me.

"No one ever tried to *shoot* me before!" she said happily. "I know it's Grace Kelly, Danny. Grace Kelly never lets John Ireland go."

Isabelle is also a thousand old movies walking around. Like a lot of slum kids left alone in a six-flight walk-up while her mother worked, Isabelle grew up in front of a television set. Later she branched out into the rerun movie houses in Chelsea and the Village. Only she doesn't leave the movies inside the TV set or the rerun house. She lives them.

"He's a hired killer, like Alan Ladd," Isabelle said, her eyes shining. "Grace Kelly hired him to kill me, and you can track him down, Danny, just like Elliott Gould."

Once, after a movie in which Ingrid Bergman was a noble

nun in China, Isabelle tried to join a missionary order. The nuns were nice about it. When she was thirteen, the city sent her to summer camp. She had to be dragged to her seat on the bus. She was Bonita Granville being sent off to a Nazi concentration camp. Now that she's twenty-six, blonde, and beautiful, she's the woman who ruins John Ireland.

"This time I know it's going to work out, Danny," she glowed. "Pauli really is John Ireland."

She doesn't mean the real John Ireland, she means the roles he plays. Not in the big movies like *Red River* or *All the King's Men*, where Ireland was as good an actor as anyone who ever stood in front of a camera, but the smaller ones. The movies where Ireland is the ex-air force officer who joins a gang of bank robbers to get money for *her*. The hitchhiker *she* picks up and seduces into murdering her husband. The ex-con going straight who is dragged back into crime so *she* can have what she wants. The gas station attendant *she* needs to drive the getaway car.

"Who," I said, "is Pauli?"

"You know," she pouted. "Paul Bambara. The manager down at the Discount Bookstore on Sixth Avenue? He's a dream."

"Tall?" I remembered. "Kind of skinny? Dark hair? Looks like he needs sleep?"

"That's him. So pale and in pain, Danny. He suffers so much. We're going to run off to Mexico. Pauli's going to do what he really wants, make things with his hands. Statues and everything. He's just bursting to be free, Danny. The wife never lets Ireland be free."

The woman who ruins John Ireland, destroys him in the end, is Gloria Grahame. For Ireland to run into Grahame in a movie is to be ruined every time. She also ruins Dick Powell the honest private eye, Robert Mitchum the dedicated young doctor, and Broderick Crawford the husband desperate to hold her.

"How long has this been going on, Isabelle?"

"Almost a whole month! He's so sensitive, Danny. He's so unhappy in that store, so unhappy with his wife. I'm going to give him a whole new life."

Because, of course, Isabelle *is* Gloria Grahame. When Grahame died tragically young some years ago, Isabelle found her best role. She looks enough like Grahame, adds the rest in as fine an acting job as the real GG ever gave. She has the wet pout, the narrow shoulders hunched as if always cold, the thin hand curved to fit the stem of a martini glass. The sleepy eyes that are naked and hooded at the same time. The limp pipestem wrists and dangling cigarette. The slender body and lazy drawl that hides the tiger.

Isabelle lives the role from her clothes to her manner and her men, hanging around with half the gamblers, drug dealers and con men in Little Italy and the Village. Only they're not really important to her. They can't be John Irelands.

"I know it's the real thing this time," Isabelle said, glowing. "Especially now."

A headache began at the back of my eyes. Isabelle's fantasies have a way of causing headaches.

"Did you happen to see who shot at you, Isabelle?"

"Well, I'm not sure, but there was this big guy in a raincoat and hat with a kind of limp, just like Robert Ryan."

I felt as if my brain were floating in some late-late show haze. With Isabelle, your reality can begin to blur.

"Grace Kelly got to have hired Ryan, Danny," Isabelle said.

"You mean Paul Bambara's wife, Isabelle?" I had a strong urge to toss a silver dollar in my hand where I sat behind my desk. Just like George Raft.

"Of course, silly," Isabelle beamed, then frowned. "Unless maybe it was Eddie. You know, jealous and drinking because I jilted him. Out to get me."

Eddie Bauer had been last year's John Ireland. A taxi driver whose wife had thrown him out after he got mixed up with

Isabelle and lost his job. Isabelle had ditched him for a short fling with a muscular type with dazzling teeth. Burt Lancaster.

"You sure any of this really happened, Isabelle?"

For a moment I felt like Jack Nicholson, feet on my desk, hat tilted down over my eyes. Except that I wasn't wearing a hat. Isabelle will do that to you.

"Dan Fortune! You know I never lie! Does this look like I made it up?"

She held out a handbag about the size of a feedbag for a Clydesdale. There was a neat hole through both sides of the bag. Big holes, about .357 Magnum. Real holes.

"Okay, Isabelle, I'll look around. In the meantime, be careful, and maybe stay away from this Paul Bambara."

She was on her feet, the indignant Gloria Grahame. "Pauli needs me! We're going to go places, do things, be someone. We have to make plans. We're going to *do* something, Danny."

I sighed. "Okay, pay me some cash before you go."

"Well . . ." She rummaged in that expensive feed bag, came out with a crumpled twenty. "I'm a little short this week, but I'll pay your regular price. Me and Pauli are going to get rich."

"Swell," I said, and resisted a nasty Robert Montgomery laugh.

Opening credits voice over: Who would want to shoot Isabelle? Why? A romantic and an innocent. A dreamer who only wanted to find her John Ireland and ruin him. Ruin him in the eyes of his normal world, that is, the dull everyday world he really hated. Ruined and free to run away to a better life. The better life of doing what he really wanted to do, being what he really wanted to be, even if he fell on his face and ended up drinking alone in some forgotten Mexican village.

For Isabelle, the losers are the winners. She's seen all the movies about all the losers and there's so much life in their misery that compared to our dull lives their suffering becomes happiness. A romantic fantasy, but where was a motive for murder?

I got my beret and duffel coat and went out. In the thin November rain I walked down to the Discount Bookstore on Sixth Avenue. Paul Bambara was out at some warehouse, they didn't know when he'd be back. I got his home address.

It turned out to be a good renovated brownstone on 9th Street near Fifth. An expensive address and he had the expensive apartment: second floor front, the parlor floor. It wasn't what I would have expected for the manager of a Sixth Avenue bookstore. I rang the mailbox bell and got buzzed in. A woman waited for me in the open doorway of the second floor front.

"What can I do for you?"

"Mrs. Paul Bambara?"

She eyed me coldly. A short, stocky woman with jet black hair and shadowed Mediterranean eyes.

"If you want Paul, he ain't home."

"Can I talk to you?"

"Me?" Suspicion was sharp in her voice. She didn't invite me in. Maybe that was just her natural brand of hospitality.

"Do you know an Isabelle Kucera, Mrs. Bambara?"

Her manner changed abruptly. The cool eyes stared hard at me, but there was a shakiness in her voice. "What about her?"

"Someone tried to shoot her."

"Shoot? You a cop?"

"Private," I said. "Working for Ms. Kucera. Can I ask where you were this morning?"

"Right here. I got three witnesses. You want me to get them?"

"Maybe later." She would have the witnesses, real or faked. "Can you think of anyone who would want Ms. Kucera dead?"

"A woman like that? Listen, Mr.—?"

"Fortune. Dan Fortune."

"Listen, Mr. Fortune, I know all about that woman and her men. All the other women's husbands." She was hugging her breasts now, looking me straight in the eye. Her full lips were sad, even trembling, and her voice had a dark throb. Not Grace Kelly, no. Ingrid Bergman. Isabelle's fantasies are insidious. "I know her, but I won't fight her. Not that way. Paul is a good man, a good husband. This is his home. He'll come back to me, Mr. Fortune. He'll find he belongs here."

"I hope he does, Mrs. Bambara," I said, which was partly true, Isabelle deserved better. "You're sure you can't think of anyone who would shoot at her?"

"No, and I'd say look into her past, Mr. Fortune."

It seemed like good advice, so I went back to my office and put out some feelers on Eddie Bauer. It was late afternoon before I located him in a flea-trap on the West Side. He was at home with a bottle for company. A long, lean type with two days' growth of beard and a haunted expression. He sneered at me.

"I don't know you, chum."

Dan Duryea down on his luck, or maybe it was my imagination. Maybe only a long day with Isabelle's shadow script, my brain going soft. My own voice lisped an answer.

"I know you, friend. I'm coming in." Humphrey Bogart.

He backed off warily, hands dangling. I hung a cigarette from my lip, snapped a match on my thumbnail.

"All right, Lou . . . Bauer," I said, "read me the song and dance of where you were this morning, and make it good."

"What's it to you, chum?" Bauer/Duryea sneered.

I told him about Isabelle and the shooting.

"Dead?" he grinned.

"You'd like that, would you?"

"I wouldn't cry too hard, chummy, only you can't hang this one on me. I was here all morning, and I can prove it."

This time I made him prove it. He did. With five poker players from the building, one an off-duty cop. By then it was way past time for a beer and even some dinner so I knocked off.

I wasn't sure I was even hearing what people were really saying by then. Maybe I was just imagining the dialogue according to Isabelle's shooting script. Maybe the holes in her handbag weren't bullet holes. Maybe if I forgot about it, had a few peaceful beers, it would all do a quick dissolve.

Jump cut: To Isabelle's apartment down on Spring Street. Monday evening. The apartment is early Warner Brothers Greenwich Village just like in *Reds*—orange crates, a covered bathtub for a table, brick and board bookcases. Except for all the photos on the walls. You could have cast a hundred Hollywood epics with the actors and actresses on Isabelle's walls.

In the apartment, just home from work, Isabelle's eyes shone like Judy Garland seeing Oz for the first time.

"They searched the apartment while I was at work!"

The place was a mess, right enough.

"What's missing?"

"I don't know. I don't keep any money around." Then she almost squealed. "Maybe my diary! That man with the limp is a private eye just like you. Grace Kelly hired him to steal my diary so she could confront John Ireland!"

"Let's take a look." I was trying hard to keep what grip I had on reality. With Isabelle, it has a way of sliding away.

The diary was where she had left it, all its pages intact. I went over the small apartment inch by inch with her, she found nothing missing for a long time. Then she gave a cry.

"My new makeup case!"

"What makeup case?"

"It's like a little suitcase, you know? It's leather, and it's got all these plastic bottles and jars inside. Pauli only gave it to me a couple of days ago for my acting classes."

"Bambara gave it to you?"

"I said so, didn't I?"

"Let's go find him," I said.

We took a cab to the Discount Bookstore on Sixth, and Isabelle got Paul Bambara to take a coffee break and meet us in the Vesuvius Coffee Shop on Waverly. A pale, scrawny man in his thirties, he wore Levi cords, a rugby shirt, and a tweed jacket with fake leather elbow patches from some cut-rate men's store up on 14th Street. Isabelle introduced us. He gave me a hard grip and tried to look tough and restless as John Ireland should.

Isabelle told him about the search and the makeup case.

"The case I gave you? Why would anyone want that?"

"Maybe," Isabelle said eagerly, "your wife wants my fingerprints! I remember one time when Ireland's wife got Gloria Grahame's fingerprints so she could check her criminal past."

I said, "Leather doesn't take prints, neither does fake leather."

"And you don't have a record," Bambara said. I didn't think he would last. Realism wasn't Isabelle's forte.

"Maybe," Isabelle chewed a fingernail, "she wanted something I'd touched, something from my body. Some hair, maybe. Like in that voodoo movie where Agnes Moorehead makes a doll of Gloria Grahame and sticks pins in it to make her die."

"You feel sick?" I asked.

"Not yet, silly. She's only had it half a day."

"Isabelle," I kept a tight grip on my psyche, "this is New York, not Haiti. That stuff only works if you believe it."

"Well," she pouted heavily, almost Shirley Temple, "maybe she just wants evidence for a divorce. I mean, it was a present from Pauli."

"Angela don't believe in divorce," Bambara said, gloomy.

I said, "Where'd you buy the case, Bambara?"

"I didn't, I got it from Angela," Bambara said. "She sells them, you know? She and her brother got a cosmetic and makeup business. Door-to-door like the Avon lady. They make a bundle."

"That's how you can afford that apartment? Her money?"

"We sure couldn't afford it on mine."

"You bought the makeup case from her?"

"Hell, no! I mean, she'd want to know why I needed a woman's makeup case, right? I swiped it when she was out. She's got so many, she never even missed it."

There was something in that. Why would Angela Bambara want her own makeup case back? One of perhaps hundreds she had for sale? If she had wanted it back. If someone else hadn't taken it from Isabelle's apartment.

"Is there anyone who could be after you, Bambara?" I asked. "Someone from your past?"

"I don't got a past," Bambara said. John Ireland all the way. "A lot of crummy jobs like the one I got. Never been out of New York. Never done anything."

"You will," Isabelle said fervently. "There's got to be some kick to life, Pauli. We're going after it even if we can't hold it. Maybe we'll fall on our faces, rot in Mexico, end up hating each other, but we'll have grabbed for the big ring."

"She's right, ain't she, Fortune?" He gripped my arm like a vulture clawing a tree branch. "Mexico, work with my hands, live if it kills us in the end."

He had that feverish pipe dream in his voice John Ireland always got around Gloria Grahame. Maybe he would last.

"You're sure you don't know why someone would steal that case, Bambara?" I said.

"Not a clue, Fortune."

I left them cooing at each other over their beers, seeing Mexican sunsets in the suds. I walked up Sixth Avenue and across to Eighth and my office. Why steal a simple makeup case? Or take a shot at an innocent like Isabelle? An internal Humphrey Bogart lisped in my ear, "Something funny going on for sure, pal," and I decided to do a stakeout—on Isabelle.

Stock shots: A one-armed man shivering in the November shadows as he watches a bright young couple have a wonderful time. The one-armed man is not having a wonderful time. The one-armed man follows the young couple. The one-armed man is cold. It becomes dark, and the one-armed man becomes aware of a short, stocky man in a black raincoat.

Camera angle over the one-armed man's shoulder. The short man is also watching the young couple. Jackpot.

There is a procession. John Ireland and Gloria Grahame hand in hand. The small man, Peter Lorre, casually behind them. The one-armed man, me, behind Peter Lorre. Until Isabelle and Paul Bambara finally reach Isabelle's apartment and go up. Peter Lorre looks up until the light goes on in Isabelle's apartment, then turns away. Fortune/Bogart lisps mentally, "Stick to this character, pal, he'll lead you to the big boy."

Six blocks later I lost him. Quick into an alley, out the other end, and gone. I didn't need a director to tell me I'd been spotted. It looked like Isabelle and Bambara were in for the night. I had nothing to do but go home. I went home.

Did you ever feel that you were sinking into quicksand? Floating away on some swirling cloud of thick fog? The quicksand of Isabelle's imagination. The fog of her fantasies.

My one-room office/apartment had been torn apart.

It took me an hour to find out that nothing was missing. But my files had been rifled, the flour poured into the sink, my toothpaste tube cut open, the sugar dumped, all my chairs upended. I felt as if I were on a roller coaster and all I could do was ride it out. What had Isabelle's make-believe gotten her into? Gotten me into?

My telephone rang.

"Danny!" Isabelle's voice cried. "Pauli's killed someone!"

Montage sequence: A one-armed detective running through dark city streets. A thin-faced blonde with a strand of perfectly arranged hair hanging over one eye, a cigarette dangling and alarm registered on the thin, drooping mouth as if painted. A man in his thirties wearing a cheap tweed jacket and a shocked expression and holding a smoking Luger. (Of course, Lugers don't smoke, but this is Hollywood.)

"Who the hell is he?" I said.

The body lay on the floor of Isabelle's apartment. The short, stocky Peter Lorre who'd been following them. Paul Bambara still held the Luger that didn't smoke, sat on the couch and stared at the body.

"Joe Ciaccio," Bambara said. "My brother-in-law. He . . . he tried to kill me."

Bambara told the whole story. He had been alone in the apartment waiting for Isabelle to return with their pizza for dinner—mushrooms, anchovies, pepperoni, the works. When he heard a knock on the door he thought Isabelle had forgotten her keys again. He opened the door. His wife's brother, Joe Ciaccio, pushed him back into the room and started to shout violently.

"Shouting what?" I said.

"It didn't make any sense, you know? All about how I was a dead man. How dumb did we think he and Angela were? A big romance, and she was just a clerk in a crummy office, sure she was. Mexico. John Ireland. Gloria Grahame. Did I think they were stupid? A hot young kid and a middle-aged

113

bum like me? Then that Fortune nosing all around. Just a small-time private eye, right? Sure he was."

Bambara stared up at us. "Then . . . he pulled out this gun. He came up close, yelled right in my face. I was scared. I mean, he was crazy, he was going to shoot me! So I jumped on him. The gun got knocked to the floor. We both grabbed for it, and I knocked him down. I got the gun, he grabbed that brass lamp. He came at me again, still yelling and cursing. I . . . I shot. I had to. He was going to kill me."

In the silence of the apartment we all looked down at the dead man.

"But," Isabelle said at last, "if he didn't think me and Pauli was in love, what did he think?"

Oddly enough, given who said it, it was the same question I was asking myself. And heard a faint answer somewhere in the back of my mind.

"Isabelle, how are you going to get to Mexico? What are you going to live on while Bambara finds himself?"

"Well, we're going to sell everything we can, and Pauli's going to sort of 'borrow' some of the money his wife makes on her business." Her eyes gleamed with cleverness. "When we get to Mexico, we'll buy a lot of pot and cocaine and sell it up here for a big profit! I know all kinds of guys will buy it."

"Guys?" I said.

"You know, silly. Gangsters and drug dealers. I know lots of them. I gave Pauli a list and he was going to talk to them, but after I got shot at we decided to wait."

"A list?" I said. "Of narcotics pushers? Where is it now?"

"I've got it," Bambara said. He produced a dog-eared sheet of typewriter paper. "We never did use it,"

"You never contacted any drug dealers?"

"No," Bambara said.

Isabelle shook her head.

"But you carried it around? Took it home? Maybe left it out

on your bureau when you went to bed, or left it in your jacket pocket?"

"I guess so, yeah."

"And you were going to 'borrow' some of your wife's money?" I said. "Did you check out her account, maybe? Find out how much she had in it? Take a look at her records?"

"Sure did," Bambara said. "Even checked with her bank."

I suppose I must have looked like Paul Newman who has just figured out how it all went wrong for him and Sundance.

"Dan?" Isabelle said. "You know what's going on?"

"Maybe," I said. "I think so."

I called Lieutenant Marx then, reported the shooting. Marx is commander of the local precinct detective squad. He arrived with his team in under ten minutes. His men went to work on the body and the apartment while Marx listened to me. His eyes glazed as I told him Isabelle and Bambara's story and my glimmer of an answer.

"Can you prove any of that, Fortune?" Marx said, his voice a little stunned.

"Piece of cake, sweetheart," I lisped.

Marx waited until the M.E. had taken the body, told his men to take Bambara and the gun to the station house, warned Isabelle to stay in town, and nodded to me.

"Okay, Fortune, show me."

As we left, Isabelle sat staring at her wall with a faraway look in her eyes. It made me nervous.

At the second floor front of the renovated brownstone on 9th Street near Fifth, Angela Bambara herself opened the door. She stared at me, and then at Lieutenant Marx. She knew Marx, covered her mouth with her hand.

"Mr. Fortune. Lieutenant. Something's happened to Paul!"

Maybe just knowing Isabelle does it to you. She was Ingrid Bergman even to the head twitching slightly sideways, the big eyes not quite looking at you.

"Mrs. Bambara," Marx took charge, "can you tell us where your brother is?"

"My . . . my brother?"

Marx looked at his notebook as if everything was down in damning black and white. We all play games sometimes. "Joseph Ciaccio?"

"I . . . I don't know, lieutenant. I mean, I haven't seen Joe for weeks. I mean . . . why are the police interested in Joe?"

"Because he's dead," Marx said. "Shot to death an hour ago by your husband."

"Because be tried to shoot your Paul," I said. "Now why do you suppose he wanted to do that, Mrs. Bambara?"

"Dead?" She blinked at Marx, at me. "Tried to kill Paul? No, I don't believe you! Either of you! I don't believe a word of it. No!"

Ingrid Bergman down to the fine quiver of the lower lip, the eyes that looked everywhere like trapped birds in a small room. Isabelle was an infection. Play it again, Ingrid. There was no way I could resist.

"You're good," I said, "you're awful good. Only it won't play, not any more. You sent brother Joe to kill your husband. You and Joe were in the whole deal together. That's where all the money comes from for this apartment. You sell all right, only it's not cosmetics or makeup kits. It's the happy stuff, the trips to shiny places. You sell drugs, sweetheart, you and poor Joe. You sell it in those makeup kits, that's why you had to get that one back from Isabelle. It was loaded with H or C or whatever you're pushing.

"You found out Paul was checking your bank accounts. You spotted that list of dope dealers. Isabelle talked about Mexico. You got scared. You tried to shoot Isabelle, had your brother tail her, searched my place after I appeared, and to-

116

night you sent Joe to kill Isabelle and Paul. Only Isabelle was out, Paul got the gun, Joe's dead, and you're cooked, sister."

That was when Robert Ryan came out of the bedroom. A tall man in a raincoat, with a limp and a .357 Magnum. Angela Bambara had a 9-mm Luger in both hands, pointed straight at us.

"I told you, Mario," Angela Bambara snarled. "Narcotics agents! That damned blonde and the peeper. Cozying up to Paul, getting the makeup case, checking my bank accounts, giving Paul that list of pushers. I told you the whole crazy run-off-to-Mexico-for-love stuff was a big act."

"Narcs," Ryan/Mario agreed, "both of them. Now we got the cop, too. All three got to be blown away."

Marx said, "Freelancing, De Stefano? The Don doesn't like freelancing."

"The Don ain't gonna know about it."

I knew the name. Mario De Stefano, a Mafia *capo*.

"The girl, too," Angela Bambara said. "And Paul."

She was a beaut. Faye Dunaway ready to blast. I tried to smile, Burt Lancaster doing a death scene. It didn't work. I was going over like a two-bit extra.

I was wrong. Never reckon without Gloria Grahame.

She came in through the outside door we'd left ajar. In a battered old trenchcoat fitted to her slim figure like skin. Hands in the pockets, hatless, her blonde hair loose, the wet pout on her lips, the cigarette dangling.

"I just had to talk to you, make you understand. Pauli needs me. Pauli has to be free. I know I'm no good, but—"

Angela Bambara whirled, stumbled into an armchair, shot wildly into the ceiling. Mario De Stefano tripped over a low hassock, shot the hell out of a lamp and a mirror. I fell on Angela Bambara. Marx clobbered De Stefano. His men, staked outside, pounded up the stairs and finished them off.

Isabelle pouted. We had ruined her big confrontation scene.

Angela Bambara glared at her before Marx's people hauled her and De Stefano off.

"She didn't fool me. Running off to Mexico with a wimp like Paul? A new life? Who did she think she was fooling? I knew she was a narcotics agent right from the start."

Isabelle raised her thin nose defiantly, let the cigarette smoke close her left eye, curled her wet GG lip at Angela Bambara. I didn't have the heart to tell Angela or De Stefano the truth.

At the precinct we gave our statements. The powder in the makeup case turned out to be PCP—angel dust. The late Joe Ciaccio, Angela, and De Stefano had been making it in a back room of the elegant apartment, selling it under the cover of Angela Bambara's cosmetic business.

Later, I sat with Isabelle at a table in O. Henry's Bar.

"A real *mafioso*, Danny! Just like Marlon Brando."

I sighed.

"They really thought I was a narcotics agent." Her eyes glowed in ecstasy. "Just like—"

I'd had enough. Her fantasies had killed one man, and next time they could kill her. Or me.

"Stop it," I said. "You're not Gloria Grahame. Bambara's not John Ireland. De Stefano's a two-bit punk, not Marlon Brando."

She didn't even hear me. "Pauli's going back to Angela. In the end, when Gloria Grahame leaves him, John Ireland always goes back to his wife."

Isabelle would always be Isabelle.

"Will she go to prison for long, Danny?" she said. "Angela, I mean?"

"A long time, sweetheart," I said. "When she comes out, Paul'll be there waiting for her, just like Steve McQueen."

Isabelle smiled, her bright eyes seeing all the way to Hollywood.

The Oldest Killer

In an hour I go to meet a killer.

Now I'm lying on the bed in a motel room in San Vicente, California, thinking about the killer and reading the local newspaper. A Saturday in April, warm and sunny. I'm enjoying the sun and the warmth of the room. Back in Chelsea it's probably raining. A cold rain. But here it's a fine, bright day and I'm waiting and reading the newspaper.

> LOS ANGELES (AP)—A lethal amount of cyanide was found last Saturday in a jar of Vlasic Polish Dills at a San Diego Safeway store with a hand-lettered extortion note signed, "The Poison Pickle Gang!"

When I was doing security at a nuclear energy conference a few years ago, I met a man who told me that we were all stupid and crazy, but not crazy enough or stupid enough to blow ourselves into oblivion.

He was wrong.

On the sunny bed I read and it was all there in the paper on this single Saturday in April. The stupidity, the insanity. From the poisoned pickles down in San Diego, to the killer who brought me back to California this time.

SAN VICENTE (Star-Press Feature)—Way Chong Won is
87 years old. He walks with the aid of two canes, and he
is the oldest accused murderer in California history . . .

I got the long distance call at 3:00 A.M. on a rainy Monday in
New York five days ago. I groped for the receiver with my
solitary arm, swearing loud enough to be heard in California.

"Who in hell—!"

"You are Dan Fortune sir?"

"You know what time it is here, you idiot?"

"I am Lee Chang. You are Dan Fortune sir?"

My mind went back twenty years. To a Black Ball Line
freighter I'd shipped out on with a skinny, happy-go-lucky
Chinese kid named Lee Chang. It explained the ungodly hour
of the call. Lee had never been too bright in the ways of the
West such as time zones. For that matter, he hadn't been any
brain trust in the ways of the East, either.

"Lee!" I said, only faking a little. I'd liked Lee Chang back
then. "How the hell are you?"

"Ah, Dan Fortune sir. Very damn fine, by damn. Old friend
in very bad trouble. You come. I pay. You come quick."

Not too bright, Lee, but loyal and a bulldog and just smart
enough to have remembered what line of work I'd gone into
after I'd stopped shipping out.

SAN VICENTE (Star-Press Feature)—Way Chong Won is
charged with killing Low Soo Kwong, 65, a fellow tenant
in a Chinatown rooming house with whom he had been
feuding.
Police found a revolver on a table in Way Chong Won's
room when they arrested him, and he is also charged
with possessing a set of lethal brass knuckles, another
felony . . .

From Los Angeles, Marmonte commuter airline got me to
San Vicente around noon. Lee Chang was working as a chef in

a Szechuan restaurant on upper State Street. He was Cantonese himself, but if the Americans wanted Szechuan, he'd cook Szechuan.

We had a pot of limp tea. Lee was sad.

"Is all wrong, Dan Fortune sir," he said, shook his head.

He had hardly changed at all. Still skinny and all grin and about as inscrutable as a five-year-old with an ice-cream cone. But he wasn't grinning now.

"Old man not violent man, Dan sir. No way. Not feud with no one. Very small Chinatown here, always old man is friend of everyone. All know old man, have respect. All like old man."

"All except this Low Soo Kwong," I said.

Lee shook his head. "That wrong too. Old man Way he fight with no one. He not know why Low Soo Kwong hate him. Kwong move into rooming house three, four year ago. Very quiet. Mind own business. Not talk with anyone. Then, last year, Low Soo start act funny, all mad at Way Chong. No one know why. Old man not know why. We think Low Soo Kwong crazy man."

"Maybe," I said, watching that incredible California April sun outside the restaurant window, "but if the old man isn't violent, why did he have brass knucks and a loaded gun?"

"Not know, Dan Fortune sir. You find out."

About then I began to wish I was back where it was raining in April the way it's supposed to.

PHOENIX, Ariz. (UPI)—Sam Jones, 14, broke into a grocery store, setting off a silent alarm. When the police arrived, the youth refused to surrender. Policeman Steve Gregory warned Jones that police dogs had been ordered, and when the viciously barking dogs arrived, young Jones gave himself up.

"No dogs I'm coming out"

His first attempt at big-time crime over, Jones walked

out to face the dogs. There were no dogs. Policeman Al
Femenia had done all the barking.

Sometimes it's funny. Stupid, yes, even murderous, but
funny.

On the motel bed in the bright afternoon April sun I count
down the minutes I have left before I go to meet the killer.

I watch the mockingbirds outside the motel room window.
I listen to the birds, and wonder if we will all be gone someday, even the mockingbirds, leaving an empty world with
new birds to sing a strange song.

After this week, now, I know it is possible. We can do it.

SAN VICENTE (Star-Press Feature)—Way Chong Won
sits in a San Vicente jail cell awaiting trial. The old man
has the money for bail, but refuses to use it. His mind
tends to wander. Sometimes he thinks he is in China.
His only explanation of the murder is that "devils"
talked to Low Soo Kwong . . .

The old man sat on the narrow jail bunk. Thin and small in a
shabby black Mao suit, high-collared and tieless. As wrinkled
as a mummy. Wispy white hair. Black eyes that watched me
suspiciously.

"No money for lawyer."

"I'm not a lawyer, Mr. Way, I'm a detective."

"No money for detective."

"What do you have money for, Mr. Way?"

"For bury. For go home. For bury with ancestors."

"In China?"

The old man nodded. "Family all bury in China."

For the first time he smiled in the small jail cell. Thinking
of his grave somewhere in China.

"Did you kill Low Soo Kwong?" I said.

"He no good man. Very bad."

"Why did you kill him?"

"He no good man. Long time I not know, not know Low Soo Kwong not like me. Not see him much at house. No one see him much, no one know him. He come, he go. Maybe year ago he begin talk bad to me, always watch me, have devils in ear. He hang around all time. Try to hurt me in kitchen. Everyone stop, but he scare me. I buy weapon, I buy gun."

"Why would he have wanted to hurt you?"

The old man shrugged. "He crazy man. Hear devils."

"What did he say about you when he 'talked bad'?"

"Say me no good man. Say I bad man, enemy. He lie. I good man. Now I old man. Go home, sleep with ancestors. Go to old village . . ."

His voice wandered off somewhere in the dim cell. Maybe to China. To the distant village where he'd been born.

> SANTA MARIA, Calif. (AP)—Joseph Vincent Marino, 37, was booked at County Jail on suspicion of burglary. Officers said that the owner of Eleanor's Flower Shop had time to phone for help because the burglar smashed the front window with a brick and had to climb carefully through the shattered glass to commit his crime.
>
> They added that the suspect could have avoided all his trouble, even his capture, by simply walking in through the unlocked front door.

Sometimes you can only laugh. Even if it hurts.

Alone on a bed in a hot motel room in San Vicente, California, waiting to go out and meet a killer.

Reading the insane mayhem and stupidity of a single Saturday in a civilized country, the absurd story of murder in a Chinatown rooming house that wouldn't have merited even a mention in any newspaper except for the identity of the accused murderer—an eighty-seven-year-old Chinaman with brass knuckles.

123

SAN VICENTE (Star-Press Feature)—Low Soo Kwong was found lying on his back in his own room with blood covering his face and body, and a trail of blood leading back to the room of Way Chong Won. An autopsy indicated that Low had been hit five times by .32 caliber bullets . . .

The elderly anglo lady had lived in the rooming house even longer than old Way Chong Won. Before it ever became part of Chinatown. She found the brass knuckles and the gun unbelievable.

"They were both such very quiet men, Mr. Fortune. Mr. Low especially kept to himself. Why, I don't think I ever saw them speak to each other before that first time Mr. Low attacked Mr. Way! I couldn't believe my eyes when Mr. Low tried to hit Mr. Way with that frying pan, or when Mr. Way came back with those brass knuckles."

"What was the fight about?"

She sighed. "These Chinese are so mysterious, Mr. Fortune. Secretive, you know? Even a nice man like Mr. Way. All I recall was that Mr. Way said something to Mr. Low about snooping in Mr. Way's room, and Mr. Low said that the old man was evil and that he, Mr. Low, would stop him. After that they yelled at each other in Chinese. A real feud."

"You told the police that it was a feud?"

"I certainly did."

"I don't suppose you know where Way got the brass knuckles and the gun?"

"I certainly do."

It turned out to be a large pawnshop on lower State Street, only a short walk from the rooming house. The owner, a middle-aged man with a sour face, was suspicious when I asked about Way Chong Won. But since the police had already asked everything I did, he gave me the answers. Reluctantly, wondering if I was up to some trick he couldn't spot. Suspicion in the air he breathed.

"The old Chink bought the brass knucks maybe four months ago. Said some guy was tellin' lies about him, threatenin' him. He wanted somethin' to show the guy and scare him off. So I sold him the knucks."

"Just the thing for an eighty-seven-year-old man."

He became sullen.

"And the gun?" I said.

"I got a right to sell handguns in this town."

"When did you sell it to him?"

"Maybe a week 'n a half ago. How did I know the old Chink was gonna shoot someone?"

"That was a week ago last Thursday, then?"

"Friday. He said the other guy had a club. He was real scared, wanted something stronger than brass knucks."

"He didn't ask for a gun? Just a weapon stronger than brass knuckles, and you maybe suggested the gun?"

"You get the hell out of here, mister."

So Way Chong Won had gone to buy a stronger weapon than brass knuckles, but not necessarily a gun. He had not planned to shoot Low Soo Kwong. He hadn't intended to kill Low, only to scare him off. But he had been sold a gun by a greedy shopkeeper. The same way he had been sold the ludicrous brass knuckles.

> SAN VICENTE (Star-Press Feature)—A homemade mace, studded with nails, was found in the hall outside Way Chong Won's room, its handle also bloody.
>
> Officer Nelson Lum quoted Way as saying after his arrest, "I eighty-seven-year-old man. Must protect self."

The young Chinese girl lived across the hall from Way Chong Won. Chinese-American. As suspicious of my questions as the pawnshop owner.

"The police already arrested the murderer."

I said, "I'm not sure he is the murderer."

"I am."

"How?"

She watched me, doll-like and cold-eyed. "Because I heard the whole fight. I heard the shots. Mr. Low didn't have a chance. I saw him stagger from the old man's room, stumble down the hall to his own room, and die there. I saw the old man come out of his room still holding the pistol. The gun was still in his room when the police came."

"Did you see Low Soo Kwong go into the old man's room with his homemade mace?"

"He knew the old man was dangerous! He needed a weapon!"

"Why was Way dangerous?"

"Because Mr. Low knew all about him."

"Knew what about him?"

She shook her head. "Mr. Low never told me. He said it was safer if I didn't know. But he watched the old man all the time, and he knew the truth about him."

"He knew the truth by watching Way Chong Won?"

"That's right."

"Where did he watch the old man? Outside the rooming house, I mean?"

"Everywhere. At the post office. At the bank. Somewhere the old man went all the time up in San Francisco. Mr. Low even saw the old man buy the gun!"

"Low knew Way had a gun, and he went to his room anyway?"

Her black eyes were bright. "Mr. Low was a very brave man. He was like a soldier. And Way Chong Won murdered him!"

ATLANTA, Georgia (UPI)—Paul R. Morris, 20, a security guard honored for helping five University of Atlanta students escape from the school's burning law library last weekend, has been charged with setting the fire himself.

Sometimes you can only cry.
We are crazy, yes, and stupid. But how?
Are we monsters, or clowns?
I think about it as I get up to shower and dress in the sunny California motel room. *Monsters or clowns?*
It is almost time to go out and meet the killer. Maybe he can tell me the answer.

SAN VICENTE (Star-Press Feature)—Public Defender Fred Walsh said that Way Chong Won fired only in self-defense after Low Soo Kwong attacked him with the mace.

"The old man fired nine shots," Walsh explained. "He emptied the pistol and hit Low three times. Low ran back to his room and returned with a knife. Way had reloaded while Low was gone, emptied the gun again and hit Low twice more. Low staggered to his room and died there."

The manager of the branch bank on lower State Street was sad.

"A terrible thing. Yes, Way Chong Won has his money with us. A small account until quite recently."

I came alert. "It changed? Recently? It's not so small?"

"It's still rather small, but considerably larger than it was."

"When did it start to grow?"

"He began depositing as much as three or four hundred dollars a month over a year ago. It's now up to a few thousand."

"Did Low Soo Kwong know about that?"

The bank manager chewed a thin lip. "I don't know how, but yes, he seemed to. He came here a few times asking about

Mr. Way's account. We gave him no information, of course, but he seemed to know about the recent deposits."

"What did he ask in particular?"

"Well, he wanted to know the total, and then something odd—if anyone else had put money into Mr. Way's account."

"Had anyone?"

"No."

"Did you tell Low that?"

"Of course not!"

I headed to the main post office. The supervisor was a busy man. He listened to my questions while he went on stamping and filing papers in the vast room behind the public windows.

"Yeh, that Low come in a couple of times asking about old Way Chong Won's mail. We don't give out information, but I guess Low found out all he wanted anyway."

"How?"

"Watching. I'd see Low hangin' around the windows every time old man Way showed up. Never thought about it until the killing, you know? Every time the old man sent anything or got anything, Low was watching."

"What kind of mail did Way send?"

"Letters 'n packages, a lot of 'em the last year or so. Mostly to China."

"What did he receive?"

"Letters from China. Rubber stamps all over 'em."

"Any money?"

He nodded. "Yeh, cash and checks both. I saw him take cash and checks out of most of those letters."

SAN VICENTE (Star-Press Feature)—"Way Chong Won fired only after he had been attacked by Low Soo Kwong," Public Defender Walsh insists. "Only in self-defense."

But the district attorney insists that it was Low Soo Kwong who was defending himself, and that "we have found no reason for Low Soo Kwong to attack Way Chong Won."

The man behind the desk of the San Francisco office of the People's Republic of China was the first inscrutable Chinese I'd met in the case. An ageless man in a neat gray Mao suit.

"People say that Way Chong Won made a lot of trips up here," I said.

"That is true, Mr. Fortune."

"Have the police talked to you about it?"

"No."

"Why did old Way come to you, Mr. Xiang?"

"To arrange for his burial in China, Mr. Fortune. He desired to be buried with his ancestors in the village where he was born. The way affairs were between our countries made this difficult. But with the reopening of relations between us, the matter became simple again, and the old man had begun to gather money to meet the cost."

"How?"

"Largely by selling small art objects and other artifacts he had accumulated over the years."

"Selling to whom?"

"Mostly to my government, which is why he came to see me so many times, and to various private collectors in Hong Kong and Taiwan, I believe."

"So that's where his money came from? Selling things."

"That is correct."

"Sir," I said, "have you ever seen anyone following Way Chong Won when he came here? Someone watching him?"

"Yes, Mr. Fortune, I have."

"More than once?"

"On many occasions."

"One man," I said. "Or maybe there were two?"

He smiled as if pleased with me. "Two."

"Both Chinese?"

His smile broadened. "No, Mr. Fortune, not both Chinese. The first, a little more than a year ago, was a definite Caucasian. A large man, very neat, very well dressed, most discreet. It was only by the sheerest chance that my secretary noticed him across the street when Way Chong Won came one day. He was clearly observing Mr. Way, but we never saw him again."

"Low Soo Kwong was the second man?"

"He was. Somewhat later on. We saw him many times." He smiled a third time. "Low was not discreet. Most clumsy."

"An amateur," I said.

Mr. Xiang nodded agreement, almost approvingly.

LOS ANGELES (AP)—The FBI says there is a good chance more than one person is involved in the Poison Pickle case. The store received a telephone call from a man who said he would identify five other poisoned items in exchange for 50 diamonds. But a later caller demanded 100 diamonds, and threatened to spike food in "every Safeway store in the area!" The next day cyanide-dosed Teriyaki Sauce was found in another San Diego Safeway.

Cry or laugh?

Sometimes you have to do both, and my time is up.

Outside in the warm sun I take my rented car and drive to Shoreline Park above the ocean. On a bench I sit and look out over the blue sea to the mountainous Channel Islands.

It has taken me two and a half days, fifty telephone calls, and more than a few threats to get the killer to agree to meet me, with no real guarantee he will actually show up. But I have a strong hunch he will.

SAN VICENTE (Star-Press Feature)—Their neighbors say that Way and Low had been enemies a long time, but

Way says it only began a year ago when Low started telling some people that Way was a dangerous man after Way took part in a May Day rally in support of the Communist regime in China.

"You killed Low Soo Kwong," I said.

He was a large man. Very neat, very well dressed, most discreet. He sat down on the bench and looked out to sea.

"Is that all, Fortune?"

"How are you people doing with the Poison Pickle case?"

"We'll take care of it."

"The old man pulled the trigger," I said, "but you killed Low Soo Kwong. You spotted Way Chong Won at that May Day rally for the People's Republic. He was a new face, so you ran him through the computer back in Washington. You came up with a blank. The bureau doesn't like blanks, so you started a small investigation. Nothing big, just routine, right?"

The man looked at his watch.

"You talked to his neighbor, Low Soo Kwong. You told him Way Chong Won could be a Communist agent, asked Low to watch the old man and report on him. That's routine too. Low saw the old man send letters and packages overseas, saw him get a lot of mail from Red China. He saw Way visit the offices of the People's Republic. He saw Way putting money into his bank account. Low had been to plenty of movies, seen a lot of television. He could add all that up—old Way *was* a Communist agent, sure enough."

The man said, "How'd you lose the arm? The war?"

I said, "Low never found out that the old man's only interest in Red China was to get buried there. That all the mail, and the visits to the People's Republic office, were to arrange his burial and to sell stuff to pay for it. Low's English wasn't good, he had little if any education, and the mighty FBI had told him that Way Chong Won was a Communist. He probably wouldn't have believed the truth if he'd been told, unless the FBI itself told him. So he believed he faced a Red agent, he saw him buy a gun, and he attacked first like a good, brave soldier."

The man stood up. "I've got to go. That all?"

"You knew that Way Chong Won wasn't a spy, or even a Communist, months ago. You're good investigators. But you didn't tell Low Soo Kwong. Maybe you got too busy, maybe you just forgot him. A nothing little investigation. So Low Soo Kwong went on doing his patriotic job, and now he's dead."

"All right, Fortune, we made a mistake. We're sorry about the dead Chinaman. We'll talk to the cops about the old man."

"Sure," I said. "You do that."

"A small mistake." He looked down at me. "It happens. We have to risk mistakes, Fortune. Our job is too important to worry about a couple of small mistakes."

"Two Chinamen," I said, "that's what's important."

He walked away without looking back. I sat there and watched the sea break below the cliffs. One man was dead, another was scared, helpless and in jail. All because the eager FBI had investigated a harmless eighty-seven-year-old man who only wanted to be buried in the land of his birth. Two victims of the oldest killer of all—insane stupidity.

Laugh or cry? Monsters or clowns?

The Big Rock Candy Mountains

They called him Rocky because of the song he sometimes sang at dusk alone on the bluffs above the sea. After the last sun had gone, and he and his old guitar were nothing but a vague shadow against the dark sea and sky.

> *Oh, the buzzin' of the bees in the cigarette trees*
> *By the rock 'n rye fountain*
> *Where the whiskey springs and the bluebird sings*
> *In the Big Rock Candy Mountains.*
>
> *In the Big Rock Candy Mountains*
> *The jails are made of tin . . .*
> *There ain't no hoe . . .*
> *And the sun shines every day.*
> *Oh, I'm bound to go where there ain't no snow*
> *Where the sleet don't fall*
> *And the wind don't blow*
> *In the Big Rocky Candy Mountains.*

Permanently bent, he walked as if he were always in pain, but his wrinkled face usually had a smile on it.

No one knew his real name. He spoke enough English to

133

get by, but rarely said more than a few words, and never about himself. Some speculated that he answered so easily to the name of Rocky because his real name was Rocco.

He lived outdoors in Summerland for thirty years.

Over those years Summerland learned only that he was Italian, had come to America in 1914, had been an itinerant field hand. He never married, happened to be working in California when he got too old for the fields. So he settled on the streets of Summerland where it was sunny and warm, and if it sometimes rained there was never any snow.

Summer and winter, in his short coat and trademark black fedora, he walked around the beach community, as much a part of it as the freeway and the sound of the surf.

Until someone beat him to death in his last home under a gnarled old oak at the age of ninety-five.

It had been raining all that afternoon, but had stopped by the time Lauri Michaels saw the old man lying under the oak in the fading dusk.

"It wasn't like Rocky to just lie around, Dan. He should have been in the laundromat or in the park on the bluffs."

Paramedics had taken the old man into County Hospital half conscious. He died two days later without naming his attacker.

Lauri Michaels was one of those who asked me to find whoever had killed Rocky. She owned the laundromat where Rocky came every Thursday to wash his few clothes, talk to the young people and transients who didn't have houses or washing machines any more than he did.

"I say you should look at all the bums we've got hanging out here now, threatening decent people," Saul Friedman said.

"What the hell are you talking about," Jess Hill swore.

"Those 'bums' were Rocky's friends. Homeless street people like him. It's you goddamn 'decent' people threaten them, Friedman."

"You're suggesting some homeowner around here killed Rocky? That's worse than the rest of your socialist idiocy."

"I'm saying maybe you should look at people who didn't want Rocky around getting in their way," Hill said.

"You mean Mario Costello?" Lauri said. "Gosh, Jess, I don't believe a businessman like—"

"I don't know, Lauri," someone else said. "The way he put up prices at The Place. He sure as hell didn't like Rocky on his veranda."

"Don't forget Terry Miken," Jess Hill said. "He's been tryin' to get old Rocky out from under that tree on the White Hole for years. Now Rocky's gone."

Another resident said, "Maybe you're all right. Anyone could have paid one of those street animals to do it."

"What about all the new people in those apartments at the end of town?"

Everyone had a theory and a suggestion.

"We're going to give him a decent funeral," Lauri Michaels said. "Put up a bench at the bus stop with Rocky's name on it. But we want to catch who did it too, Dan. For Rocky."

Sheriff's Sergeant Jaime Villa shook his head.

"He couldn't tell us, Dan. We asked every hour on the hour, but he just sort of raved."

"Raved?"

Villa read from the report, *"Young is hard . . . no damn chance . . . die soon . . .* Stuff like that. *Old man . . . too damn old . . . no damn good . . .* You know how Rocky used to talk. Only word you could understand sometimes was *damn."*

"English?"

"Sure, English. Do I know Italian?"

"Sounds almost like he was remembering when he was young. But I think he'd remember that in Italian."

"I guess maybe. Anyway, all we got out of him was raving."

"What about the crime scene? Around that tree?"

"Footprints all over in the mud, it'd rained hard. Nothing clear, you know people tramping. Nothing else we could find. No one saw the attack. None of the stolen stuff has shown up yet."

"Stolen?"

"Sure, people gave old Rocky money and stuff. He always had some bucks, a big portable radio he carried around, even a signet ring that looked like gold but wasn't. They're all missing. And Lauri Michaels says she gave him a brand-new storm coat someone left at the laundromat. It's gone too. His hat and his guitar."

"His hat?"

Villa shrugged. "Someone needed a hat."

Who steals a hat? Bums? Street people? Kids?

"Not much to kill a man for."

"You never know about thieves. Maybe some drunk. A hophead street punk. I've seen junkies desperate for anything to sell. That ring looked real."

"If it was any of those people you should have found some of the stuff by now. On the streets or pawned."

Villa nodded, rubbed his jaw. "We figure the thief didn't mean to kill the old man, or even hurt him. So when he hit old Rocky too hard he panicked, grabbed the first way out of town. We've got word out from San Diego to the Bay Area."

It was three days since the attack on Rocky. Contrary to what people think, homeless transients are the easiest fugitives to spot. They move in limited areas in any city, are usually known to the police.

"A transient with any of the loot should have shown by now."

"Maybe he was so scared he dumped the stuff before he ran."

"Then it should have been found around here, right? If he was going to dump it, he'd have done it fast."

Villa only shrugged again. People don't always do what they should, or what you expect.

The White Hole was the irreverent but accurate and symbolic name for a piece of land at the edge of Summerland owned by Terry Miken, one of the largest developers in Santa Barbara. The focus of a long debate over its use, it had no zoning designation so appeared white on county planning maps—the White Hole.

It was a large overgrown slope that came down to the road from the steeper slopes of the high hills behind. Wooded on the upper half, it had developed over the years into a kind of local park with paths and rustic benches where the residents liked to walk, or sit and look out at the spectacular view of the sea and the distant Channel Islands. Its lower part was brush and brown wild grasses with a few twisted old native oaks. Under the largest of the old oaks Rocky had lived and died.

Two people came out of their houses to stare up at me as I walked around under the old tree. They would call the sheriff's office, Summerland was that kind of neighborhood. It was good I'd told Sergeant Villa I was going to the tree.

The mud had hardened, showed the ruts and gouges of many feet tramping around when it was wet. No particular shoes were identifiable, no marks indicated a struggle. How much fight could a ninety-five-year-old man have put up? There was an orange crate Rocky had used for a table, cleared spaces close to the tree where he had slept, cooked, read and dined. When he was there. Time and place had meant little to Rocky. He moved when and where the urge hit him.

I walked slowly around the tree in widening circles. None of the grass had been trampled, there was no indication of any kind of struggle. Only three discoveries caused me to bend, pick them up, or think about them.

The first was a tiny, cheap, lead-colored oval of metal with a ring at the top. A St. Christopher medal. The tiny ring was bent open as if it had been pulled off a chain.

A few strands of thick, stiff grass lay almost hidden in the lighter wild grasses around the tree. After a time—studying and feeling—I decided it wasn't native to the field. It was straw.

As I held the tiny medal that had been just about invisible in a deep rut in the mud, and the easily overlooked strands of straw, I noticed the house. A dilapidated cottage on a steeper slope next to the White Hole. The closest building, it was the only house higher than the tree. Its upper windows would have a direct view of anything that happened around the tree.

Paint-peeled siding, tattered shingles, broken panes covered by cardboard. An overall grayness. The house had no doorbell. I knew the man who answered my knocks.

Jess Hill glared at me. "You find out who done it yet?"

"Not yet."

Inside, the cottage was neat and warm, the old furniture shabby but clean. The oak tree where Rocky had died was visible from the side window.

"Where were you that afternoon, Mr. Hill?"

"Right here."

"In this room or maybe upstairs somewhere?"

"In this room. It was raining, I don't heat upstairs."

I walked to stand at the side window. The line of sight wasn't far enough down to see a body lying under the old oak, but maybe enough to have seen an attack. And certainly close enough to have heard a fight.

"You didn't see or hear anything?"

"Not a damn thing."

"No shouting, no struggle?"

"I told you, no. What is this? The police have some damned stupid idea?"

"They're investigating the idea of robbery."

"Shit!" He sat down on the worn-out couch, shook his head angrily. "That the best those monkeys can do? Rob what, for Christ sake?"

I told him what seemed to be missing. "Could he have had something more, Mr. Hill? Money? Something valuable we don't know about?"

He looked around his shabby living room. "You know what I was once? Union organizer. In the fields up in Washington, Oregon. I got burned out with all the lyin' and cheatin' and exploitin'. My uncle left me this place, I come down to do nothing 'cept live in the good weather just like Rocky. Forget it all."

He sat for a time as if thinking about what he had come here to forget. The distant sea and islands clear on the far side of the old oak in the bright sunlight beyond his window.

"Lemme tell you about Rocky. He don't have much English, but I know him ten years, speak Spanish, can pick up Italian. He was a field hand: lemon picker, strawberry picker, cauliflower, whatever they got to pick. Stoop labor, the short hoe down in the Southwest. You ever use a short hoe? Break your back."

139

He shook his head in a kind of wonder. "You get up in the dark, work all day, come back to a bunk or a shack, go to bed. That's it. When you're young you get drunk before you go to bed, that kills you faster. You work, you get old, you die. If you get married your wife gets old faster than you do, your kids don't go to school because you follow the crops. You never save a dime. You get old you got one suitcase, leather skin, and a crooked back. You got no pension, no social security, no nothing. You die or disappear. Way out on the edge where no one even sees you. Where you ain't dead yet, but you're dead."

"Rocky didn't disappear."

"Sure he did. Thirty years he lives here and nobody sees him. Nobody knows what he thinks about. Nobody even knows his name. Then he gets real old. He's a character, a freak to talk about, a pet like an old lame dog or a one-eyed cat. No one knows who he really is, no one cares one damn."

"They care now."

"They care about themselves, Fortune. Somebody took what belonged to them away from them."

"Who do you think that was?"

"I already told you. Terry Miken wanted him off the White Hole and that's how he got killed. That's all that makes sense. He didn't have no enemies, nothing anyone could want. That Mario Costello's no saint, but Rocky on that veranda was even good for business."

"What about the big portable, the ring, his guitar, the coat Lauri Michaels gave him?"

"Smokescreen. I seen it before, believe me."

Rain clouds were building out over the sea. At the side window I still looked at the old oak where Rocky had died.

"What about the hat?"

"Hat?"

"His hat was missing too."

"Some people got funny ideas, I guess."

"Did Rocky wear or carry a St. Christopher medal?"

"Not that I ever saw.

"How about you?"

He laughed. "Radical ideas don't go with superstitions."

"From a black hole not even light escapes," Terry Miken said. "With the White Hole a hell of a lot of money goes in and less than nothing comes out."

"You wanted old Rocky off your land?"

Miken was a big, lanky man who'd once been a TV talk-show host in Los Angeles, had taken the proceeds of his high salary, perks and some judicious payola, moved up to Santa Barbara and invested in real estate. His office was attached to his private apartment on the top floor of his flagship building in downtown Santa Barbara, had a great view of the steel skeleton of one of his rising projects.

"What do you think?" He scowled out at the towers of steel that warmed his heart and his pocketbook. "I've had that land ten years. I apply to build on it. Nice low-density residential and low-density commercial. But it's not zoned, so I have to go to the Planning Commission every time, have a goddamn hearing. The locals want it left wild so they can sit on it and write poetry. The supervisors think visitor-serving facilities would be nice. The do-gooders want low-income housing for bums. And every goddamn time they trot out the old man. Where would poor Rocky go? Look how he enhances the community, blends in with the scenery and lifestyle. We need free space like that. Shit!"

"Why not just fence it and throw him off?"

"He was a fucking institution." Miken swung around in his big high-backed swivel chair to lay his glare on me. "I'm not dumb. I build a fence I've got the whole community down on

141

me. I try to bring in a bulldozer with him there I've got a war. That's not how to get what I want."

"He's not in your way anymore," I said. "Are you a religious man, Mr. Miken?"

"I go to church."

"Mind telling me what church?"

"Trinity. The Episcopal Church. Why?"

"They sometimes have St. Christopher medals, right?"

"If you believe in that sort of protection. I think it's mostly Catholics that carry them." Another swivel to admire the bare steel of his building and maybe even the sea behind it. "I don't murder people, Fortune. I haven't been out to Summerland in months. Anyway, don't the cops say it was a robbery? Those street bums?"

"Nothing stolen has surfaced, the robbery could be a ruse," I said. "A lot of people work for you."

"What the hell does that mean?"

"You know the story of Henry II and Thomas à Becket? *Will no one rid me of the old man?* The police think the killing was an accident. Someone manhandled Rocky too hard."

When he swivelled back this time, he didn't smile. "That's pretty close to slander, Fortune, but I'll let it pass and tell you something you might want to think about. There are those who say that old bum was as much a miser as a hermit. Bank accounts, or maybe cash in a box in some hole in the ground. Maybe you should look into that? Next of kin. His friends. Those street bums out there."

❧

Mario's Place was a large and popular seafood, hamburger and spaghetti palace in an old house with a porch all around where Rocky liked to sit and watch the passers and patrons. It had been through many guises and many owners, with Rocky there on the veranda the whole time. He greeted everyone, played his guitar, never panhandled. The patrons liked him. He was, after all, a local landmark.

"Sure," Mario Costello nodded, "when I bought the place, found the old guy almost living on the goddamn porch, I told my manager to tell him to take a fast hike."

Costello was a wiry little man who hadn't lost his New York accent even though he'd been on the Coast for twenty years. He'd bought the place a year ago, immediately got the community's back up by raising prices, banning bathing suits at lunch and shorts at dinner to favor the upscale trade from Santa Barbara and Montecito, and trying to banish Rocky. For a time there was talk of a boycott, and there had been some nasty scenes.

"So I found the guy was a goddamn institution, part of the community, right? I told my manager let him stay, just be sure he don't worry new customers maybe didn't know who he was."

He'd rescinded the dress code too, but not the high prices, and there were many in Summerland who felt Rocky had been on borrowed time on the veranda. There had even been renewed talk of a boycott when Costello's manager had tried to move Rocky down to the foot of the veranda steps because they were glassing in part of the veranda to make an extra room.

"Was he here the day he was killed?"

"Not that I remember."

"Mind if I look around?"

"Why not?"

I found nothing on the veranda, or around the kitchen where the cooks and chefs were moving crisply through all those precise motions. In a rear storage shed I did find some crates that had been lined with straw to insulate or protect whatever had been shipped to Mario's in them.

≀❧

"No family we can find," Sergeant Villa said. "He talked some about sisters and brothers in the old country, but he figured they was all dead."

"How about money?"

"We checked the banks. Nothing there."

"Any evidence of digging anywhere out at the White Hole?"

"No. But that doesn't mean he didn't have a box hidden away. Or that the killer didn't find it and take it."

≀❧

Lauri Michaels dispensed change from behind the counter of her laundromat. "I never saw any box, Dan, and he sure never acted like he had any money."

It was raining again outside, the laundromat crowded with street people. That didn't bother Lauri. She watched them all talking, reading, sleeping out of the way of real customers. But the talk was muted, the reading distracted, the sleep restless. One of their own had been murdered, and somewhere out there was a killer. Out there or among them.

"Rocky used to come in a lot when it rained, they all miss him," she said sadly, then smiled. "I remember this guy from the newspaper came to interview Rocky once. The jerk asked Rocky where he went when it rained. Old Rocky looked at him as if that was the stupidest question he'd ever heard, and said, 'Where it isn't raining.' "

"Was he here the day he was attacked?"

She shook her head. "No. That's one reason I looked under the tree when I went past that evening."

I talked to the transients who sat around in the haven of the laundromat. None of them admitted to having seen

Rocky that day, or being near the White Hole. One man remembered a derelict who wore a St. Christopher medal.

"Joey Luna. He was Italian, you know? Used to come through with this real young *chica*. They both got them medals roun' their necks, you know? Rocky he like 'em, talk all the time wit' 'em."

"Was this Luna around when Rocky was killed?"

"I don' know."

Another looked up in disgust from his copy of *Decline of the West*. "Joey Luna hasn't been through for a year. He's in jail down in Mexico."

None of them admitted to wearing a religious medal. Some were belligerent about it.

"When it rained, he went where it wasn't raining," I said to Jess Hill in the shabby living room of his cottage. The rain was heavy again on the White Hole and the old oak tree through his side window. "Where was that besides the laundromat or Costello's veranda?"

"Here, but not that day. I wish to hell he had."

"Where else?"

"Under the freeway. The maintenance shed in the beach park. A couple of caves up above the White Hole. In the railroad culverts. All kinds of sheds people got behind their houses." He sat on his couch and looked out through the rain to the old tree. "I told the cops all that, Fortune. They got to have checked all those places."

I showed him the St. Christopher medal and the straw I'd found near the tree. "You ever see these? Who would wear a St. Christopher who knew Rocky? How did straw get under the tree?"

"Costello's Catholic," Hill said. "I seen straw around his place."

145

"But you don't think Costello wanted him out of his hair that much. How about Terry Miken?"

He shrugged. "I don't know what religion he got. He maybe got straw somewhere around some goddamn house he owns. But he wouldn't have hit old Rocky himself. He'd have sent people. Maybe one o' them wore a St. Christopher."

"Terry Miken's already rich as hell. Why would he have old Rocky attacked just so he could make more money?"

Jess Hill continued to look out at the rain. "I told you I used to organize workers. I got to see a lot of rich guys owned a whole county. Some people can't stop working for money even when they don't need it and don't like the work all that much. I've seen guys who wanted to do something else, but the money wasn't as good so they went on doing what they hated. The work don't matter, just how much money does it make. They get rich and they still can't stop working for the money."

He nodded toward the White Hole through his window. "That land oughta be a park or cheap houses, but Miken owns it and got to make all the money he can squeeze on it. It don't matter if he don't need the money or'd rather be fishing." He looked back at me. "Rocky used to say he'd seen them back in Italy. The princes and dukes who grabbed everything, never cared if the peasants lived or died. That's why he squatted out there, to stop Miken from building, and Miken knew it. Rocky hated the rich, loved the field workers, especially the kids he used to say never had no hope for better unless they got out. That they—"

"Kids? What did he say about kids?"

"How it was hard to be young in the fields. How they had no chance, died too soon, had—"

"Most field hands around here are Mexicans."

"Yeah."

"But there's no picking now. What would they do when they weren't picking?

"Get some kind of job or go back to Mexico."

"Where would they get a job after the picking season?"

"Hell, I don't know. Probably on the estates. Gardening. Maybe the horse ranches. Some of them're good with horses."

I said, "Horses. Barns. Straw."

He looked at me.

"Jess, if he went somewhere out of the rain, would he take his things with him?"

"He wasn't crazy enough to leave stuff behind under a tree."

I started with the ranches inland from the beach in Montecito. The rain had blown away by the time I walked into the fifth barn.

Rocky's hat lay in the corner of an empty horse stall near the back. There was blood on the hat, and on the wooden corner post. The fake gold signet ring was trampled in the dirt, some small change had been missed in the straw at the back where there was more blood. There were only three horses in the small barn.

At the house they told me they'd hired two day men to muck while their regular man was away in Mexico. The two men worked three days and then vanished. They had hired them through their regular man's cousin who lived on the lower east side of Santa Barbara. The cousin had come to feed and groom the horses until their regular man was back, but he didn't muck. They hadn't looked in the barn since the two men left.

I picked up Sergeant Villa on the way.

No one answered at the rundown cottage on Voluntario Street. There were no cars in the driveway. But inside a voice droned, and pale light flickered from somewhere at the back.

Villa had his gun out. I pushed the back door open.

147

The light was a television set across the kitchen in a back bedroom. The droning voice was on a cooking show.

The man lay on a narrow bed and watched the television. He was wrapped in a heavy storm coat like the one Lauri Michaels had given old Rocky. There were dark stains on it. The man spoke without looking at us, as if he knew we would come, had been waiting.

"Me an' Esteban we pick the lemons. The old man he come aroun', you know? He say he was picker long time ago. He say it no good, we got to get better job. He say look at him: old, no house, no one give a damn. He buy us tacos, some beer. We pick, but cost too much up here. No more pickin', we clean out barn. Esteban hear his wife sick, he got to get money take home.

"This day it rain, the old man come to barn. He got radio, coat, fine guitar, gold ring, money buy beer an' tacos. The old man is old, he got no wife, kids. Esteban tell old man to give him money. Esteban say he take radio, guitar, coat, gold ring. Old man better not give him no trouble. The old man he look sad, give money to Esteban. He says somethin' we don' know what it is, some funny words. The old man is talkin' all the time, you know, on'y we don' know what he say when he talk funny."

A small young man, and on the narrow bed he seemed to listen to old Rocky in that barn as they took his money and possessions. "Then he talk English. He say, 'Is hard for be young.' He say, 'Steal . . . die soon.' Esteban is scare. 'Hey, shut up, old man. You don' tell no one.' The old man talk more stuff we don' know what it is. Esteban is more scare an' he hit the old man. He don' mean to hurt, on'y make him keep quiet. But old man hit head, there is much blood. We got to get him out of barn. We put him in cart, take to tree so people find him. Then we run."

He lay there in silence, looked at the wall. "Esteban go home with money, radio, guitar."

Sergeant Villa said, "How much money?"

"Twenty dollar. The ring is no good." The small man on the bed closed his dark eyes. "We don' want hurt. On'y he die."

I said, "Why didn't you go home too?"

He shrugged. "Got no family. Got no home, got no money. Got nothing. You come, I wait."

Villa took him in. His name was Jesus Rocha and he was nineteen. They picked up Esteban Sanchez in the small town in Mexico where his wife and children lived. He'd sold everything, the Mexican authorities never found the money. Before they could extradite him he hanged himself in his cell.

I got Rocha a lawyer. He hadn't killed old Rocky, there were no witnesses, so they let him plead guilty to second degree and sent him to Soledad for twenty years to life.

Lauri Michaels and Jess Hill had the bench and plaque put up to Rocky's memory. Mario Costello says he misses Rocky on his veranda. Terry Miken is still having trouble getting the White Hole zoned for residential-commercial.

Everyone misses Rocky, and the bench and plaque remind us all he was here. I don't think that would have mattered to him. I think what would have mattered to Rocky, I told Sergeant Villa, was Jesus Rocha and Esteban Sanchez.

"He said the same things in the hospital he said to those two field hands," I said to Villa. "It's hard to be a young field worker. You die inside. You're dead but you go on."

"So?" Villa said.

"He wasn't raving, he was telling us he knew why they had attacked him and it was okay, he understood and forgave them. He could have told you who they were anytime."

Villa shrugged.

Resurrection

The only two things that cannot be looked at directly are the sun and the truth.

SPANISH PROVERB

1.

The light is white and soft. Translucent and luminous. A giant white pearl that surrounds me like a soft fog. Clouds of light blown on swirling fog. A great black hole that grows larger, comes closer.

"Dan? You're safe, darling. You're fine. Dan?"

I don't answer. I'm not a fool. They want me to speak, let them find me again. But I'm too smart. Clever, I say nothing. I hide inside the light of the giant pearl.

"I love you, darling. We all do. Sybil is here, and Sergeant Chavalas. Can you hear me? You have to get well, darling."

They are out there beyond the thick clouds of white light waiting for The Preacher. I know the answer. *I know!* A voice tells me the answer. Which voice?

"Can you hear me, darling?"

I try to hear the voice that tells me what I must know. Will tell me what happened to George Rogers. What happened to me.

ॐ

George H. Rogers, 47, winner of three Pulitzer Prizes, flies to the high grassland of East Africa to report on the great relocation of Michael Sarguis, The Preacher, and his fervent followers, The People.

It is the most massive movement of religious fervor in search of the promised land since the Church of Jesus Christ of Latter-Day Saints went west to find their great salt lake. They, The People, build a modern town in the interior far from where the rivers that begin in the Mountains of the Moon finally flow into the sea. Journalist George Rogers is sent to report to the American people what nearly two years of massive mission have done to The Preacher and his flock, to the natives and the land.

For six months his reports come. Skeptical and fair, then equivocal and ambiguous, and finally enigmatic and repetitious. When none comes at all, the national news magazine makes phone calls, wonders in bold print what has happened to its prize reporter. Before anyone can answer, the world hears the report of the bloody battle between The People and the army, the death of The Preacher and all but a pitiful handful of The People. George H. Rogers is not heard from, cannot be found, and, presumably, has been killed in the crossfire.

The powerful news magazine does not accept "presumably," neither does the United States government. George Rogers is an important man, has friends. No stone is unturned, no pressure is unused, but George Rogers isn't found.

Perez Medina is.

Almost a year after the battle, Medina, former disciple of The Preacher, emerges from the bush where his wounds have been tended by tribesmen. Whisked backed to the States, Medina is welcomed joyously by the other six known survivors. He is interrogated with equal intensity, and what he says

151

rocks the survivors, if not the nation. He no longer believes in The Preacher or any religion; and The Preacher, George Rogers, and perhaps others of The People whose bodies have not been found, are still alive.

Five of his six fellow survivors are confused. They know, of course, that The Preacher and all The People can't die, as The Preacher had told The People. But they loudly denounce Perez Medina for his suggestion that The Preacher is hiding from the world and the survivors, and for his apostasy. They know The People have the truth. They know The Preacher is alive and will come for them.

The sixth survivor, Gabriel Sarguis, son of The Preacher's dead older brother, comes forward and makes his own statement: Perez Medina is hiding his own evil deed. He had murdered The Preacher and George Rogers after the attack, had fled into the bush in fear, there were no other survivors.

He, Gabriel Sarguis, through the pain of his own wounds had seen the murders, had then passed out. For a long time he had doubted what he had seen, had thought his memory was a delusion brought on by pain and being near death. But now he knew he had seen real murder. Perez Medina has invented his story to cover his guilt.

My office is at the rear of the house where Kay and I live in that part of Santa Barbara called Summerland. Kay Michaels, who makes my life, who is tall and auburn-haired and has her own modeling-theatrical agency. Sybil Rogers had been a model when she was younger, they keep in touch. Kay was at the wedding of Sybil to George Rogers years ago while I was still in New York.

"Perez Medina says George is alive."

Sybil Rogers could still have been a model. Trim and slim in my office, wearing a blue sheath dress that set off both her body and her blonde hair. The dress did nothing for her puffy eyes and face ravaged by grief, or the death grip she had on Kay's hand where they sat together on my couch.

"Medina says he saw George after the attack, and now I'm sure George tried to call me. He's alive, Mr. Fortune. Perez Medina isn't like the others. He's educated, a teacher."

"How do you know George tried to call you?"

"There were calls where no one spoke. A lot of noise on the line. As if from a long way away."

"How many calls? When?"

"Three. The day of the attack or soon after. I don't remember exactly when. I didn't have any reason to pay much attention then."

"What do you want me to do, Sybil?"

"Find him. Talk to Perez Medina, the others."

George Rogers, who everyone said had been dead for a year. Except Perez Medina, a man who had been wounded, disappeared into the bush to hide with primitive tribesmen for the same year, and who another survivor said had murdered George Rogers.

"Medina is accused of murdering him."

"They haven't arrested him."

"It happened too far away, in too remote a place. They have no evidence one way or the other. Just the stories of two men. No witnesses, no bodies."

"Find evidence. That's what Kay says you can do. You're a detective."

"I'm a detective, not a miracle worker."

"He's alive. It won't be any miracle."

"If your husband is alive, Sybil, why hasn't he come home? Why hasn't he been seen since the attack?"

"I don't know."

Kay said, "Perhaps he's lost in the jungle, Dan. Wounded and being taken care of by some remote tribe the way Medina was."

"Like David Livingstone? You want me to be Stanley?"
"Find George, Mr. Fortune," Sybil Rogers said.
"You mean find the truth?"
Her hands in her lap were as rigid as claws. "George is alive. I know he is."

෪

The seven survivors were scattered across the state. Max Pugo, Cosimo Baltieri and Gabriel Sarguis in San Francisco where The People had begun. Honoria Ebersole in Santa Barbara, Matthew Soames in Barstow. Perez Medina in Los Angeles. He was the one I needed to talk to most, but the last, Samuel Justice, was on the way.

In California even the mental hospitals are gentle to look at in the sun against the distant mountains. A pleasant building set on green grounds thick with flowers and trees and shrubs. Soothing as you parked and walked toward it. The bare rubber room was neither soothing nor pleasant. Without toilet, washbasin, furniture or anything else hard or sharp. Only a high window and a drain in the center of the padded floor.

"Why the rubber cell?"

"He's suicidal, Mr. Fortune," the doctor said. "It's part of the whole god thing."

"Because Michael Sarguis failed The People?"

"Because they failed him."

He sat in the corner of the rubber room. An old black man, his knees up to his chin, motionless. Small, emaciated, the skin of his narrow face like a carved wooden mask. His whole thin body rigid in the institutional jump suit like a seated statue placed to guard some sacred tribal shrine.

I squatted to speak into his face. "Mr. Justice? What happened to George Rogers? The reporter down there with you?"

The doctor stood behind me in the silence of the room. "Does he hear me?"

"He hears you."

I reached to the old man with my lone hand, looked up at the doctor over my shoulder. "Can I touch him?"

"He's not really dangerous, but I can't say how he'll react. I believe they practiced the laying on of hands, it could help."

The jump suit was coarse and harsh to my touch, the shoulder as hard as a statue. Flesh that quivered and jerked away from my hand as the old man's eyes flew open in the wooden mask of his face. Dark eyes focused on something far from the rubber cell, light-years away from the corridors of the mental hospital.

A hoarse voice that came from nowhere. "We got to be free. From the money, the cities, the chains we got on us. No one kills the sky. No one kills the truth. The earth hides us, the sky makes us invisible, the trees stop the bullets. They can't kill the truth. No one dies. No one . . ."

His voice didn't stop as much as fade into a silence. Only his hoarse breathing. The heavy breathing of a man who had run a long way. Who was still running. Rigid again in the corner of the rubber room without anything but the walls and a drain in the center of the floor, but running where he sat.

"Is he hallucinating?"

"He's had a complete mental breakdown," the doctor said, "but he's telling us what he believes is true, real."

"That none of them could be killed?" I said. "Even when he saw them all blown away in the attack? The bodies lying around? Has he forgotten, repressed it all? They never fell?"

"He saw them fall," the doctor said. "He remembers what he saw. But he saw them get up, too. He watched them all get up, go off hand-in-hand to where they're all still alive."

The old man began to rock against the rubber wall of the bare room. A slow, rhythmic rocking.

"He thinks he saw all the dead get up?"

"He *did* see them all get up. As real and solid and rational to him as looking at you and me in this room. More real than you and me and this room."

The old man began a low moan that turned into a singsong chant that matched the rhythm of his rocking.

"If they're all alive, why is he suicidal?"

"Because he's irrational, confused, guilty and afraid. He wants to be one of the flock again, be safe. Most of them do, the survivors. They confuse life and death. Death becomes life. Death ends life so it isn't death. It's life."

"They all believe that those killed in the attack are still alive?"

"Except the few who left The People before the attack, or were shocked by it back to our reality. Even they feel guilty."

The old man's voice filled the gray room. "They alive and I be with them. With The Preacher. We all take The Word around the world. Nobody dies what got the belief. That The Word."

The hoarse old voice faded into nothing. The old man rocked on. Sometimes he smiled, his eyes open like tunnels into a great distance.

2.

I hurt. The great black holes of pain float in the luminous white fog. A fog that blows away faces. The black hole is a face with giant eyes.

"I think he's awake."

The black hole grows and breaks and grows again. The pearl of fog swirls violent.

"His head moved."

"He shouldn't move too much."

If I move they will see me.

"Dan? Can you hear me?"

I hurt.

"Sybil's here with me, Dan."

I lie rigid, motionless. The heads move in the soft, blowing fog. I hear different voices. Distant voices that know the answer. A voice that tells me what I have to know. I have to find George Rogers. I only have to hear.

"He can't hear you, Kay. I better go."

George Rogers runs through the white fog where the bobbing black holes have eyes.

Tall and thin, Perez Medina lay on the bed in his mother's house, his face turned up toward the ceiling. The cracked and peeling ceiling of an unpainted house in the *barrio* of East Los Angeles.

"You saw them alive, Medina?"

"I saw them."

"The Preacher himself, and George Rogers?"

"Yes."

"All the others too? Are they all alive?"

The former disciple's sunken eyes didn't seem to see the cracks on the ceiling above him, or hear my voice. His emaciated body lay on the bed like the effigy of a medieval saint with the eyes fixed on some vision.

"I saw two men alive. I saw thousands of dead."

"The other survivors all say—"

"The other survivors talk belief. I'm talking fact."

A small bedroom. Narrow, with a single window and little furniture. The single bed, a bed table, a bare bureau. Empty walls where things had hung but were all gone. A monk's cell without a past or even a present. The past removed, the present bare, and no future. As isolated as the man who lay motionless on the bed.

"Tell me everything you saw."

"They were at the tents, the trucks."

"Tents?"

"Where we'd spent the night."

"What were you doing there?"

"Hiding."

"The attack was over?"

"I don't know." He rolled over on the bed, faced the wall, his back to me. "I ran. I ran away from the attack. I was there with The Preacher and all the others, then I panicked. I knew we'd all die. To stop the bullets you had to believe, and I didn't believe. I ran. Nothing seemed to work inside me. Not my mind, not my will, not my body. I ran all the way back to the camp. The tents and trucks we'd marched out from that morning."

On the narrow bed his back moved like a man running as fast as he could run. "I heard the guns, the explosions. No one around me, no movement anywhere. I listened for a long time. I knew they were dying, The People. The Word was dying, and The People, and I sat calm, and then I got up and started to walk into the brush and they saw me."

"The Preacher and George Rogers?"

"Soldiers. Looters. Some rogue officer and his men looking for what they could steal. Or a force sent out to be sure there was no one among the tents who could harm them. It doesn't matter. They were there at the camp. They saw me. They shot me. I was bleeding, I ran again. Fell and passed out. When I came awake I couldn't move my left arm, my right leg was all blood, my head was bleeding. I was in thick brush. I listened, heard nothing. I got up and walked and found I was back in the camp. The tents were burning, the trucks."

He turned on the narrow bed to look at me. "They were there, The Preacher and Rogers. Their clothes were torn and dirty, they looked exhausted, but I didn't see much blood and they walked fast among the tents and trucks toward the brush. Rogers had The Preacher's arm, pulled him along as if he were blind. Like Oedipus being led from the city. But The

Preacher's eyes were open, I didn't see any injury on his face. Only shock and horror. A horror I'd put there."

"You? How?"

"I didn't believe. Everyone had to believe, or The Word would fail. That was what The Preacher said, and I hadn't believed. I had never believed enough, and they were all dead because of me."

"You didn't go out? Speak to them?"

"No."

"What did they do?"

"I don't know. It was almost night by then. They walked on past where I hid. I heard no shots. No soldiers came. I passed out or slept, I'm not sure which. I wanted to kill myself, escape the shame and the fear. Instead I went to sleep and woke up in a hut. I was too weak to run again, and they saved my life, the tribesmen. They gave me back my life in all ways they could. They were a gentle, honest, practical people. They believed in themselves and the sky and the rivers and the animals. In nature. They know what a bullet does. Death is something they don't want, nothing else."

He sat up on the edge of his bed. "They taught me to see reality, Fortune. The Preacher and George Rogers are alive. Or they were after the attack was over."

"They healed you, but you lie and stare at the ceiling. An educated man, a teacher, alone in your mother's house."

"They healed all they could."

"What couldn't they heal?"

"What took me to The People in the first place. What took us all to The Preacher."

"What was that?"

He looked at me for some time in the small, bare room where he had grown up. "Need. Pain. Fear. A need you don't even understand yourself. A black force inside as powerful as a black hole in space." He looked away toward the wall. "I remember a couple who joined us late, just before we went over there."

Lisa MacSweeny, born into a poor family of miners with little education and less opportunity, grows up with all the anxieties of an uncertain and terrifying world. She tries many faiths and finds them all lacking before she meets Ben Rudman at a service of Seventh-Day Adventists.

A pastor in the strict sect, Rudman has grown up the only son of an overeducated family with no religious roots at all. Or with roots that had long been rejected and forgotten in the arrogance of their belief in their own knowledge. He finds their answers to the dark questions that come to him inadequate. He feels none of the strength his father and mother have, seems to himself to be alone in a world where he has no control of what will or will not happen to him. He comes to distrust the answers of everyone around him. He wants a rock to live by free of the fear of emptiness. He finds it in God, but finds that none of the forms of God offered by the churches of his ancestors, his friends, or his searchings, are the God he looks for.

At the time Lisa meets him, Ben has already begun to doubt that the God of the organized Seventh-Day Adventist sect is the one he seeks. For a time, Lisa's fresh belief in the new church rejuvenates Ben and maintains them both. They have a fine family of two boys and a girl, Lisa serves as his assistant in his pastoral duties, they build their entire life around the church. But as time goes on and the children grow, both Ben and Lisa become suspicious of all the civil authorities who want to teach the children lies and errors, and they also come to distrust the church that tells them they must obey the secular laws made by nonbelievers.

They leave the church, shun the outside world, withdraw

into themselves. An isolated and close family wrapped in their own fears and answers. Cold and withdrawn, they do not get along well with outsiders at school or on the job. They stand aloof from everyone, are unpleasant to be with. When times of hardship and recession strike the country, they are always among the first to lose their jobs. They alienate employers with their isolation. Finally they can't find jobs at all. They run out of money, have barely enough to set aside the ten percent they always offer to God.

They gather the family in prayer, discuss their plight and decide that they must all go on a fast so that they can continue to make their offering to the Lord. They know God will come to their aid as long as they maintain their faith and devotion. They fast for over a month. The money set aside for God is untouched. The family weakens. The younger boy becomes very weak. The family prays again, asks if they can use the tithe money for food, but Ben and Lisa cannot take what belongs to God. That would be stealing. They would be thieves against God.

The fast continues. No jobs come. After two months the younger boy dies.

Ben and Lisa are arrested. The other two children are put into the hospital where they are saved from the malnutrition that killed the younger boy. Their lawyers defend their right to exercise their religion, the right of their children to exercise their religion. It does not help. Ben and Lisa are convicted and sent to prison for ten years. The surviving children are placed in foster homes.

Released after seven years, Ben and Lisa move to California, find jobs, regain the two surviving children, and hear of The Preacher. They join The People, are among those who make the long retreat to the new home in the distant African country where they can live with their God as they wish.

❧

Kay sat silent over dinner for some time after I told her Perez Medina's story of the Rudmans.

"They died in the attack. Ben and Lisa and their two children. They were lucky, their bodies were identified."

"Those poor children." Kay poured wine. A nice Carmignano. Life goes on. "That's criminal, Dan."

"The jury thought so. And the judge. I'm not sure those children did, and I know Ben and Lisa and all the others in The Preacher's flock didn't."

"How can they justify killing their own children!"

"Their faith couldn't justify to themselves, or to their children, not killing them under those conditions. They have The Word, and they must live by it. Most of the survivors still believe in The Preacher."

"They must have lost all touch with reality."

"Not their reality. That's just what they can't lose."

3.

The giant pearl of luminous light is gone. The clouds of fog are gone.

The pearl has become a light in the ceiling of a pale green room, or the sun beyond the windows of what must be the same pale green room. The white fog is now only a line of light under the door of the dark room at night. Light from whatever world is on the other side. The bustle of morning light ushered in by the chattering nurses from that world outside the pale green room.

Kay smiles. "You look so much better, Dan."

I lie propped up in the bed. "How long?"

My voice startles me. I look all around the bright room. No one is there. Only Kay.

"Three days."

Three days. An eternity in the white fog, and no time at all.

"Does it hurt very much?"

"Not too much."

I look around again. But it really is my own voice.

"Is something wrong, darling?"

Kay looks too. There is no one else. Only Kay and my voice. But there are other voices. The voices that tell me I know the answer.

Voices without words.

The Church of the Universal Resurrection was in a white frame house set back from a side street in San Francisco. Its bare yard was littered with rusted junk. The house itself was in better condition, with a new front door and windows and a fresh coat of paint. Signs were mounted on the porch posts on each side of the front steps up to the open door.

On the left the sign proclaimed the name of the church and its pastor—Rev. Gabriel Sarguis—and the hours of the daily prayer meetings, readings, class instruction and services. On the right the simple lettering announced AIDS Counseling and Hospice, Drug Rehabilitation, and Neighborhood Networking. I climbed the steps between the signs and knocked on the door that was ajar. My knocks echoed in an empty space. Somewhere inside there were voices, but no one came to the door.

Inside, the interior walls and ceiling had been torn out to leave a long, high room with rows of folding chairs that faced a raised platform and lectern. There was no center aisle, nothing to kneel on in front of the rows of chairs, no bibles or hymnals, no altar or crosses or decorations on the platform.

Only the lectern and three chairs. To the left of the platform there was another door. The voices came from behind it. I went through.

The man who faced me from behind the desk in the sunny office smiled. "How can I help you, friend?"

The other man with his back to me turned in his chair, stared as if I were a species he'd never seen. A small, skinny latino in tight jeans, decorated shirt, and colorful woven vest. He looked me up and down, fixed his gaze on my empty sleeve.

"Reverend Sarguis?"

The man behind the desk nodded. "I'm Gabriel Sarguis, yes." He put on the serious but carefully neutral face of all clergymen about to try to help someone with a problem. "The Reverend isn't really official, sort of a courtesy from our church, but I'll be glad to try to help, Mr.—?"

The Preacher's nephew was in his early thirties. Stocky and going to fat over the muscles of a man who had worked hard with his hands at some time. Black hair long and straight to his shoulders, he had the calm eyes of someone who knew what he had to do. He wore well-tailored gray slacks and a black and silver Guatemalan *jaspe* shirt without a tie.

"Dan Fortune," I said. "It's Mrs. George Rogers who needs your help. I'm a private investigator she hired to find out what did happen over there to her husband. If we could—"

"Sure, of course." He stood behind the desk. "Let's go back to my digs. Angel, we talk some more later, okay?"

The skinny latino shrugged. "No sweat, man. Pass the word to Rafael, okay?" He slouched past me, pointed at my pinned-up sleeve. "How you lose it, man?"

"Shark."

"Jesus."

He crossed himself and went out.

Gabriel Sarguis half smiled. "The Catholics are always the hardest to change." He opened a rear door out of the office, led me down three steps to a long, narrow backyard. "I live in the cottage over there."

Around the yard there were three buildings hidden from the street. The small cottage where Sarguis lived was on the left, the other two buildings on the right. They were like one-story barracks with bars on all their windows. A high chain-link fence surrounded the whole yard.

"Why the bars?"

"Don't have a clue. They were here when we bought the property. We use one for an AIDS center and hospice, the other is our drug rehabilitation unit. It's probably good we have the bars, we keep methadone and other drugs." He looked back toward the big house. "Angel's one of the first to come here for drug help. He's close to going clean. The Preacher always said there were a lot of ways to save a lost person. 'Many roads to resurrection.' He had the gift of words."

In the living room of his cottage he told me to sit down, went into the kitchen. It was a comfortable room. A large futon love seat and two leather armchairs, a long teak coffee table, a large color television set and a big desk. He returned with two Bohemia beers, dropped onto the futon love seat. "What can I tell you except what you already know if you're here, Mr. Fortune?"

"There's a lot I don't know and Mrs. Rogers doesn't know. For instance, how did you happen to survive?"

"I wasn't there."

"Why not?"

"He'd sent me on a mission."

"The Preacher?"

He nodded. "A last mission. One more shot at negotiation, no stone unturned." He stretched out his legs. "I went to the provincial capital. I was supposed to go on to the national people, but the army brass wouldn't let me. They were going to handle us alone, make big names for themselves. They beat the hell out of me to get me to tell them what The Preacher was doing. They don't play polite games in Africa, or worry much about diplomatic relations even with big old Uncle Sam." He took a long drink of the Bohemia. "Then they took me back to the camp. We didn't get there until the attack was over, they were all dead. Or almost all. Some of the survivors think The Preacher sent me away because he wanted me to survive and go on with the work. I've decided that if he intended that or not, I'd try to go on with all he did that was good, stay away from the bad. Maybe he did send me off on purpose. Had some doubt right there at the end. That maybe he didn't have the whole truth."

He pointed at the bottle in my hand. I shook my head. When he returned from the kitchen he had two more bottles of Bohemia. "The bodies were lying everywhere out across the grassland and brush. Floating in the river, stacked in the *barrancas* on top of each other. The soldiers were already bulldozing bodies into mass graves. The vultures were on the ground. Scavenging animals I can't even name."

He drank the beer like a man who wants to drown something. "You ever watch people you know being eaten by animals, their flesh torn off in strips by the vultures? The soldiers were looting everything they could find on the bodies. Eyeglasses, gold teeth. The soldiers who'd brought me back ran to get in on the loot. The officer told two of the soldiers to shoot me too, but he didn't stay around to see them do it. They shot me, but they were so anxious to get their share they only wounded me and ran off after the others, left me alone at the tents and trucks. That's when I saw them."

He went to work on the third Bohemia. "I was in a kind of trance from the pain. I was sitting against the wheel of a truck, saw them between two tents. Two of them had their backs to me. The third I saw clear. He had one arm hanging down like it was broken, his good hand carried one of the AK-

47s The Preacher got for us. It was Perez Medina. How could I miss him? Our college man, our scholar? He was screaming at the other two. They tried to run, the other two, and that's when I saw who they were. The Preacher and the journalist Rogers. Medina cut them down like rabbits. I tried to get up and must have passed out."

He held the empty bottle in both hands. "The next I knew I was in some hospital. The day was over."

"Why didn't you tell anyone about what you saw then?"

He turned the empty bottle in his hands as if it hurt. "At first I was too weak to think. When I did, they all said Medina, my uncle and Rogers had died in the attack. For a long time I thought what I'd seen was all a delusion. No one else had seen Perez Medina. They said they were all dead, bulldozed in one of the mass graves or ripped up by the animals. Then Medina reappeared, told his lying story about The Preacher and Rogers being still alive. There was no way The Preacher would have run away, hidden out. He'd have contacted the world. He'd have contacted the other survivors. He'd sure have contacted me."

"Maybe something else happened down there. Something he doesn't want known. Maybe he doesn't want to be resurrected."

"He's dead, Mr. Fortune, and so is George Rogers. I'm sorry for Mrs. Rogers. If they were alive, why wouldn't Rogers come home? Medina is lying. When he came out of the jungle two weeks ago he had a healed broken left arm, just like I'd seen. He had a scar where I'd seen his face bloody. He didn't tell his lies until after he found out I was a survivor."

"What was his motive?"

"All I can figure is when he ran out on The Preacher he told those soldiers something he shouldn't. The Preacher and Rogers knew it, he was scared of them."

"But you're not sure."

His dark eyes were steady. "Perez Medina killed them

167

both. No one's going to prove it, but he knows it, I know it, and The Preacher knows it. He'll have to live with me in this world, and with The Preacher in the next."

Michael Sarguis, The Preacher, had had his first vision in a frame house in a nice area of San Francisco beyond the Castro. It wasn't an official shrine. No commemorative plaque for an unsuccessful god. But flowers in vases lined the front steps. Offerings.

Inside, there were more flowers under a giant photo of The Preacher. Rows of small statues of a figure in a black robe stood on a shelf next to the photo. A hand-lettered sign pointed up the stairs to *The Window*.

"Are you interested in The Preacher?"

He was a short man in his mid-thirties, heavy and nervous. He pulled at his gray polyester suit, adjusted the knot of his tie. One tip of the collar of his cheap white shirt was bent under. Sweat shined on his high forehead in the cool day.

"Mr. Max Pugo?"

"Who are you?"

"Dan Fortune. I called you earlier. To talk about George Rogers. You live here?"

"Yes. I don't know anything about George Rogers."

"You're one of the survivors. Did you see him or The Preacher after the attack?"

"I was sick. In the tents. Someone found me in the tents. He'll come for me."

"Who?"

"The Preacher."

"He's not dead, Mr. Pugo?"

"He died there with The People. They'll all come for me."

"They died but they're not dead," I said.

"That's The Word."

He wasn't Samuel Justice in the asylum, but he wasn't that rational either.

"Is Cosimo Baltieri here too?"

"He comes later. You want to buy a man in black?"

I declined a man in black, whatever it was.

4.

I am in Santa Barbara. I know that. I have been told.

I am in a hospital in Santa Barbara, California. I'm not sure how I got here, but it is Santa Barbara and Kay is here.

"Too tired to see Sybil? She's in the waiting room. She's been here four times."

I hear footsteps in the corridor. They startle me. No one comes in with a gun. No one comes in at all. I stare at the door. I want to hear the voice tell me what I can't remember.

She nods, Kay. "All right, just rest now, Dan. Sybil will just have to wait until you're stronger."

I know the answer, but I don't know what I know. Who is lying? Medina? Sarguis? The Colonel and the government in Africa? Sybil Rogers? I try to hear the voice that tells me why they all wait and die.

In the house at the edge of the desert, blood had pooled in the kitchen, dripped a trail out across the dirt and dust of the unfenced back yard to the desert itself. The body lay out back with its empty eye sockets up to the sun.

Spread-eagled, arms and one leg in a cross as if crucified against the desert floor. One leg was missing. Not missing a long time like my arm, but hacked off and hung from a stunted tree across the yard. Black candles had burned out at the head and arms. A half-smoked cigar rested on the bloody chest.

I couldn't see what had killed him, there was no weapon in the yard or in the silent and dusty house. Inside the house his papers were in the upper left-hand drawer of the bureau in the bedroom. Mr. Matthew Soames, recipient of social security and Medicare, with a heart condition and no next of kin. Without driver's license or telephone.

I drove to the diner down the road, called the Barstow police. They said go back and stay in the house, they would be out in five minutes. I sat in the living room and felt the ache I get in my missing arm when I think about it too much. The leg in the tree outside made me think of it. I still wonder where it is, my lost arm. They never told me when the surgeon had to cut it off back in New York when I was seventeen.

I thought of something else. The living room. It was as austere and bare as Perez Medina's room. A hard couch covered in fake black leather, two upright chairs with wooden arms. A cheap pine coffee table, a tarnished brass lamp with a torn shade. A drab room so clean and neat it looked untouched by human hands. As if the dead man out in the desert had not really lived here. Passing through on his way somewhere else. Or waiting.

Nothing that was him except the large photograph of The Preacher on the living room wall draped in black and gold. Waiting for a hope, myth, delusion. What was out in the backyard was neither delusion nor hope. It was real death. A real murder in a real world.

Two Barstow police appeared and took a quick look around. One made a fast call back to headquarters. The other sat with me until the major crimes detectives and coroner's team arrived. They sat with me too, the detectives. The coroner went to work in the back yard.

"Let's hear it, Fortune."

They did, from the move of The People to Africa, to Sybil Rogers hiring me, to my talks with all the survivors except Cosimo Baltieri and Honoria Ebersole.

"You think this is part of what happened over in Africa? To that preacher and his people?"

"I don't know."

"Are they psycho? This sure looks like the work of some loony-toons chopper."

"One is, but he's locked up and the doctors say he's not dangerous. The others are traumatized, but I don't see a motive for any of them."

"What motive you need for what's out there except a brain like the inside of a butcher shop?"

"You know what killed him yet?"

"Blow to the back of the head with some kind of large knife or sword. The blood on the chest was carved for fun."

Their search of the house and grounds turned up nothing that meant anything to them or to me. They would dig into the past and present of the dead Matthew Soames, but that wasn't where they expected to find the answer. "All kinds of psychos in and out of the desert. We'll find this one sooner or later."

৵

Mr. Walter Ebersole lived alone in the large white Victorian house on Santa Barbara's upper east side.

"My wife died ten years ago, Mr. Fortune. Thank God for that small blessing. She saw the beginning, but not the end of the travesty Honoria has made of her life."

A slender man in his seventies, Walter Ebersole wore a dark gray suit, white shirt and tie in mid-afternoon. His living room was large and comfortable. His voice was narrow with scorn.

"I thought your daughter lived with you now?"

"We did not get along. We have never gotten along since she left high school. Neither her mother, God rest her soul, nor I."

"Why, Mr. Ebersole?"

"She chose a different lifestyle, Mr. Fortune." The sharp edge of disgust as hard as steel. "A monstrous lifestyle. Neither my wife nor I could ever understand why, whatever possessed her. I still don't, and I have tried."

I tried to imagine what his idea of trying to understand his daughter would have been.

"What was so monstrous about her life?"

"Everything! We entered her in a fine women's college up north. Mills, where my wife had gone. She refused to go." He took a deep breath. "She did not want to go to college, she wanted to play music. We had given her piano lessons with the finest teacher in town, encouraged her music, even held recitals here at the house. Do you know what she had done? Behind our backs she had learned to play the guitar. Had met this man who lived in a trailer, played the guitar on streets, took drugs, had been in prison. Secretly for over a year, lying to us, stealing from us to give him money, learning to play the guitar with him."

Ebersole looked old. "She left her home to go with this man. To sing songs on streets and in taverns like a homeless vagrant." His steel eyes warned he was about to speak such horror I had better brace myself. "To live with this man like a whore. Take drugs, lie and steal, beg for money. No home, no family, no morality."

"Did she ever tell you why she had to leave? Find a different life?"

He dismissed that with a flick of his wrist in the immaculate suit. "Nothing that made sense. Our life made her feel empty, alone, afraid. Whatever that means. We did everything because it was right, not because we wanted to do it. We were liars inside. I slapped her for that." He looked down at his

172

thin hand with something like satisfaction. "She knew there was an answer, but we didn't know it. What answer? We'd sent her to Sunday school, church, high school, taught her right from wrong, what decent people did and did not do. She found her answer—a depraved and godless life."

"Not godless, Mr. Ebersole. Her own god."

"That madman? Yes, that is the god she deserves. A mad god, and now a dead one."

"She still believes in The Preacher? That he's alive?"

"From what I can tell, both alive and dead. I told you she made no sense. Then or now."

"Alive metaphorically? Or really?"

"Really, I should say. I've heard they all do, the few survivors."

"Believe, Mr. Ebersole? Or know?"

"There doesn't seem to be much difference in her mind."

"Could she have seen The Preacher alive?"

"I thought it was a known fact that the madman died with all the others over there."

"One man says he didn't."

"Then perhaps Honoria did see him. She speaks such nonsense I'm sure I couldn't tell you if she did or didn't."

"Where can I ask her myself?"

His laugh was as contemptuous as his voice. "Do you know where The People, as they called themselves, had their first so-called mission here? In the *barrio* slum? She moved down there to be near it."

I left him with his contempt firm on his thin face, drove down to the address on Cacique Street. It was a weathered gray house across from an abandoned church with a sign so faded I could barely make out the lettering: MISSION OF THE PEOPLE.

Honoria Ebersole's apartment was at the rear. I walked around the gray house, up the broken driveway, and knocked on the door that had been repaired with two lopsided and

unpainted boards. There was no answer. The door was unlocked, I looked in. A tiny apartment. One room and a
kitchen. This time the killer had left her in the kitchen.

She lay on her back, her eyeless face up to the peeling paint
of the ceiling. A still-young face slashed with geometric de-
signs like some ancient fetish. Her arms were out in the
cross, she had both legs. The candles were there, still burning
at the tips of each outflung hand.

She was naked. Her throat had been cut.

The same large photo of The Preacher hung on her living
room wall. I called Sergeant Gus Chavalas. Whatever I had
been doing for Sybil Rogers was now something else.

They had taped off the gray house, shooed the curious away
at least as far as across the street, removed Honoria Ebersole's
body. The lab team still worked over the house and grounds.
Sergeant Chavalas brooded in a butterfly chair in the spartan
little room under the photo of The Preacher. A room like
most of the others where the survivors lived.

"They didn't go for the good life," Chavalas said.

This kind of murder depressed Chavalas. From the dark
places inside some solitary, tortured mind you had to hate
but couldn't. Not if you dealt with crime and violence every
day, had a mind yourself.

"No one killed her for what she had," he said.

"Maybe for what she was," I said.

Chavalas listened to his men working outside and in the
kitchen. "It's exactly like the other one in Barstow, Dan?"

"Not exactly, but close enough."

"Barstow's not so far away."

"Too far."

He didn't like that either. Two senseless killings were no
better than one. "I called Barstow. Nothing. Soames was

alone, not a relative they can find. Hardly ever even went out."

"Waiting," I said. And two senseless, grotesque murders were better than one. "There's a reason, sergeant. Two at the same time."

"You think all the crazy stuff is a cover? Make them look like some psycho?"

"I think someone's trying to cover something. Maybe head me off."

Chavalas got up. "Let's check on the names in your case."

Three hours later Chavalas had our answers. Gabriel Sarguis was in Mexico City to help start a new Church of the Universal Resurrection. He could prove it. Max Pugo and Cosimo Baltieri hadn't left San Francisco, had ten people to say so. Samuel Justice was still in the corner of his rubber room. Perez Medina hadn't left his mother's house in two days, but he'd been alone most of that time.

5.

I watch the city outside the hospital windows. The red roofs and white walls, the pastel pinks and blues and yellows. The sea and the trees.

There are a lot of trees. Tall blue-gum eucalyptus and red eucalyptus and a hundred other varieties of the Australian tree brought across the Pacific by forgotten sailors. The white of silk floss and orange-yellow of silk oak. Lavender of jacaranda. Olive and pepper and tall pine. The dusty green of native live oak. Red fire tree and tulip tree and bottlebrush. All flowing down with the red roofs to the blue sea and distant islands.

It is peaceful in the sun, Africa is far away. The mass graves and the river floating with bodies are in another country. The vultures and small animals tearing at the flesh of the dead are somewhere else.

At night I wait for sleep. I lie awake, think of Kay and the sun and the sea of Santa Barbara where I have lived some years now, I can't remember how many. New York was my home, but I left New York. For Santa Barbara. For Kay. There comes a time when you have to face the truth of what you need.

I think of George Rogers, of Sybil Rogers. What do I know to tell Sybil Rogers? Of The Preacher. Of Perez Medina and Gabriel Sarguis. Someone is lying. I know, but don't know.

Perez Medina sat in a wicker chair against the broken fence of his mother's back yard. Clay pots stood on a wooden box in front of him. He painted flowers on the pots in bright enamel colors.

"Someone killed two of the survivors. The police can't find a motive in either case. Savage killings. Why?"

He finished a gaudy blue leaf on the clay surface. "Someone doesn't want The Preacher found."

"Or maybe they knew he was dead, you were afraid one day one of them would face reality and tell the truth."

"He was alive after the attack, Fortune." He painted a yellow flower on the blue leaf.

"Why would Gabriel Sarguis say he saw you kill them both?"

"I suppose he thinks he saw what he says he saw."

"If he's lying, why would he?"

He concentrated on the outline and placement of a new red leaf. "He always made me think of Saul of Tarsus. Paul the Apostle. He didn't really believe in The Preacher. Only in what The Preacher could become. In what The Preacher could be made into. What he could get out of The Preacher."

The woman's voice called from the ramshackle house. "Perez? Is another friend to speak with you."

The man who knocked Mrs. Medina aside as he pushed through the open door was short and heavy, dark and disheveled, wild-eyed, dressed in stained gray polyester slacks and a dirty white shirt. Max Pugo.

That was all I had time to see before he fired the big forty-five automatic held out in both hands. I dove for cover, tried to get at my new Sig-Sauer. Perez Medina was slammed back against the wall as his mother screamed.

The LAPD detective behind his desk was a short man with neat curly blond hair and a boyish face. In the corner of the office an old man in a black suit looked at my empty sleeve.

"Sergeant Paul Knight. What's your version, Fortune?"

I told him my version of the shooting, how I had captured Pugo. "It wasn't hard. He emptied the forty-five, mostly at the sky, sat down in the dirt and covered his face. I called you."

"You know this Max Pugo?"

"He's one of the other survivors."

"Survivors?"

The sergeant listened uneasily to my brief summary of The Preacher and The People and the attack in Africa. It wasn't the kind of event he wanted to have to deal with. Not at the East Los Angeles Division.

"Seven? That's all? Out of how many?"

"Two thousand, give or take."

"Jesus Christ."

I watched the concept of two thousand people killed in a single attack work through his mind. The concept of one of seven survivors trying to kill another.

"Why the hell would this Pugo want to kill Medina or you?"

"What does he say?"

"I'm not so goddamn sure he knows. We've been talking to him, getting shit for answers. Maybe you can get us something."

The interrogation room was small and crowded. One detective talked, two leaned in weariness against the walls around where Max Pugo sat under the light. Pugo was the first one to see me.

"He is liar! Him and Medina, all liars!"

The older of the detectives looked at me. "Who the fuck's this, Knight?"

"Dan Fortune, lieutenant. The other guy Pugo tried to shoot up. He's a private snooper. Maybe he can get something."

The lieutenant stared at my empty sleeve. "Why the fuck not? Be my guest, Fortune."

Max Pugo's thin hair was matted with sweat in the hot room. His heavy face full of anger and something else: fear. It wasn't fear of the police.

"Liars?" I said. "That's why you wanted to kill us? You don't want anyone to think The Preacher didn't die down there?"

Naked fear in his eyes. "They want to come back, but the lies don't let them. The Preacher says, Max, we can't return because Medina lies, the detective blasphemes with his questions. The Preacher says—"

"You heard The Preacher? His voice?"

"Medina won't let him come back. Medina and you."

"Medina says The Preacher is alive, survived the attack. Why is that bad, Max?"

"The Preacher does not abandon The People! He does not run away! He lives with The People. He wants to come for us, but the lies won't let him."

178

"Where did you get the gun, Max?"

"Medina he is liar. You are liar. Medina don't let The Preacher come to us. He is devil, anti-Christ."

Sergeant Knight said, "The SFPD is tracing the gun."

A wall of fear behind Max Pugo's eyes as he looked up at me. I touched his shoulder. "It's okay, Max."

The lieutenant watched me. "That's it?"

"That's all you'll get now, lieutenant. By our standards he's not rational."

"Was he ever?" the lieutenant said. "Let me be sure I get it. This man Medina says he saw the Preacher guy alive when he's supposed to be dead. Another guy from down here says Medina murdered The Preacher, and The Preacher is really dead. This Pugo and some others say The Preacher is dead but he isn't dead."

"That's about what Pugo believes."

"What about the guy who says Medina murdered The Preacher? Why aren't they mad at him?"

"He doesn't count. The Preacher can't die, so if he was murdered it doesn't mean anything."

"So what is Pugo's motive to kill Medina *and* you?"

"Fear," I said.

"Fear of what? What the hell's he afraid of that makes him grab a gun and go shoot another survivor?"

"Fear of losing The Preacher. Fear that his belief in The Preacher isn't true."

"Who does he think this Preacher is?"

"God."

In the room they all looked at me. All except Max Pugo.

"You want me to tell the D.A. that Pugo tried to kill two people because he was afraid to lose God?"

"That's the truth."

"They're going to love it at City Hall." The lieutenant pointed to Sergeant Knight. "Go talk to Medina, maybe he can give us something better. Take Fortune, sounds like you

179

could need an interpreter. And tell that old man he can see Pugo now."

In his office, the sergeant nodded to the old man in the black suit. "You can see Pugo in a couple of minutes."

The old man said, "He is okay? Max?"

"If going to prison or a mental hospital is okay."

"That don't matter. He'll be free soon."

"Free?" Knight said. "You're not thinking about anything crazy, are you, Mr. Baltieri?"

I said, "He means The Preacher will come and take him. Mr. Baltieri is another of the survivors. Do you want to kill Perez Medina and me too, Baltieri?"

The last of the survivors ignored me. I walked to him.

"If Medina is lying, is Gabriel Sarguis telling the truth?"

"They both liars."

"Why would they lie? What do they gain?"

"Medina got to hide he run away. That Gabriel I never trust. Out for himself. Start his own church. I can see Max, officer?"

The sergeant took Baltieri out, came back for me. The LAPD wanted an answer they could file and label. Greed or lust, hate or jealousy. A fact to write up in a report, a place and date to point to in court. *On the twenty-second of June last, at five-twelve P.M., Perez Medina did do . . . to Max Pugo, causing Mr. Pugo to . . .* At the hospital we had to wait.

"He's in his room now, sergeant. Ten minutes."

In the room, Perez Medina lay bandaged thick across the chest under the hospital gown, his left arm strapped tight.

"Mr. Medina? I'm Sergeant Paul Knight, LAPD. I'd like to ask you some questions if you feel up to it."

Medina nodded.

"His name's Max Pugo. You know him?"

"I know him."

"Fortune says you and Pugo survived this Preacher thing. You have any trouble with Pugo before today?"

"No."

"Did you know him over there?"

"Not so well."

"You were one of the leaders? But you didn't know everyone in the organization?"

"It wasn't an organization. It was a mission, a faith. There were no leaders except The Preacher. I knew most of The People by sight, fewer by name. Names weren't important. We were The People, all part of The Word."

"You got to know him better after you all got back?"

"No."

"Seven survivors? I'd think you'd know each other pretty damn well. I mean, after what you'd all been through."

"The People weren't a club or a fraternity. Each of us was there alone with The Preacher, not with each other. We survived alone with The Preacher, not with each other."

"He knew you well enough to try to kill you."

"Not me. Who I was, and what I am now."

Knight looked at me, silently asked if either of us knew what we were talking about? Couldn't we give any answers that made sense?

I said, "Mr. Medina was a disciple of The Preacher. He no longer believes in The Preacher, but says he's alive somewhere. Physically alive and hiding from them. Max Pugo doesn't want to hear either statement. He's afraid to hear them. They might be true, and he can never admit that possibility."

"Why are they mad at you?"

"I'm asking questions. They live in their own world with their own answers. What I find might make them question those answers. They've committed their lives to those answers."

"You mean they're fanatics."

Perez Medina said, "A lot of people don't want to hear the truth if it doesn't support what they believe."

6.

The solarium is warm. I've been in the hospital four days, Kay comes only in the evening hours. Rules are important now that I'm better. Sergeant Chavalas doesn't have rules.

"You have no idea who shot you, Dan?"

"I have ideas, more than one, but that's all. Someone we know or someone we don't know."

"Who the hell are you a danger to?"

"If I knew that, I'd know what I don't know. You've found nothing on who shot me? Honoria Ebersole or Soames?"

"Barstow's a dead end, everyone connected to Soames is clear. The Ebersole woman didn't have any life of her own we can find. Not a clue in her place."

"And me?"

"Two people saw a late-model dark blue Japanese car pull away from outside the parking lot right after you were shot, but no one got the make, model or number. No one saw you or the shooter in the lot. No one heard the shots."

"How was I found?"

"You got lucky. A guy came for the car next to yours, spotted you down between cars."

When Chavalas leaves, I look out at the towering silk oak with its mass of orange-yellow flowers a block from the hospital. How do I tell them I know the answer, but I don't know? That somewhere someone gave me the answer, but I can't remember who or where? What do I tell Sybil Rogers, who waits out there with her binoculars?

Sybil Rogers lived on her ranch in the Santa Ynez Valley, forty-five minutes over San Marcos Pass from Santa Barbara. I could see her on the redwood deck. Sun glinted off binoculars. She watched me all the way along the dirt road, sat on the porch swing with the binoculars in her lap when I walked up.

"Have you found him?"

"No." I sat on the rail with my back to the view. "More of the survivors have been attacked. Including Perez Medina."

"Is he dead?"

"No, but Soames and Ebersole are. Medina was shot by Max Pugo. Pugo's over the edge, so is Justice. That rules them all out except Cosimo Baltieri, Gabriel Sarguis and you."

"What's happening, Dan?"

"What do you think?"

Her eyes were focused on the vast view. "You sit here and look at the sun, the trees, the flowers, and it's hard to believe people would kill for anything."

"People have never needed to work hard to find reasons to kill other people. Almost anything will do. God's always been one of the more popular reasons. A little out of fashion the last few centuries in the Western world, if not the Eastern."

She said, "If The Preacher is alive too, perhaps George is a prisoner."

"If George is alive," I said, "maybe he doesn't want to be found."

Some horsemen rode across a field far off like distant toys. A haze all but hid the range of mountains on the far side of the valley. Like the shadow of a killer.

"What possible reason could George have to not come home? To hide from me? There isn't any reason."

"Maybe it's not you he's hiding from."

She got up, walked along her deck. "Do you have any other theories, Dan?"

"Revenge has always been a popular motive."

"You think George could want revenge? On The Preacher? On The People?"

"Maybe."

"Or perhaps I want revenge?"

"That too."

"Why?"

"What they did to your husband."

"But they did nothing to my husband. He's alive and well."

"He's not with you."

"He will be." She walked back toward me. "Why would I hire you if I were about to go out and massacre all the survivors?"

"Maybe you didn't know then you were going to do that."

"I'd have to have gone insane."

"Temporarily."

"Then I could be dangerous. Even to you. But I'm not dangerous and I'm not crazy. I want to know what happened to my husband, Dan."

But she didn't want to know. She wanted to believe. That her husband would come back to her.

The man behind the desk in the pastor's office of The Church of the Universal Resurrection was older and heavier than Gabriel Sarguis, but there was a strong resemblance. An older face, more like the photos of The Preacher himself.

"If you want Gabe, take a seat in the church. He'll be back."

Behind the desk he added figures in an account ledger, tallied them on a hand calculator, ignored me. But I had seen the glance not at me, at my empty sleeve. He knew who I was.

"Uncle or brother?"

"Rafael Sarguis, uncle."

"The Preacher is your brother?"

"He was my brother." He pushed away from the desk. "Gabe says you're snooping for some *loco* woman doesn't think Michael or that writer who went down there to dig dirt are dead."

"My snooping for the crazy lady is turning into something nastier than it started out."

"It's a nasty world," Rafael Sarguis said.

"Someone's killing the survivors. You have any ideas about who that could be?"

"Not a one. I came back to San Francisco after the trouble over there, after Gabriel got home. I never was with Michael, never been the religious type."

"What type are you, Mr. Sarguis?"

"An accountant helping out my nephew with his books and finances. The church operates on small contributions. That's an accounting nightmare with Uncle Sam on your back."

"*Mucho grande* nightmare, Fortune, believe me." Gabriel Sarguis came in from the church. In running shoes, he made almost no sound as he walked.

"Back from Mexico?" I said.

"Today. I tell you, they've got the faith down there."

I said, "Perez Medina was shot yesterday."

"Dead?"

"Not yet. Max Pugo shot him. Pugo's gone psycho, if he wasn't already."

Rafael got up. "I'm going to check inventory in the drug rehab and AIDS units, Gabe."

He left through the back door, Gabriel Sarguis sat down at his desk. "Why would anyone want to kill the survivors?"

"That's my question, isn't it? Why would anyone? What did they know? See? Hear? Guess? Or what were they doing or going to do that could be trouble for someone?"

Gabriel shrugged.

"Or is it hate? Revenge? For those who died because of the

185

beliefs of The Preacher and The People? Or is it maybe to cover something you survivors know from down there? Something the killer doesn't want known by anyone else?"

"Such as?"

"Maybe The Preacher did come back to all of you and someone doesn't want you to tell me that."

Gabriel smiled. "You're going in circles, Fortune. If he didn't want anyone to know he was alive he wouldn't have come to tell the survivors he was. And if he was alive, why would he hide? Why would anyone care who knew he was alive? No, my uncle didn't come back to me or to anyone else."

This time the shots smashed the window behind the desk and Gabriel Sarguis. The first ripped past my ear. I hit the floor, took a hard blow to the armless shoulder from the desk. The second shot came with a cry, "Ahhh!" A slam of weight against the desk, and a burst of more shots from outside.

I rolled, crawled to the window behind the desk. A man lay on the baked dirt of the back yard a few yards from the church building. He wore what looked like a black suit, black shoes run over at the heel. There was a gun in his hand. Blood on the grass and dirt.

Rafael Sarguis stood over the man in the black suit. His gun was pointed at the dirt.

"Fortune?"

Gabriel Sarguis's voice was almost a whisper. He sat in his desk chair, half turned away from the desk and away from the window. His face was pale. His left arm hung over the chair arm. The blood ran from his shoulder down his suit jacket to his hand and dripped to the floor.

"You going to pass out?"

He shook his head. "How bad?"

The cloth of the jacket had been ripped open, not punctured. A bullet passing, not entering.

"It's a deep flesh wound. More blood than damage."

Outside people had run out of the other buildings around the rear yard. They all looked at the man on the ground and at the church building. One was the skinny latino I'd met the first time here, Angel. Others were women in white smocks like nurses. One of the women hurried back into a building. Rafael came toward the church. I went out to meet him.

"Gabriel's hit. Not serious, but a doctor wouldn't hurt."

"They're already calling 911."

I looked at the man on the ground. He hadn't moved since I'd first looked out. He wasn't going to move again.

"You shoot him?"

Rafael didn't look back at the dead man. "I have to handle big money. Bonded."

"You know him?"

"No."

"I do." Gabriel held his left arm with his right hand to keep it motionless as he looked down at the man on the ground, at the automatic in his hand. "So do you, Fortune."

I went to the fallen man, bent down close. The old man who'd come to the police to help Max Pugo. Cosimo Baltieri. The last of the survivors.

"It leaves only two alive outside a mental institution. Perez Medina and Gabriel Sarguis, and they've both been shot."

Kay lay in bed and watched me undress. "This Baltieri tried to kill Sarguis?"

"The two bullets in the office were from his gun. The San Francisco police are trying to trace that gun, too."

"Did Pugo and Baltieri kill the others?"

I lay down beside her. "I don't know. They might have mutilated Medina and Sarguis the same way as the other two if they'd shot better and had the time. But what's the motive?"

187

She had turned off the overhead light, left only the single table lamp on, when the telephone rang. We both looked at it in the dim light of the bedroom. It went on ringing. My work has its frustrations. I picked up the receiver.

"Fortune?" It was the voice of Rafael Sarguis. "Gabriel got a call from Washington."

I looked at our clock radio in the dim bedroom light. "It's two in the morning in Washington."

"They just got the word from Africa."

"What word?"

"Another survivor came out of the bush two days ago."

"George Rogers?"

"Some guy named Crispin Brown. He saw Perez Medina kill my brother and that writer. He's been hiding out ever since."

"Where is he?"

"Still in Africa."

I hung up, lay back and listened to the night surf.

"I guess I go to Africa."

"Tomorrow," Kay said. "Tonight I have other plans."

I liked her plans better.

7.

You always leave a hospital in a wheelchair. Liability.

Five days since I was shot, three weeks since I took Sybil Rogers's job, a month since Perez Medina walked out of the bush, when they wheel me out to Kay's car. She drives, I sit in the back where there is more room for my leg, for my shoulder that is still bandaged.

I see the car as we leave the hospital. A dark blue Honda Civic that pulls out when we do. I am aware of it on the freeway two or three cars back, but it does not take the Summerland exit. Kay parks in front of our house so I don't have to make the longer walk from the garage in the alley behind the house.

I watch for the Honda at all the corners while Kay goes to unlock the front door. I watch in the rearview mirror. The car does not appear. Kay helps me inside, makes a high tea.

I call Sergeant Chavalas, ask if he has anyone watching me, a bodyguard. He says no, asks if I need one. I tell him I'll call back, ask if anything new has turned up for the police in any of the cities. He says no. I hobble in to have my tea.

"I'll bet they had high tea in Africa," Kay says.

I smile. "Ex-British colony."

I think about Africa, and about the dark blue Honda.

In that vast area of East Africa drained by the Nile and former Congo rivers, high grassland, thick bush and rain forest all blend and separate over millions of square miles that still belong to the animals, adventurers, guerrillas and ivory hunters. To soldiers in the provincial towns.

I made my contacts in the capital, without much blessing from the U.S. embassy. But they didn't stop me. I was there for Sybil Rogers, they didn't want a fight with the widow. I flew inland from the coast. The dry bush country stretched to the horizon, snowcapped mountains off in the distance. Hemingway country. The jungle appeared and disappeared. Stanley and Livingstone. Burton and Speke.

From the dusty airfield of the provincial capital, a car took me to the army headquarters where the latest survivor was being held. The town was hot. Army headquarters was hot. The young colonel who sat behind his desk and fanned himself was hot.

"Mr. Crispin Brown, from Miami in the Florida of your country. He has confirmed the report of Gabriel Sarguis," Colonel Abner Ngane said. "He saw the murders, was fright-

ened, ran into the bush, has been living across the border
with a small tribe in our neighbor country. He came out now
because he was sick with fever and wanted to go home."

Crispin Brown was a tall black man in a white gown. He
lay in the military hospital bed. His pupils were pinpoints.
He smiled at me, didn't seem to notice my missing arm.

"Mr. Brown? My name is Dan Fortune. I'm here for Mrs.
Sybil Rogers. I wonder if you can tell me more about Mr.
Rogers. About what happened the day of the attack?"

"He kill them. Mr. Rogers he come to find the dirt, he stay
to be with The People. He fight for The Preacher. He love The
Preacher. He kill them. That Perez Medina."

His voice moved like a slow recording, the dilated eyes not
seeing me. A voice with a strong West Indian accent. Jamaica
or even Trinidad.

"What happened after Medina shot them?"

"They was dead. Medina he run."

"Did you check the bodies?"

"Sure I check, what you think?"

"Medina ran, you checked, then what?"

"They was dead."

"And you ran?"

"Man, like a big-assed bird, you know?"

"Where were you when you saw Medina shoot them?"

Whether it was the fever, or the drugs against the fever, he
seemed to have difficulty concentrating on what I said.

"The trucks they was burning, but I was under this here
truck wasn't burning, you see? I see them, three of them. Two
of them have their backs to me. The other one is all bloody
and dirty. His arm it hang down, he hold the AK-47 in one
hand. He screaming, out of his mind, you see? He shoot them
down. That is when I see who they are, man. They are dead, I
run."

"After you checked to be sure they were dead."

"I see they are dead, then I run."

"And Medina didn't see you? When you checked on them?"

"He gone, man. He run off."

"He ran, too? Before or after you ran?"

Brown licked his thin lips, looked at the colonel. Smiled. Frowned. He was like a man in shock. Or in withdrawal. Closed his eyes and went to sleep. We left the room. Back in his office, Colonel Ngane took a bottle of Scotch from his desk, offered it to me. I shook my head.

"Is he an addict?" I said. "Brown?"

Ngane poured the whiskey, splashed water from a jug. No ice, English style. "Yes, he is an addict."

"In a native village in the bush?"

The colonel shrugged. "Those you call *natives* had all manner of drugs long before so-called civilized society, Mr. Fortune. Then, no village, no matter how remote, is too far for narcotics to reach today if the demand and money are there."

"Does he have money?"

"It would seem not now."

"What would make a believer in The Word turn to drugs?"

"The death of belief. Despair. Exile, self or otherwise."

"Do you believe him?"

"He says the same as Gabriel Sarguis. We have not found The Preacher or Mr. Rogers alive."

The attitudes of colonialism die hard. He wanted the whole affair swept out of sight as much as any official out from Whitehall. "He took a long time to come in, colonel."

"But he is in. He has changed nothing, revealed nothing we did not know."

"He's made what you think you know more probable," I said. "And there's another change. We know there was another survivor. If there's one, there could be more."

"We have made exhaustive inquiries at the site of the attack among the tribesmen and settlers. We have searched. We have found no trace of Mr. Rogers or Mr. Sarguis." The colo-

191

nel swirled his drink. "Besides talking to Crispin Brown, what did you come here to do, Mr. Fortune?"

"Satisfy myself I can go back to Mrs. Rogers and tell her George Rogers is dead. Maybe how he died."

"How do you propose to do this?"

"Look at all the reports and testimony of the investigation you and the U.S. people did. You do keep records and reports, right? They're available to me?"

"Of course. But I can do better. I can let you speak with the officers, men, civilians and tribesmen who did the actual work. It was most thorough, Mr. Fortune. When would you start?"

"Now?"

"Let me arrange for the files to be opened, and a driver. You will stay in my quarters, of course."

I got the documents and the driver. The documents were detailed, complete and numerous. It took me two days to learn that one-hundred-and-ninety-seven of The People were unaccounted for and presumed to have fallen into the river, been eaten by animals, or buried by tribesmen. They had exhumed all the mass graves, and, with the insistence and help of the U.S. government, identified all they could. A search and interview with everyone in the area had turned up no witnesses to anyone who might have left the area alive beyond the seven.

Yet at least one more had left the area alive, survived undetected within a few hundred miles for almost a year.

It took less time to interview the officers, soldiers and civilians, but the result was the same: no one had seen anyone beyond the seven known survivors, no one had heard a report of anyone who had seen anyone else walk away, but everyone admitted the whole one-hundred-and-ninety-seven could have walked away unseen in the blood and confusion of that time.

"We will never know the final fate of them all, that is my

opinion, Mr. Fortune," Ngane said. We were in his house the evening I finished the last paper and interview. A large, airy, whitewashed house high above the dusty provincial town where the night breezes blew through. He was relaxed, I had found nothing to compromise him or his country, the sun was almost down behind the nearest mountains, and the beer was cold.

"I'd still like to visit their town," I said.

"I'll arrange it in the morning."

"What happened to them, colonel? The Preacher and his people? How did it end in so much violence and blood?"

"He did much good when he came here, Mr. Fortune. My government welcomed him and his people. The area was a source of trouble trying to control the tribesmen and adventurers who flew in. He brought money, civilization. They built their town, paid taxes and fees, planted crops, stabilized the area."

"Then?"

He touched a bell, the orderly appeared with two fresh beers. "How much do you know about The Preacher, his history?"

"Not much."

"I have made it a point to know all there is to know since I was sent here."

Michael Sarguis's father comes home to his family in Fresno, California, at the end of the Second Great War. Adnan Sarguis's own father had fled Turkey with the mass Armenian escape from terror after the First Great War—despite being not an Armenian at all but an Assyrian from the ancient race of conquerors fallen to a tiny remnant. Adnan's father and the Armenians were aware of the difference, but it had not seemed to matter to the Turks.

Adnan returns from serving his country wearing the uniform of all American soldiers, sharing the triumph, at last a real American. He shares the pain too, with a plate in his head from the vicious treebursts of the Huertgen Forest. Michael's mother welcomes Adnan home in the traditional style of women who have waited in wars, and then tells Adnan that she and their three children want to leave Fresno because the Armenian community has not been hospitable to the mixed marriage of even an Assyrian with a Mexican—who is actually only half Mexican but that matters to the Armenians no more than the difference between Armenians and Assyrians had mattered to the Turks.

Maria Sarguis, née Bello, came with her Nicaraguan father and Mexican mother north over the border in the early thirties, but her roots in California go back to the eighteenth century when a maternal ancestor had come north with Captain Don José de Ortega and Father Junípero Serra. (At the time, in 1785, the good captain had been plain José Ortega. It was only later, when his descendants had achieved land and status before the Americans arrived to take it all away from them in turn, that the captain had become Don José de Ortega, the first honored hidalgo of Alta California. For all the settlers in the new land, latino or anglo, there was a strong urge to recreate in the new land the world of the aristocrats they had left back home.)

The family moves to the San Francisco neighborhood where Maria's family lives. Adnan goes to work in her Uncle Paco's used-car lot. Michael Diego Sarguis is born nine months later, the product of the welcoming home. Adnan does well as a salesman of cars, is much in demand in the community as an interpreter and translator between the latino world and the large, frightening anglo world beyond, and for a time the family prospers in San Francisco. Michael has the normal childhood of a baby brother in the family-and-church world of latino immigrants in the northern city with the Spanish name and past, anglo power and present.

Young, lighter-skinned and speaking English, if with a latino accent, Michael is bolder than most, ventures farther afield beyond the boundaries of custom and language. He wants to see the ocean. From high windows in the *barrio* he has seen the bay, but the ocean is beyond the horizon. He is eight the Sunday he decides he will go alone to the ocean. To conserve the little money he has saved, Michael decides he will walk. It is a long walk, but everything is new and he walks happily.

He finally reaches the coast road, the broad white beach across it, and the amazing blue ocean. He is washed by the sights and sounds and smells and touches of the sun and air and wind. The wind that bends the beach grass, whips at his face. The gulls that circle above. The white foam of the breaking waves. The expanse of the beach itself, without a house or a tree. The sky and the distance. A distance of beach and water and sky he has never imagined.

The ocean.

Michael climbs over the low wall and onto the white sand. He runs through the sand, falls sprawling, laughs. He has never tried to run in sand. It is soft yet heavy, like a thick liquid that sinks his feet and weighs them down. He falls laughing, rolls in the sand, kicks, and hears the angry voice:

"What the fuck you think you're doing with that sand?"

The anglo boy isn't much older than himself. Fully dressed in dirty jeans, black sweatshirt with red words that look like blood, heavy hiking boots. Tall, his dark blond hair is dirty and uncombed, and he has two friends behind him. He also has sand on his shoes and legs. His two friends laugh. They are the same age, wear the same clothes, have the same belligerent manner under their laughter.

"He don't look like he's from around here, Deano."

"We never saw him before."

195

The big boy, Deano, steps toward Michael, fists clenched. "You like kicking sand, guy?"

Michael stammers, "I . . . I . . . don' mean I kick . . . I don' see you *gringo* . . ."

"Jesus, Deano, he's a goddamn *spic*."

"What's a *beaner* doing out here?"

Deano stares at Michael. The enormity of the challenge to his position as leader paralyzes him. Deano is not yet old enough to be instant with a violent response. He hesitates. Michael, from the less sure world of the *barrio*, knows instantly what he must do. He runs.

"Get the fucking *greaser!*"

The three boys howl like wolves in a pack. Michael is on the concrete, runs across the road through the sparse traffic, gains some distance on them. But they are bigger and maybe faster. Michael knows he must be smart, looks back. They run at an angle across the road. Michael plunges into the yard of a big house that faces the ocean. He finds a low fence, climbs over into the back yard of another house with a long driveway out to the next street. He runs across the new street, through more yards, until he is four blocks from the ocean. They have not been fooled. They appear, run toward him once more.

The church is almost directly across the street.

A church of gray stone without the high tower of the beautiful church of Santiago de Compostela where his mother takes the family. There are no statues of the saints over the wide doors, no young Father José to greet him in the doorway, but there is a cross and stained-glass windows. He slips inside the strange church.

Two hundred faces all turn in their rows to look at the intruder in their service. Michael has forgotten it is Sunday. He stands alone, and over all the faces turned toward him sees the figure in black. A giant figure that towers high above the faces. All in black. Tall and powerful. Where the altar should be. Where the flowers, the gold crosses and the tapestries have always been. Where Father Hidalgo and Father José in their gold robes intone the magic words.

The figure in black is like nothing he has ever seen in the holy church of Santiago de Compostela. The church where the figure towers is nothing he has ever seen. Without pictures or candles, without color, the silent people solemn and pale. A single cross on a plain table behind the figure in black.

"Young man, come forward." It is a strong voice, yet soft and pleasant. "Ushers, bring him here to me."

Michael feels the hands on him, and the two men take him down the long aisle among the faces that stare but do not smile. To the low platform and the table with the single cross and the austere figure all in black. He sees that the black is a suit, but a suit like none he has ever seen in a church, without gold or color or jewels or decoration.

"Don't be afraid, we'll talk after the service." The black giant even smiles. "One of you stay with him in my office."

The hands guide Michael through a door at the side, down a corridor and into an office with high windows. The windows have thick, heavy drapes pulled back to let the sunlight in, and long shelves of books in all colors to the ceiling. There is a garden with trees and flowers outside the windows, with benches and paths where he imagines the tall figure in black walks alone to decide what the world will do. Michael likes the beautiful garden. He thinks he would like the tall man in black. The black figure has so much more power than Father José, or worn-out old Father Hidalgo. The tall man in black could take him to the ocean. Deano would run away if they saw him with the man in black.

"You must be a long way from home, young man."

The man in black is in the office. He is not alone. Behind him there is another man. A man in uniform. A policeman.

"What's your name, son?"

"Michael Diego."

"Well, Michael Diego, would you like to go home now?"

"I want to go to ocean."

"I think you'll be a lot happier back where you belong, Michael. We'll leave the ocean for another time, shall we? When you're older. Officer Detko here is going to take you home in his car. You just tell him where your people live, you'll soon be back where no one will harm you."

The tall figure in the black suit smiles, and his hand rests on Michael's head as he nods to the policeman. They go out a side door to a patrol car where he is pushed into the back seat behind the metal grill. There are no handles on the doors in the back seat.

"Lucky that reverend's a nice guy or you'd be in real shit."

At the edge of the *barrio*, the policeman pushes Michael from the car and drives away. Michael runs all the way home. His father is angry, wants to borrow a car and drive Michael back to the beach then and there, but the ocean would not be the same thing with his father. His mother says it is better he stay near home, makes him his favorite enchiladas.

That night, the tall austere giant in black towers in his dreams. A monolithic figure he both fears and loves.

When Michael is twelve, his father becomes sick from the wound in his head where they put the metal plate in the war. One day his father runs through the hospital smashing everything and they have to put him in a special hospital where the doctors don't think he will ever get better.

His father's Assyrian family in San Jose blames Maria, will have no more to do with her and her half-breed children. Times become hard for Maria and the four children. If she goes to work, she is afraid the boys will get into trouble, especially young Michael. There is little work in San Francisco anyway for a latina mother who can barely read English and knows no skill beyond cleaning a house. Maria writes her father who has long ago returned to Nicaragua after the death of her mother. He tells her to bring her family home to the town where she was born. They will be welcome, there are cousins and aunts to help her, she should never have married an atheist *norteamericano*.

It is a large town with electricity, running water, and factories for making textiles and processing the coffee that is grown on the plantations of the landowner where most of the men work. Maria gets a job at the textile factory, the oldest boy, Frank, goes to work at the coffee processing plant. Children do not go to school as long as in the States. The girl, Josefa, is allowed to continue in return for teaching English, but the middle boy, Rafael, is apprenticed to learn to build houses. Only Michael does nothing but go to school where he has some trouble with his American *barrio* Spanish and his name, but he soon learns Nicaraguan Spanish, the trouble passes. It is not San Francisco, but they are better off, Maria feels safe and children are resilient if they have to be. Except for Rafael, who had dreamed of being an astronaut in America and doesn't want to be a carpenter, they are not unhappy in Nicaragua.

The children become comfortable in their new town and country, begin to forget they are American. Somehow they are less outsiders here than in San Francisco. The town becomes their home, and while it is a poor life without all they had in America, it is a slower and easier life too, and everyone is the same except for the plantation owners who they never see except on church holidays and feast days, or sometimes driving past on the road in a cloud of dust.

They might all have settled in the country forever, but it is the time of the Sandinista rebellion against the government of President Somoza whose father was president and whose son will be president as long as the army and the landowners are in control. Michael is fourteen when the Sandinistas appear in the town and the plantation.

It is Easter Sunday, the landowner and his family come in from the plantation hacienda to the town church that stands by itself in a dusty field at the edge of the town where it towers over the houses. Not all the men go to the church—the younger men get drunk and play cards when they aren't working, and there are many not-so-secret socialists among the young men who accuse the Church of being too tied to the army and the landowners—but most of the women are there every Sunday, some every day. On the days when the landowner and his family come, on Christmas and Easter and saints' days, the church is always full even in the heat and dust of summer.

The landowner's great-great-great-grandfather built the church. It is one long room like a cathedral, the bell and the stained-glass windows came from Europe. The building itself is of local brick, and there is a high wooden roof it must have taken all the slaves and peasants who worked on the plantation back then to build. The altar at the front is gilt on oak, with a railed sanctuary. In front of the altar are the pews. There are twenty rows that fill a quarter of the church. They end in another rail and gate, and outside that gate most of the people of the town stand. The pews belong to those from the plantation. The back fifteen rows for the overseers, the skilled workers and their families. The next two rows nearer the altar for the lesser relatives and visitors. The front three rows have gates, are for the landowner, his immediate family and official guests.

The landowner is a good Catholic, goes to some church every Sunday without fail. He makes his entrance only minutes before the mid-morning Mass is to start, walks through all the people like Moses parting the Red Sea. He looks neither right nor left, goes into the first row of his pews, the first seat on the aisle. There he kneels in prayer for a full two minutes, telling his beads. When he sits back it is the signal to start the service. He is always the first at communion. Comes to the rail, kneels alone, and takes communion alone. Only then do his family, guests, the ranch hands, and finally the townspeople come forward. When the Mass is over he walks out first.

On this Easter Sunday morning, the landowner and his family have made their entrance, most of the townspeople are inside the church, when the Sandinista units arrive in the town. The old priest, Father Geronimo, is about to offer the communion. The landowner has come to the rail to kneel alone. The townspeople at the rear smell the dust, hear the feet all around the church. The back door is flung open, the people at the rear step aside and a young man walks through them to the gate into the pews. No older than Frank, who is at the rear of the church that day, he is dressed in camouflage fatigues, has a Russian AK-47 slung over his shoulder. He stops at the gate into the pews. His dark eyes look over everyone, look at old Father Geronimo, look at the landowner at the rail who has not even turned around.

He opens the rear gate, walks straight down the aisle between the rows of seats, opens the gate at the front, and kneels at the communion rail beside the landowner. Not to his left, but to his right. In effect taking the landowner's exact place—the first one at the rail on the right. The landowner finally turns his head to stare at the young guerrilla beside him. They look at each other. The landowner is at least six inches taller than the young guerrilla even kneeling, yet it is as if they are the same height. Perhaps because the Russian assault rifle juts that far above the young man's head there at the communion rail. Or perhaps it is the anger in the guerrilla's dark eyes.

The young guerrilla leader nods to old Father Geronimo. He wants the priest to continue with the communion. His voice shaking, Father Geronimo asks the young man when he last confessed. The guerrilla only stares at the priest. The church is full of women and children and old men, the guerrillas are all around the church and at the windows. Father Geronimo gives the landowner and the young guerrilla communion side by side. When it is over, the young man stands and walks up the aisle and out. The people part for him as they always do for the landowner, follow him out without waiting for the landowner and his family and retainers. The plantation people and the family are left in the pews, the landowner himself alone at the communion rail.

On the plantation, the guerrillas burn the warehouses of coffee, the coffee processing plant, the radio transmitter and the hacienda. In the town they destroy the telephone exchange, cut all wires to the outside. They do not touch the town itself or the church. They take the landowner's private aircraft and helicopters, all the trucks and weapons, the food and clothing they can carry, some men from the town, and disappear.

Frank Sarguis is one of the men from the town the guerrillas take with them. He asks the guerrillas to take him with them. In the church that morning he has had a vision.

"He's like the first Christians," Frank tells Maria and his grandfather. "He's not like the rest of them down here, nothing more than two-bit slaves. Back in San Francisco I remember the history teacher telling us the great strength of Christianity in the early days was that all you had to do was be a Christian and you were as good as the emperor. Slaves, workers, farmers joined the church and were as good as the emperor in the eyes of God and in their own eyes. That's what he is, the guerrilla—the equal of the landowner, and that's what I'm going to be."

His mother says, "He had a gun. They are atheists. God is not served by men with guns who do not believe in Him."

"There are bandits with guns," young Frank says. "They're

not like him. No, it isn't the gun, Mother, it is what he believes, what he is doing."

"Barbarians. Scum," his grandfather says. "Desecrating the church. Burning and stealing!"

"They did nothing to the church. The landowner stole all he has from the people. People can't eat coffee. The coffee only makes the landowner and the generals rich on our work."

"You will be killed," Maria wails.

"No. It was a sign, what happened in the church this morning. It was God telling us what we must do. God showed us what He wants from us."

"That is blasphemy," his grandfather says, crosses himself.

But Frank goes with the guerrillas to fight for the sign from God and against the tyranny of *El Presidente* Somoza and the generals and the landowners who own the nation.

The government troops catch up with the Sandinistas two days later. There is a small fight. Two guerrillas and four soldiers are killed, fifteen soldiers are wounded. The guerrillas escape into the bush, there is no count of their wounded. Frank Sarguis disappears into the mountains with them. The landowner gets most of his trucks back.

The soldiers return to the plantation with the landowner's trucks but not his private plane and helicopter, none of his food and weapons. They stay to help the landowner rebuild what was destroyed on the plantation. The landowner does not forget how the townspeople parted for the young guerrilla, how they followed the guerrilla leader out of the church and left the landowner and his family alone in the pews. The leaders of the town must be removed and new leaders selected by the landowner and military commander, and the people must rebuild the warehouses and the coffee processing plant.

The landowner does not forget how old Father Geronimo gave communion to the guerrilla leader. Father Geronimo retires to a retreat house, the bishop sends a new priest of good family.

The families of the men who went into the mountains with the guerrillas must be dealt with.

Some, whose vanished men were whispered to be socialists, disappear. Most are warned and avoided by the townspeople. Maria and her family, because her father is known to be a pious and law-abiding man who respects the rights of the landowner, and perhaps because the children are American, are only watched.

Michael is sixteen when Frank returns to the town.

Josefa has married a cousin of the landowner and gone to Managua. With the help of the landowner's cousin, Rafael has joined the National Guard and been sent to guard the borders against supplies coming across for the Sandinistas. Frank comes alone in the night with his wife and son. His wife is another Sandinista soldier, keeps watch while Frank goes into the house to leave his son with Maria and Michael.

"His name's Gabriel, Mama. We can't keep him with us in the mountains. After Somoza and his soldiers are gone, we'll come back for him."

Maria grips his arm. "They are too strong, Francisco. Stay here with me. You and your wife and your son."

Frank smiles, seems so much older to Michael, has been so much farther away than the mountains. His wife comes to the door. She too carries a rifle. "The soldiers are coming."

The soldiers follow Frank and his wife into the mountains. Maria has Michael take the baby to her father. The soldiers fail to catch Frank and his wife, return to town, take Maria away. Nothing Michael's grandfather can do this time will save her. Her body is found shot in the head, her hands tied behind her back. The soldiers do not know about the infant Gabriel, but look for Michael. In the night he escapes from the town.

In Managua, Michael goes to the United States embassy,

tries to tell someone he is an American. By now his English has a Nicaraguan accent, his passport is lost, he has no other papers and no one to be a witness to his claim. He is turned away by the first person he speaks to. When he begins to shout and object violently, the police are called and he has to run. He knows the police and National Guard keep a record of anyone who is wanted anywhere by any of them, ask few if any questions.

Alone, with an accent as alien to the Nicaraguans as to the Americans, Michael drifts into a gang of homeless teenagers who live by their wits on the streets of Managua. He sees true poverty, true suffering, true rage, true savagery. He sees the poor go to the churches that tell them their suffering in this world will be forgotten in the next. That they must endure what is God's will. That prayer is the answer to guns and violence.

He dreams again of the towering figure in black. A giant above the whole world with a pale face and a sad frown. A face of sorrow. In the dreams, Michael wants to speak to the figure but can get no words out. He wants to touch the black shape, but it is always too far away. He dreams of the silent black figure, and learns survival. Learns to lie, rob, cheat and steal. He finds he is a natural leader. Perhaps because he has never until now been as afraid as they have been, always had more hope and dreams no matter how foolish they would become later.

The National Guard is waiting for them one night. Someone has told the guard that they are going to loot the warehouse of a *norteamericano* company. They will never know how or who. The guard is there and only by the sheer chance of Michael seeing the black shape high above the warehouse does he escape.

It is the first miracle.

Michael sees the black figure in the sky with the low moon behind it, freezes as the others run ahead. He is behind when the guard opens fire, is only wounded in the arm and neck, gets away unseen, runs once more. It is still dark when he can run no farther. Half-conscious, delirious, he knows somehow that he cannot be found on the street, climbs a fence on the edge of the city, falls into a garden. In his delirious state he sees the garden all in color in the black night. A beautiful garden like a rainbow. And before he loses consciousness a tall black figure grows from the center of the rainbow, towers over the garden and the city in the dark night.

It is the second, the disputed, miracle.

For a time Michael feels only pain, and hands that hurt him. Sees the tall black figure that grows and fades and grows again. Then the pain is less, and when he opens his eyes he is in a bed in a room with banana trees outside a single window. It is not the beautiful garden of last night outside the window. A man stands over the bed. A tall man in a black suit like the giant figure so long ago, but not all black. There is a white collar turned backwards.

"So, how do we feel now?"

It is good Spanish but not Nicaraguan Spanish and with an accent Michael knows.

"Where is this?" Michael says in English.

"You speak English, young man? You're from the Bluefields area? Or perhaps not Nicaraguan?"

He speaks in English with a funny accent, his voice is almost afraid. Michael knows what is wrong. This man has found a Nicaraguan boy who has been shot and has sheltered him. This could be trouble, but probably not much. But if Michael is more than a simple Nicaraguan teenager, it could be something far more complicated and far more dangerous.

"I'm American."

The man sits down. "What's your name?"

"Michael Diego Sarguis."

The name clearly means nothing to the man, which means he has not read it or heard it lately in the government media, and that is a relief. "I'm Bishop Smith of the Anglican mission in Nicaragua. Perhaps you had better tell me everything."

Michael tells him the story of his family, of San Francisco and the town where his grandfather still lives. It is both better and worse. The immediate problem is not dangerous to the Anglican mission. Michael is one of thousands of teenagers who hustle in the slums of Managua, nameless and of no special interest to the authorities. They will not be looking for him.

The long-range problem is much more. Michael is American, has rights the bishop, in his own eyes, is bound to protect, insist on. But the Somoza government will not want him to return to America with his stories of murder by soldiers and guardsmen and death squads. To approach the government on his behalf without total proof and powerful support would be suicide for Michael and the mission.

"For the time being, Michael, let's forget the question of your citizenship, concentrate on your full recovery. Those were rather nasty wounds and are by no means healed."

Michael becomes a gardener at the Anglican mission. After a time he is allowed to help the bishop at the Sunday services. No one notices the boy in the Anglican robes who follows behind the bishop to carry the wine and the wafers for communion. Michael comes to love the aura of the church, the odor of dust and robes, flowers and incense. He feels safe inside the walls and shadows of the church. (Later, the bishop will say how often Michael sat alone far at the back of the empty church and stared at the altar. How Michael listened to the bishop talk of the religions found in the New World and brought from the Old World. Even from Africa and Asia. How Michael loved to read the bishop's books of the world's religions.)

In the end, the bishop writes to his Episcopal colleagues in San Francisco and obtains the statements and official papers to prove Michael's United States citizenship. The bishop and the papers make it a routine matter, the officials of *El Presidente* Somoza are very polite to the United States ambassador. Michael is issued a passport, the embassy contacts Josefa and Rafael. Josefa and the landowner's cousin want nothing to do with Michael. She renounces her U.S. citizenship, is proud to be a Nicaraguan. A sergeant now in the National Guard, Rafael does not renounce his citizenship, but he will stay in the guard. No one mentions Frank or Gabriel.

Michael is eighteen the day the bishop puts him on the jet and he flies home to San Francisco alone.

The *barrio* has changed. There is greater militancy in the air, confrontation with the anglo landlords and city leaders. As a survivor of the U.S.-supported tyranny of *El Presidente* Somoza, the murderer of his mother, Michael is welcomed by Maria's brothers and uncles. He becomes fiery in the demands of the *barrio* for their rights as Americans. He goes to night school to improve his English, to understand more of the anglo world, becomes a leader among the younger militants in the *barrio*.

He marries, fathers a son, learns in night school he has an ability to draw, and becomes an artist and a commercial artist. As an artist he paints walls in the *barrio* with large murals of his people and the people of Nicaragua where the Sandinistas are growing more powerful. As a commercial artist he makes enough money to buy a small house outside the *barrio*. He does not turn his back on the *barrio*, but fights to bring the *barrio* out into the whole anglo city.

The years pass, there are more children. In Nicaragua the Sandinistas win, and *El Presidente* Somoza and his National Guard flee the country. His grandfather dies before he can see this tragedy against the world God had intended. His brother Frank dies in the struggle before he can see the triumph of the people against the tyranny of man and Church. Josefa and the cousin of the landowner fly to Miami. Rafael escapes with *El*

Presidente Somoza to Argentina. Gabriel remains in his great-grandfather's town with a new family.

In San Francisco, Michael lies awake nights in his house and feels a power within him that is more than the cause of the *barrio*. When he walks alone through the night city, stands at the edge of the sea where he goes often after he has finally reached the ocean, he senses a force driving him. He does not know what this power is, but he can feel it there like a great snake coiled restless inside.

A snake coiled around itself that struggles with its own weight and the weight of the sun and moon and earth and trees and sleep and laughter and anger and hate. He feels the snake, but does not know where it comes from or how to use it. (He will say, later, that something else within him told him to escape the snake, to run, but he did not know how.) When the snake finally tells Michael what he must do, he is twenty-seven years old.

He wakes up that morning in his small house and thinks of his Assyrian relatives. He has not gone to Fresno since his return. His children have never seen their grandfather. Michael hasn't seen his father since the day his father's mind snapped in the illness of his war wound and they shut him away. He hasn't thought of his father since he returned from Nicaragua. Is his father alive or dead? Something in the room tells him his father is alive and he must go to him, speaks inside his mind and tells him his father waits to be set free.

His father's family in Fresno doesn't welcome him. He has chosen the heritage of his mother. They tell him Adnan Sarguis doesn't even know he has a family, won't know Michael, it is too late for Michael to come looking for a father. He tells them he will not go away until he sees for himself that it is too late. They finally tell him where his father is, he goes to the private sanitarium. His father is the youngest patient there. Adnan Sarguis sits on a wooden bench in the sun of the green, wooded grounds, looks up at a noisy mockingbird in the nearest tree. His face is vacant.

"He doesn't suffer, Mr. Sarguis," the doctor assures Michael. "Most of the time he has no idea who he is and doesn't seem to care. At times he recognizes me, or some others on the staff. The next day he may think we're soldiers in World War Two or even the enemy. He might think one of the female staff is your mother. He doesn't seem aware that he has any children, yet there are times when we feel he looks at young visitors as if looking for someone."

"There's no chance he'll ever recover?"

"There's always a chance. To be honest, we know so little about the mind and its workings we can only grope for labels and understanding of even what exactly is wrong with his mind."

"Does he hear you when you speak to him?"

"We never know for sure."

Michael walks around the bench, faces his father. "How are you feeling today, Father? It's me, Michael."

His father continues to look up at the noisy mockingbird, then turns to Michael. "You liked the mockingbirds when we visited Fresno. You missed them in San Francisco. I'm sorry, Michael."

It is the third miracle.

Within the month it is as if Adnan Sarguis had never been ill. With the daily company of Michael and his wife, Adnan rebuilds the lost years, cries for Maria and Frank, returns to the world. He is the first to call Michael's visit a miracle, and when, a month later, Michael has The Vision, the first to believe.

Michael is again awake in the small house outside the *barrio*. He hears his father downstairs. After all the missing years, his father sits like Lazarus with his face up to the sun or the moon until he drops into sleep from exhaustion. Michael feels the coiled snake inside himself. This time he knows he doesn't want to escape. He knows the snake is good, the snake is his destiny, and the cage that holds them both bursts.

The tall black figure appears in the room.

"You have the power, go out and help the poor and sick."

Michael becomes aware of himself where he stands in the dark room before the black figure. "I'm not a doctor, how do I help?"

"Help the sick in mind, the wounded in spirit, the lost in soul, the desperate in fear and need. Help your own people."

"How can I do that? I'm not a priest."

"You have the power. The time is now."

The figure sweeps off the great black cloak. Michael can see the city outside the window through the tall shape. "Gather the people and heal the hate, the fear, the death with the power of the trees, the animals, the world, the universe."

The figure's arms reach from far across the city to place the black cloak over Michael's shoulders. "The only path honored now by man is the path of triumph over other men. The time has come to lead down a new path of help for all that live."

The cloak descends over Michael's head and shoulders and the light of the city vanishes for an instant. When it reappears, the black shape is gone. Michael stands alone on a mountain with the city spread in sunlight below.

He lies awake in the sunny bedroom and knows he has not been asleep, yet the night has ended and the sun come without transition. There was night, now there is sun. He doesn't know how he knows he has not been asleep, but he knows he has not been. He feels the black cloak on his shoulders, even sees the cloak, but knows no one else will see the cloak. Not until they join him and his mission.

He sells the small house outside the *barrio* and rents a

storefront in the heart of the *barrio*. He quits his job, hangs a sign on the storefront with large letters: BRING YOUR ANGER AND HATE AND PAIN AND NEED. WE WILL HEAL TOGETHER. Michael and his wife and children live in the back of the store.

Nobody comes.

In Fresno, his father proclaims the miracle that returned his sanity in the flash of a second, the miracle of the voice of his son Michael who speaks to the people.

In San Francisco, Michael wanders the *barrio* and beyond and ponders again and again the words of the message of The Vision. *"Help the sick in mind, the wounded in spirit, the lost in soul, the desperate in fear and need."*

In the *barrio*, the wound is poverty. The hate is drugs. The fear and death are poverty and drugs. It is work and food the people need, help to turn away from drugs, help in the real world to dispel the fear of each day. He opens the store to the jobless and homeless, begs through the *barrio* and beyond for contributions and food to feed and shelter the poor and homeless. In Fresno, his father hangs a sign: MISSION OF THE PEOPLE. Michael begins to preach on streetcorners to the rich and comfortable: the sickness is poverty. The hate is drugs. The healing is work and no hate or fear.

Money comes. He buys food and beds, finds jobs. More people come. They come in Fresno where the man who was brought back to hope by a miracle talks to them of the resurrection of their empty lives, tells them the word of his son, the preacher. They listen and ask when will the preacher himself come to speak to them?

Michael goes to Fresno to talk to the people.

In San Francisco, others join from in and out of the *barrio*. People who want to help against the drugs, the poverty. Find jobs, heal, bring hope. People with skills to do these things, and the storefront becomes too small. A hall for preaching the word to everyone is needed. A dormitory for the homeless. A drug rehabilitation program. A dining hall. An abandoned Episcopal church that lost its congregation when the *barrio* became the *barrio* is found. (To some this is the fourth miracle. Michael was saved in Nicaragua by the Episcopal mission. Now his mission is saved. At least it is a sign from God.)

His father paints the large letters over the doorway of the renewed church: MISSION OF THE PEOPLE. Another empty church is found in Fresno: MISSION OF THE PEOPLE. The work of drug rehabilitation is a great success in the *barrio* and in Fresno. The work of shelter and food. The work of jobs. The work of help for the poor. The People's Missions, as they come to be called, are honored by the *barrio* leaders, by the city itself, the churches. The work goes on, the years pass.

Michael is thirty-two years old when it is not enough. The Vision is clouded in his mind. Many come for help but few hear The Vision. The work is good, why does he feel incomplete, even empty? Something is gone from The Vision. He walks again by the ocean, calls for the figure in black to speak to him once more.

He hears the voice. *"You have the power."*

He hears the voice above the beat of the surf and the song of the sea wind. He realizes it is his own voice: *Gather the people and heal the hate, the fear, the death with the power of all the living, of the world, of the universe.*

What is missing is the power to change the world. He is on the wrong path. A path that will not heal the hate, the fear, the death. A good path, but a partial path. The meaning of the giant figure in black he has carried inside for so long has been weakened. He has seen the trees and not the forest. He has forgotten the voice of the universe.

It is the Rebirth.

The word is recovered.

Michael gives the drug rehabilitation, the dining hall, the dormitory, to those who came to the mission to do those things.

He will preach the word.

If you feel the word, there will be no hate or fear or death. Believe in all as one and you will be healed. The world does not believe in all, that is what has been wrong. What is wrong with religions. They do not believe in all, only in one. That is why they have not succeeded in saving man, why they can't lead the people out of hate and pain and death. The word will do what the tired old churches can't do.

In the *barrio* and in Fresno and on the streets they come to listen and join. The missions grow in the *barrio* and in Fresno. The word becomes The Word. The people become The People.

The *barrio*, the city, the churches are alarmed. They no longer honor Michael. They give him no more money, they don't help. His wife goes to the church of Santiago de Compostela and prays for him. Father José tells her Michael is blasphemous, a heretic, she must renounce him. Michael tells her she must believe in The Word and The People. She is afraid to believe in anything but what she has always believed in. She leaves him.

Believe with The People. The People will bring you out of drugs and poverty and pain and hate and fear and death.

Believe in The Word and The People.

The missions expand beyond the *barrio* and Fresno. Michael must travel from mission to mission. To preach The Word. The People wait for hours for Michael to preach The Word. They wait to believe with the preacher.

They come to believe with the preacher.

To believe in the preacher.

The Preacher.

Michael is thirty-seven when he becomes The Preacher.

Converts flock to The People, to The Preacher. In Los Angeles. In San Diego and Santa Barbara. San Jose. Oakland. Phoenix. Flock to The Word: All you have to do is believe in The Preacher and everything will be good, right, safe and eternal.

The Preacher holds the first mass preaching in a park on a night when the fog does not come to San Francisco, the wind is calm. A miracle, the newspapers laugh. The People do not laugh, do not call it a miracle. There are real miracles. Many that night at the park hear the heavenly music. Two of the lame walk. Not by the touch of The Preacher, but simply by The Word. Those who search for truth, find it. Isn't that miracle enough? The sad and confused are no longer sad or confused. The figure in black appears to many of The People. Only the figure has the face of The Preacher. The Word is in the voice of The Preacher.

Gabriel Sarguis, far down in Nicaragua, hears the voice and comes north. Gabriel is the second disciple after Adnan.

When there are over a thousand of The People across the Western states, The Persecution begins. There are attacks on The People and The Missions. The Preacher himself is shot at by a crazed parishioner of his old church in the *barrio*. The Preacher denounces the hate and violence of the unconverted, demands the police, the state, protect The People. The attacks continue, and The Preacher accuses the authorities of conspiracy. In Fresno, Adnan is beaten to death on the street in front of The Mission.

The Preacher orders The People to bring all they own and takes them into the mountains behind Santa Barbara. They buy an old camp and establish a commune where all who hear The Word, believe in The Preacher, will live in peace and eternal life. Soon there are over two thousand. They buy all the land around the camp. They will be self-sufficient, live The Word.

They are opposed, hated. The newspapers rage against them. The churches hound them. They are reviled, attacked,

sued. The Preacher is sad. Those who cannot hear must destroy. It has always been so for those who discover a new
Word. It is time to find a new land for the new Word.

The Preacher is forty years old when he flies to preach in
Africa and sees the broad grasslands and forest below, un-
tainted by the hate, greed and violence of the enemies of The
People.

8.

The age of anxiety is what W.H. Auden called the middle of
the twentieth century. Anxiety leads to tension and stress
and need. To the end of the twentieth century. To the age of
need for a cigarette long after you have quit smoking, don't
really like cigarettes and never did.

After dinner, while Kay does my job with the dishes, I
stand at the front window of the dark living room and watch
the street in front. I look for a shadow across the street, under
an old oak in our neighbor's yard, in the light at the corner.
There are no shadows. No one on our street, no cars parked
with the glow and fade of a cigarette inside, the shape of a
head through the windshield.

I limp back to my office, sit at the window on the back
yard, finally light a cigarette where Kay can't see me. I watch
the yard, the alley behind the house, the thick bushes in the
next yard where an army could hide. I listen to the night. To
the sound of the surf beyond the loud, laughing voices of
some neighbors on their way home.

The answer could be out there in the night, too.

A black night, the moon not yet up.

I will get no help, no easy shadows. I check the Sig-Sauer in
my desk, smoke and look for movement. I can't run far with
my leg and shoulder, or even walk. If there is anyone out
there, they will not spare Kay.

❧

Colonel Ngane rode beside the pilot of the helicopter. "He brought much good here, Mr. Fortune, but he could not let well enough alone."

We flew low over the dry bush and high grassland after leaving the provincial capital before coming to country with more forest. A river that curved through the trees on the edge of the grassy plain. I saw no sign of human life below. Only the crocodiles that sunned themselves on the mud banks of the river.

"The good intentions of a dreamer," Ngane said, "joined to the dark places of the imagination, considerable stupidity and much delusion, Mr. Fortune. A bad mixture for my country and for The People."

The colonel was telling me about the massacre of The People, would do it in his own time and way.

"What happened to George Rogers down here?"

"We have never found—"

"I mean before the attack. Brown said Rogers came down to find the dirt, but joined The People. He said Rogers fought for The Preacher, loved The Preacher. That doesn't sound like the George Rogers I've read about, the great investigative reporter."

"No, I suppose it does not."

"When I read what he wrote down here for his magazine, his first reports were fair but skeptical. The kind of work that won him his Pulitzers. Then they became ambiguous, without any bite. Then they were repetitious, he wasn't really saying anything. Finally they stopped. A week or so before the attack."

The colonel continued to watch the land below as it became greener. "When Mr. Rogers arrived he seemed more with us than with them, went to the capital quite often. Then he did not. He changed, dressed as The People did, seemed to work for them."

"He became a convert."

"So it would seem."

I saw the buildings below. A small city of wooden houses spread across the brushland at the edge of the forest. A town that had literally sprung up overnight almost four years ago. I saw the medical building and hospital, the meeting hall under its geodesic dome, the dining halls, the facilities building for electricity, for water and sewage treatment. A small city like a miracle in the wilderness where no one lived now.

The helicopter came down in the dusty square between the dome of the meeting hall and the low administration building. A pair of four-wheel-drive vehicles appeared. Three soldiers rode in one with a military driver, the other carried a driver and one soldier. Colonel Ngane and I got into the second.

Ngane said, "I have something to show you."

We headed into the forest on an unseen surface as good as any blacktop. An invisible road.

"It is a blacktop," Ngane said. "The jungle has grown back, but the road is still there underneath. Not for long, but it has been only a year since the town came to an end."

"Why did it?" I said. "What made it happen?"

"What you will see is part of the answer."

It was another town, much smaller. The land had been cleared, frame houses built like those back in the town of The People. With streets and a small geodesic-domed meeting hall. A village as empty as the town of The People.

"The Preacher built it for the local tribesmen," Ngane said. "He built many villages. The tribesmen would not live in them."

The colonel got out. "Perhaps it must be that the leader sooner or later becomes the god. Perhaps it must be that the leader also comes to believe that he is a god. That he is God."

With the shafts of sunlight that filtered down like the light from high stained-glass windows, the clearing could have been some medieval Gothic cathedral.

"Perhaps it is always that God expects believers to live only for him. That they must be isolated from evil, error, and false beliefs. I know it is inevitable that a new god is opposed, perhaps hated, and comes to believe that everyone who does not believe in him is the enemy. So everyone must believe."

"Is that what happened to him, colonel?"

"He came down here already paranoid and messianic at the same time, Mr. Fortune. A dangerous combination my government was unaware of. Ridiculed and attacked in your country. In his own mind, persecuted. Perhaps the death of his father was the trigger." Ngane looked at the silent forest. "We gave him the land, but we charged him and taxed him for everything. The materials for his colony did not come this far cheaply. We did not flock to his vision. He came to feel we were trying to block him, destroy him as he saw us destroying the tribes, the innocent children of the cosmos.

"We have tried to protect the tribes in this region from contact with a civilization they are not ready to understand, but the forces of need within our country bring many adventurers to search for wealth in the tribal territories. As it was not so long ago in your own country. The adventurers see the tribesmen as obstacles to their wealth. To the tribes the adventurers are intruders killing their brother totems. The Preacher saw the tribes as converts, the adventurers as agents of our government."

The colonel paced among the shadows of the narrow clearing. "The People shipped in arms hidden in crates of bibles and food. Before we knew it, The Preacher had barred every white man from his area by force, moved the tribes into his villages, preached The Word to them in the meeting halls. Our tribesmen think of themselves as part of nature. They are practical people, direct. Superstition and animal totems to

219

protect them, a few myths to explain what they cannot explain. But they do not spend much time thinking about what they cannot explain. They had no idea what he talked about when he preached.

"The moment The People left they went back to their own villages. The adventurers continued to enter the area. There were clashes. We had to intervene. The Preacher ordered The People to keep us out. There were confrontations, our local authorities asked what they should do. The government told them to bring The People under control without using any more force than riot tactics—blank ammunition, tear gas, rubber bullets. We were to avoid injuring anyone. How could we have known what that would lead to?"

Michael Sarguis, The Preacher, knows at last that they want to silence The Word, destroy The People. The way they want to destroy the native people and their beautiful land. The way they had killed Adnan Sarguis and tried to destroy The People in San Francisco. The way the soldiers, the landowners and the Church had wanted to destroy Michael Sarguis in Nicaragua. The way they tried to destroy a boy who had only wanted to reach the ocean.

They have turned the tribesmen against The People. Only if the tribes are free will they hear The Word. The People must be free to spread The Word. The beautiful land must be saved while there is still time. The evil that would destroy The People and the land must be stopped. The Preacher tells The People it is time to take up arms and sweep away evil. Armageddon is near, when all will follow The Preacher to The Word and eternal life. The Preacher takes The People to stop the soldiers from entering the beautiful land that belongs to The People.

There is violence. The People are not soldiers, have some

guns but not many, are beaten back, retreat to the town where The Preacher meditates with his disciples. There are bruises, broken bones and burns. But there are no deaths. None of The People die from the bullets of the armies.

It is the final miracle.

The figure in black comes to The Preacher once more. "None can die who follow The Word, believe in The Preacher. The time has come. The transformation has occurred."

And the figure in black goes down on its knees before The Preacher. The figure kneels, head bent. The Preacher hears his own voice as a different voice from inside the earth, the sky.

"Is The Preacher now The Word?"

The kneeling figure in black smiles. "Yes."

"The People are invulnerable?"

"Yes."

The figure vanishes, leaves only the vast sky over the land. The Preacher gathers The People, tells them of the miracle and the visitation.

"The People cannot be killed by the soldiers! By anyone! We will save this beautiful land, the countries, the continent, the world, the universe!"

The Preacher sends a message to the capitals of all the nations of East Africa. The universe belongs to The Word, to The People. The rivers and the tribes. The nations and the continents.

They send the soldiers.

At dawn of the third day The Preacher leads The People out of the town toward the capitals of evil. In trucks and on foot. With tents and food and the few weapons they have. On the third night they meet the columns of soldiers, camp on the grassland at the edge of the bush and forest. In the morning they leave their camp and their trucks, advance on the soldiers.

The soldiers fire over the heads of The People.

"We are invulnerable to bullets!" The Preacher intones. "Attack! Save the land! Save the soldiers!"

The People attack, weapons high over their heads. They laugh, almost dance to bring The Word to the soldiers.

The soldiers fire.

The People fall.

"They will rise!" The Preacher intones.

The soldiers shoot.

"You cannot harm us!" The Preacher intones to the soldiers. "Save yourselves!"

The soldiers continue to fire.

The People fall in their blood.

The Preacher falls.

The People run.

The soldiers run after them. The soldiers shoot and hack and club and slaughter.

All across the brush and grassland The People lie dead and dying as the soldiers shoot, stab, bludgeon and laugh in a frenzy of rage and blood.

Colonel Ngane looked across the grassland from the rotted tents, the hulks of the trucks, at the last camp of The People. "We will never know how many died, Mr. Fortune. They kept advancing as if in a trance. Even when they fell they would crawl until they died."

"Could they have been drugged? A lot had been addicts."

"No trace of drugs in the bodies. Your own American doctors performed many autopsies. The drug was euphoria and exaltation. They believed. Only the machine guns, the cannon fired point-blank from the armored cars finally stopped them, made them run. The few that were left to run. The soldiers pursued them, killing and looting. We are not proud of that, but there had been too much blood to be turned off like a spigot."

On the plain the grass moved like a pale brown sea on the wind, where no trace remained of the deaths of two thousand people. Of two hundred soldiers. The sun and heat, birds and beasts, had returned the land to itself.

"And no trace of The Preacher or George Rogers?"

"No, Mr. Fortune."

"There was no trace of Perez Medina either, but he came back. No trace of Crispin Brown, but he's come back."

The helicopter that would take us back circled looking for a place to land. Ngane said, "Most of them were found the first day. A few were brought in late by tribesmen or walked in on their own after three or four days like Sarguis."

"Gabriel Sarguis?" I said. "Then you can't be sure The Preacher and Rogers didn't survive too. They just haven't walked in yet."

Ngane shook his head. "Say it is possible The Preacher might have a reason to continue hiding, what could possibly keep Mr. Rogers from returning to his country, his magazine, his wife, if he could?"

"Guilt," I said. "Guilt that he had joined The People, believed in The Preacher, abandoned his magazine, his work, his objectivity, and maybe his sanity."

"He was still with The Preacher after the attack," the colonel said, "according to both Medina and Sarguis."

"Then maybe he had even more guilt."

Ngane watched the helicopter settle, its rotors still turning. "So much guilt he would abandon his former life entirely? Abandon his wife? What could have caused that much guilt? That he felt shame, yes. A fool, ridiculous. But abandon his entire life? An intelligent man does not do that."

The pilot stepped out of the helicopter. Colonel Ngane bent down to go in under the turning rotors. I followed. The chopper rose over the remains of the last camp of The People, the brown grassland blowing on the wind, the emptiness that seemed to stretch a million miles.

"Where's the nearest telephone, colonel?"

"You can make a call when we return to my quarters."

"No. Where could George Rogers have called his wife from after the attack?"

"There is nowhere. The nearest would be thirty miles away at an outpost we keep to watch for poachers."

"His wife insists he tried to call her."

"Impossible. The People had radiophones at the town, but I doubt they had them with them. If they did they would not have been operating." Ngane shook his head as we flew across the barren bush and plain. "I do not believe he could have made such a call. An illusion of Mrs. Rogers, a hope."

9.

Kay is brushing her teeth when I hear the faint sound below in the rear yard, turn off the bedroom light, limp to the window.

I watch for some time. Until Kay is ready for sleep. In bed I listen. It has been more than two weeks, but I make no move toward her.

Kay's eyes shine in the dark bedroom. "Try to get some sleep. It's been a long two weeks, you've been shot."

A long two weeks, a lot of miles and a lot of lost blood. Long days and too many unfamiliar rooms. Too much death. Now I'm home in this house we share, and it isn't over. The questions have all been asked, but the answers are still locked inside my mind where I know the voice has told me what I need to know. But which voice or voices?

"I'm tired."

That isn't why I lie in the bed and make no move toward

her. Someone could be out there who wants me dead. I don't know who or why, and I can only listen in the night.

"What are you going to tell Sybil Rogers?"

"That I still don't know if her husband is alive or dead. That if he is dead I still don't know who killed him."

"But you think he's dead."

"I don't know what I think. I don't even know what I know."

When I returned from Africa, the hospital in L.A. told me Perez Medina had been discharged the day before. His mother said he had gone to Venice to a bookstore, to smell the sea. I found him on a bench near the bookstore, reading in the sun. A book about Africa. His arm hung in a sling.

"Going back?" I sat beside him where the gaudy people walked and skated past on the oceanfront walk.

"I could do worse. What did you learn over there?"

"Where could George Rogers have made a telephone call from after the attack?"

"Wherever he went."

"The day of the attack."

"Who says he did?"

"Sybil Rogers. She had three calls with no one on the line. She's sure it was George trying to reach her."

"There was nowhere. We had no phones, no radio. The army picked the spot to stop us because it was as far from any village or outpost as possible. If he made calls, they were from somewhere else, on another day."

"He could have done that only if he was alive."

"He's alive."

"There's another survivor who says he isn't."

"What survivor? They're all dead or in asylums except Sarguis and me."

"They found a new one. He came out just a week or so ago. I talked to him over there."

"Who?"

"Crispin Brown."

Medina closed his book. African history and culture. "I remember him. A heavy addict who came to us from Miami less than a year before The Preacher took us to Africa. Worked for drug dealers. Terrified of death. As close to the edge as I've ever seen a man. The Preacher rehabilitated him. He wasn't doing much of that by then, but he plunged in on Brown. Brown seemed to think it was a miracle, and I guess in a way it was. He became devoted to The Preacher. Totally loyal."

"He says he also saw you shoot and kill The Preacher and George Rogers. Exactly as Gabriel Sarguis did."

"If he had, he would have killed me then and there."

"He ran away and hid for over a year with tribesmen. Would a loyal man have done that if The Preacher were alive?"

"You never know until the moment comes. A flood of naked reality like a scream in your head. You come out still believing, or you don't. You can never know which it'll be. I came out knowing I didn't really believe in a god. I could be wrong, but my reason told me in that moment that I couldn't believe. Maybe Brown had his moment, looked too close at the sun. Then he had an illusion that The Preacher was dead to help him face himself. The Preacher was dead, so he could run away. But alone he couldn't deny, reverted to what he had been to hide from himself. I hid by doing nothing. He went back to drugs."

"Gabriel Sarguis had an illusion too?"

"Or a delusion."

"Or they're both lying," I said. "Coincidence of illusion, conspiracy, or maybe the truth."

"Which one, Fortune?"

The mental hospital was as green and peaceful in the sun among its flowers and trees as it always was, the violent crime wing as locked and guarded as it always was.

"You want to see Max Pugo this time?"

The doctor had the framed picture of his children in their confirmation clothes on his desk.

"I want to see Justice too, but Pugo first."

In the same institutional jump suit they all wore, Pugo sat in a straight chair with his back to the window and the sunlight beyond the bars. He faced the pale green wall of the small room. We were alone in the room, they didn't want me to disturb the other patients.

"How are you, Max?"

His manic state in the interrogation room of the East Los Angeles Division was gone. The hate and the anger too. But not the fear. A fear that was as much a part of him as his hands folded in his lap with the knuckles white from the pressure of their grip on each other.

"Still waiting for The Preacher to come for you, Max?"

His eyes never flickered, the manic replaced with the silent depressive, the absent depressive.

"Where are they, Max? The rest of The People who're alive?"

His head twitched.

"Why did you shoot Medina? Try to shoot me?"

"Liars. Blasphemers."

"Who told you we were liars, Max? Blasphemers?"

"Liars. Blasphemers."

"Did someone come to you, tell you to shoot Medina and me?"

The fear a film on his eyes in the sunlight.

"The Preacher himself, Max?"

227

On his knees in front of the chair he prayed not to me but to the wall. So low I couldn't hear the words.

"George Rogers? His wife?"

Not in English. Maybe Russian. It sounded like Russian.

"Someone else, Max? Came to you and Baltieri, told you The Preacher couldn't come for you unless you killed Medina and me?"

That was when he began to cry. Soft at first, then louder, and the attendant came in and took him out. The doctor came and took me along the antiseptic corridors to the old man, Samuel Justice, in his rubber room with its drain in the center. The old man sat against the wall as he had weeks ago. He rocked and smiled like both the child and the singer of the lullaby.

I squatted before him again. "He came to you. The Preacher. It wasn't something you could face, so you hid."

The emaciated face like some ancient African tribal mask.

"When did The Preacher come? Was George Rogers with him?"

The old man's dark eyes stared into nothing.

"Sarguis or Medina came to you. Said The Preacher needed you."

Like a puppet held by an unseen ventriloquist, the old man spoke in a monotone, "No one kills the sky. No one kills The Word. No one dies with The Word. They all alive. All of us with The Preacher. Praise The Preacher, amen. Praise The Word."

"It was The Preacher himself?"

"He come for us. All of us. Tomorrow he come take us home to The Word. The People go home tomorrow. We all sit with The Preacher an' The Word. Hallelujah."

The doctor took my arm. We went out of the rubber room. He walked with me along the scrubbed corridors. "You're right about one thing, Mr. Fortune. He's hiding far away inside. You want to know what triggered it, but he can't tell you. We think it was what happened over there, unable to face that trauma once he was safe here but alone without God. You're suggesting there was something more recent, a sudden shock he couldn't face. We have no knowledge of anything like that, but it is possible."

"He really saw them all get up? Believes they're all with The Preacher?"

"Yes."

Outside in my Tempo I thought about what people can see, believe.

On Saturday, March 19, 1988, a total eclipse of the sun drew a curtain of darkness across land and sea in a one-hundred-and-eight-mile path that moved across the Indian and Pacific oceans.

Scientists came from across the world, set up their instruments to study and analyze the natural phenomenon that occurs when the moon's orbit around the earth positions it between the earth and the sun. The first recorded total solar eclipse was reported by the Chinese in 2137 B.C.

Thousands of Indonesians prayed and beat drums to herald the start of the eclipse in the island nation.

Young Filipinos shot rifles and tossed firecrackers at the blackened sky to drive away the spirits of the dark. In Baguio City, one hundred and thirty miles north of Manila, pregnant women rinsed their hair with water dripped from burned rice straws. If they do not do this, the locals believe, their babies will be born deformed.

In northern India, a million naked men and women waded or dived into huge sacred pools to cleanse their souls in a massive Hindu ritual. Amid the chanting of hymns and the blowing of conch shells three thousand naked Hindu holy men were the first to enter the pools at 6:30 A.M. Massive waves of men and women followed. The bathers pushed and shoved their way into the pools that can accommodate 125,000 people at a time; divers and lifeguards in boats had to keep watch on the mad crush in the half-hour of the total eclipse.

The scene was repeated in smaller numbers at rivers and pools across India, but the giant pools at Kurukshetra are the most popular because the god Lord Krishna once appeared there during an ancient battle.

10.

I am almost asleep when I hear the light steps down in the yard beyond the windows. Quick steps, there and gone. The faint sound of wood being struck.

I listen to the night, the drone of the freeway, the soft pound of the surf. I wait for it to be my imagination in the night. A trick of the wind. An echo from the next block.

It comes again. Soft like a cat. Not an echo or the wind. I slide my bulk of bandage from the bed.

At the windows there is nothing below but the dim yard and alley, the path of the moon that has come up now over the dark houses. Again I am ready to believe it is my imagination, the vulnerable fear of a wounded man.

The shadow crosses the path of moonlight directly below. A slender shadow.

The second shadow is larger.

I slip from the bedroom, limp as fast as I can down the stairs. I hurt, hold to the banister. In my office, I take the new Sig-Sauer from my desk drawer. I call Sergeant Chavalas. He is off duty. I leave a message on his machine at home.

I call the sheriff's office, tell the dispatcher to send the patrol deputies. I give her my name and address, that someone is outside my house. That I have been shot. That I have a gun.

I sit in the doorway where I can see the side door in my office and the front door of the house.

❧

In the cottage behind The Church of the Universal Resurrection Gabriel Sarguis played casino with his uncle. He lay on his futon, still bandaged.

"You go over there to Africa to talk to Brown?"

"I talked to Brown," I said.

Rafael studied the cards on the table and in his hand.

"I talked to a Colonel Ngane," I said. "He was there when The People attacked. He was there after The People were dead. He thinks George Rogers and The Preacher are dead, too."

Gabriel watched his uncle play.

"Ngane has no evidence Perez Medina killed them. No evidence that anyone killed them. His view is that they died in the attack and reprisal."

Gabriel considered Rafael's play. "He didn't see what I saw. I'd think the same as him if I hadn't seen it happen with my own eyes. Brown saw exactly what I did, right?"

"Almost to the letter," I said.

Rafael Sarguis said, "That mean something, Fortune?"

"I wonder about where Crispin Brown has been since he vanished, was thought to be as dead as everyone else except the seven. Where he got the high-grade horse to keep his habit in check? The colonel over there says no tribal village is too remote, and they have their own narcotics anyway. But I wonder."

"I fought in Nicaragua with the Contras," Rafael said. "I've been in enough villages. I've seen the reach of drugs."

"It doesn't surprise you that Brown's an addict? Relapsed to

231

what he'd been before The Preacher saved him? Lost his belief so completely?"

"They all came out damaged. All except Gabe."

"All except Gabe," I said. "How do you account for that,
Reverend Sarguis?"

Gabriel sat back, winced from the wound. "I had more belief, and less belief. A stronger belief in what The Preacher
wanted to do for the world, and less belief in him. I never
believed he was really God, so when he couldn't do all he told
The People he could, my faith in him wasn't shaken as bad.
But I believed in his hopes, and they weren't changed because
he'd gone crazy, so I didn't lose as much, could regroup and
try again the way we're doing. Helping the community, reha-
bilitating the drug addicts, comforting the poor and beaten
down, serving the lost."

"Sort of like Saint Paul," I said.

"I never thought of myself that way, Fortune. But if you
mean continuing the work of The Preacher, why not?"

"And you came to help him," I said to Rafael. "From Argentina? After you heard of your brother's death?"

"From Miami," Rafael said, gathered the cards up with one
hand. "I haven't been in Argentina for a long time."

"Since the murder of Somoza?"

He boxed the cards. "Soon after."

"Then to Miami?"

He slipped the boxed cards into his pocket, sat back in his
chair too. A man who carried a deck of cards to pass the time,
keep his hands busy when his work required long hours of
waiting. "Not to Miami, Fortune. I told you I was with the
freedom fighters in my country. After we liberated my country, I laid down my arms so there could be peace and joined
my sister in Miami. When I heard of the tragedy in Africa,
and that Gabriel had survived, I came to help him continue
what was good in my dead brother's dream."

"Why not go home?"

"We who were ex-National Guardsmen were considered too provocative."

"Or too involved with drugs? To support your war?"

His brown eyes were almost yellow. A hard yellow.

I said, "Who got The People's money, property?"

Gabriel said, "A lot of the money was lost over there, the rest was claimed by their government. Reparations. The camp in Santa Barbara was sold. Most of the other buildings in this country had been sold before we left. I got the house where he had The Vision. He'd bought it back for The People. I keep it as it was in his memory."

"Someday a shrine," I said. "Baltieri and Pugo ran it for you?"

"We let them live there, yes."

"You weren't aware Crispin Brown had survived? Never saw him down there that last day?"

"I wasn't seeing too well that day, Fortune. But I saw Medina, and I saw them, and I saw him murder them."

"If Brown is alive when no one knew it, there could be others. They could be who is killing the survivors. The question is, why?"

"Why do there have to be more, Fortune? I'd say it was amazing there was one more."

"Even more amazing he saw exactly what you did, came back to tell us about it."

Rafael said, "Lucky for us and you. You'd never of known what was the truth."

"No," I said. "Could George Rogers have made telephone calls to the States before you saw him?"

"Telephone calls?"

"His wife thinks he called her after the attack. Where could he have called from in that area? Did you have radiophones with you in the trucks?"

Gabriel played a card. "Possibly, I'm not sure. We had them at the town. The Preacher could have brought one."

Rafael said, "Maybe this Rogers had a phone with him. I mean, he was a journalist, right?"

"That's possible," Gabriel agreed, smiled at me. "He would have had plenty of time to call before I saw them."

❧

Had she always watched everyone who came to the house with binoculars? Or was it only now, looking for someone she expected. Hoped would drive up the long, narrow dirt road to her ranch. Hoped or feared. George Rogers? Me? The police?

"What did you learn?"

In her riding clothes—jeans, twill shirt, boots, spurs, wide-brimmed Akubra brought back from Australia by George Rogers on one of his trips.

"I saw where it happened. I saw the town and what The Preacher tried to do. I heard what he came to believe and what killed him. I saw where they all died."

"But not George."

"Maybe not," I said. "I talked to another man who said he was dead, that Perez Medina had murdered him and The Preacher."

"He's lying. Did you see any proof he was dead?"

"No."

She had her horse tethered in the shade of a large old oak. She had been about to ride her land before she saw the telltale dust on the road, got her binoculars.

"I met a Colonel Ngane over there. George had become a convert, a follower of The Preacher. One of The People."

She shook her head. "No. He wouldn't."

"The new survivor over there, Crispin Brown, says that George had joined The People."

"George fooled them."

"Colonel Ngane noticed the change too. When George first

arrived over there he was much closer to the local authorities. Then he changed. He rarely left the town The Preacher built, dressed the way The People did, seemed to work more for them than his magazine. Ngane thinks he did become a convert."

"It's not possible, Dan."

Her horse pawed the ground in the shade, swished its tail against flies, impatient to be moving. A New York boy, I'd never learned to ride.

"It's possible. When I started this job for you, I saw something odd about his reports, but I didn't know enough then for it to mean anything. Now I do, and so do you."

A large bird soared in the cloudless sky above the oaks and western sycamores where the creeks ran in winter.

"His first reports to the magazine were his usual style of in-depth reporting. Then they became tentative, fuzzy and without any bite. That wasn't like him. Then the reports were repetitious and empty, essentially saying nothing. Then they stopped entirely. None of that is like him, and you knew it when you hired me. It is like a convert, Sybil. You know that, too."

The great bird rode the air currents in circles high up, had to be a buteo. Red-shoulder or red-tail hawk. Until it came closer and I saw the pronounced dihedral of its wings. Only a turkey vulture. Then it swept lower down the sky to pass over where the horse waited for Sybil Rogers. It was a hawk after all. A harrier. The only one in the West: a marsh hawk.

"You think that's why he hasn't come home? He's still one of them? Is with The Preacher?"

"It could be. Or it could be the reverse. Reversion seems to be sudden and difficult for The People. The trauma of the attack creates a conflict so strong it breaks their hold on reality. Was George a religious man, Sybil?"

"No."

"When he was young? Was his family?"

235

The harrier sailed past, large and low, and out of sight on the far side of the ranch house.

"They're Catholics. Not emotional Mary-Mother-Of-God type Catholics. English Catholics. Reserved, cool, but proud and very stubborn. George rejected the Church, called it hollow. All empty ritual. He turned his back on it completely."

"His family is still Catholic?"

"As far as I know. I've never met them."

A man who doesn't introduce his wife to his family?

"Was there some reason he turned his back on the Church?"

"He had a younger brother. I think they'd been very close, and the brother—his name was Dennis—ran off to Mexico to be a priest or something. George was twenty-one or so, Dennis was nineteen. I think it was a big blow to George, and he seemed to have felt that the Church took advantage of an immature boy, blamed it for the loss of his brother. When I met him he was, if anything, antireligion."

A man raised in a strong religious tradition, who lost his religion in anger and became actively antireligion. Who then succumbed to a messianic new religion. What would the stress of the destruction of his new religion do?

"Colonel Ngane over there, and Perez Medina, say it would have been impossible for George to make a phone call from where the attack occurred."

"I don't care what they say. I know those calls were from George."

"How long after the attack? What day were the calls?"

"I don't know what day the attack happened. I mean, I do now, I didn't then, did I? We didn't hear about it right away."

There was a long time difference between Santa Barbara, California, and East Africa. Twelve, fifteen hours, I didn't know exactly. With the delay in the report reaching the States, perhaps a matter of as much as three days. At least two days. Only Gabriel Sarguis said George Rogers had died on the day of the attack, would have to have made the call from the area.

"You know George is alive," I said. "You think others are alive, maybe The Preacher himself, and holding George prisoner."

"I know he's alive, and that's one explanation of why he hasn't come home."

"You hate The Preacher."

"Yes."

"You hate The People."

"Yes! I hate them all! What do you think that means?"

"I don't know what it means."

11.

In my chair in the open doorway, the dark office bright now with moonlight, my Sig-Sauer in my hand, I listen for the cock of a hammer, the click of a safety. A magazine that locks home.

Across the office the fierce stone head is all curving fangs in the light of the moon out in the night through my windows. A replica of an ancient stone head from Mexico, the feathered serpent, Quetzalcoatl. Lips and teeth in massive gray stone. Great stone teeth that curve up and down like scimitars behind lips that grin as if the monstrous serpent sees its meal in front of it. The four middle teeth rest on the thick lower lip between the six recurved fangs that could be the legs of some ancient crab that moves toward me. An eating machine.

"Is that what's outside, Dan?"

In the hall to the living room, Kay stands behind me.

"Perez Medina gave it to me. He saw the real Aztec head in Mexico. Lips, jaws and teeth, all that was left to us. The ancient Aztec god from Tenochtitlán. Medina collected the images and stories of the ancient gods of his country, brought them with him when he came up here."

"What kind of people have a god like that?"

I hear the shiver in her voice.

"Frightened people."

I listen. There is movement out in the night. Somewhere close to the house.

"Isn't everybody frightened, Dan? Inside? Afraid of something?"

The stone fangs move, gnash in the silver moonlight, a sound like the grinding of ancient stone.

"I suppose so."

What were they afraid of out there in the night?

Perez Medina wanted to see me. He sat in the wicker chair in the yard of his mother's house.

I said, "Sybil Rogers uses binoculars to watch everyone who comes up the road long before they get there. Is it because she keeps hoping it'll be George, or because she's afraid it'll be someone else?"

"Like who, Fortune?"

"Me. The police."

"You think she's been doing the shooting and killing?"

"She's got a lot of money. She hates The Preacher, she hates The People. Maybe she hates the survivors."

"And the killings have the look of hate. Anger at what we all did to her husband."

"She hired me as cover. It happens."

"So does human sacrifice, ritual killing." He stood. "Come inside."

His mother was in the kitchen, her hands busy in a bowl with a mixture that smelled hot and pungent. Rows of fresh tortillas were ready on the worn old table. She watched us go past, the anxiety in her eyes not quite hidden.

Medina took me into a room even smaller than his bedroom. It was a storage room with walls of cabinets that hung over narrow counters on top of more cabinets. It might have been a homemade pantry at one time, built by someone who had lived in the days before refrigeration had come to Mexican villages.

"In the hospital while you were gone I had time, had to come all the way back from Africa, finish the job those tribesmen started for me. I've thought about Max Pugo and why he shot me, about Baltieri, about the two murdered survivors. I've thought about The Preacher and what happened over there, and about how The Preacher and Rogers looked after the attack. As if more than the world had ended for them."

"What's more than the world?"

Medina leaned against one of the cabinets above the counter, his back to the window and the light.

"Have you ever been to Mexico, Fortune?"

"I've been to Mexico."

"I grew up in Mexico City. Did you know there isn't any such place? Mexico City? Only Mexico. Mexico, D.F., Mexico." He thought about all the people of the world outside Mexico who believed there was a Mexico City. "When I was a teenager my mother took me to the main celebration of the holiday of the Virgin of Guadalupe. Millions celebrate with masses, fireworks, parties, dances, but the real devotion comes at the Basilica of Guadalupe in the northern part of the city. The basilica is at the spot where an Indian peasant saw the Virgin Mary back in the sixteenth century. Pilgrims by the thousands come from all over the country to the basilica on that day, crawl on their knees across the whole plaza to the entrance to the basilica. She's Mexico's patron saint, the Virgin. Successor to Quetzalcoatl. Or maybe that is really all the statues of the bloody Jesus. I don't think there have ever been any more harrowing statues of the Crucifixion than those in the churches of Mexico. Nowhere else is there such a fixation on the broken bodies of the saints, on so much blood and torment."

"Is that what made you reject it? Turn to The Preacher?"

"I didn't reject it. I was as good a little Catholic as anyone in Mexico or East L.A. when we came up here. Sacred Heart, Sodality, morning Mass every day, the whole thing."

"How did you lose it?"

"What do you know of the Aztec religion?"

"They built big temples, liked to cut hearts out of human sacrifices."

"Blood and temples." He looked toward the single narrow window. Maybe for the light. "Massive monuments to ritual murder. Cutting hearts out was the least of it. The Aztecs were a totally structured society, stable and orderly, with a central religious rite of human sacrifice. Not a virgin or prisoner here and there, but thousands and thousands. We don't really know how many. Men, women and children collected for the sole purpose of being butchered in religious celebration. Whole rooms full of children slaughtered for the sun. Flowers a metaphor for murder, wars planned just for the sake of death, jewelry and sculpture designed to hold still-beating human hearts. A whole society with great sculpture, poetry, painting, astronomy, mathematics, but committed to cosmic regeneration through human sacrifice."

He shook his head in mystified wonder. I realized it wasn't for me, or even for the Aztecs. It was for himself.

"Human murder on a scale almost unknown, at least until our own time. The twentieth century of advanced, civilized Europe. And all of it to keep the world in motion. To keep the world alive. Because Aztecs believed the world, the whole universe, could stop at any moment, the way every single human life could be stopped at any moment without any apparent reason or cause. Ended, snuffed out in a second for no reason except that the gods wanted that life. The universe as they saw it was always balanced on a knife edge seconds from vanishing, just like an individual life. But if the universe died it would take *all* life with it. Because the gods lived on blood. So, give them blood and they wouldn't end the world. Life, the whole universe and its cycles, could only be maintained by human sacrifice. It lived on blood. Death was all that sustained life. Without streams of blood, the sun would not rise tomorrow over the lakes of Tenochtitlán."

He half-smiled at me. "They died so often, so young, the only logical answer they could think of was that the gods needed people to die. When you think about it, that makes the Aztec religion damned logical. Octavio Paz has said their beliefs were senseless and sublime. A horrible, tragic vision."

I waited, but he didn't go on. He'd stopped shaking his head in wonder at himself and the Aztecs, had finished what he wanted to tell me. Or part of it.

I said, "You learned about the Aztecs, put them together with your Catholicism."

He opened the cabinet he'd been leaning against. It was full of squat little clay statues, stone carvings, grotesque pottery masks, dazzling tile paintings of intricate figures that seemed to be made of colored mosaic, black-and-white and color photos of pyramids and giant statues. He touched one horrible but beautiful painted clay mask of a grotesque face with the ears and horns of a bull, staring human eyes, a nose of fire, great protruding teeth in two savage rows, and smaller horned gargoyle faces growing out of it like a second set of ears beneath flame nose and eating mouth.

"I started collecting all this when my family decided to leave Mexico. I didn't want to leave, needed to be even more Mexican. But we left and came up here. I was maybe twenty, at UCLA, when I realized that the Aztec religion and the religion I'd grown up with weren't all that different. Maybe it was being here in L.A. where people sneered at Mexico and laughed at religion, or maybe it was just growing up in the modern world, but a time came when the Church and the Aztecs looked pretty near the same, so I left both, left the *barrio*, became a real American."

I said, "Why The Preacher? The People?"

"Maybe when you've grown up in a place where in the past there were gods for everything, and a God that is everything in the present, you never get over it. When times get bad, when you lose a wife, a child, a job, you need something to believe in. I lost my son, then my job, then my wife. My son drove me to the bottle, the bottle cost me the job, the job cost me my wife. All I had left to lose was my life. The bottle would have done it, but I guess I wasn't ready for suicide, even the slow kind, so I found The Preacher. The People saved me from the bottle."

He reached into the cabinet and took out a gray stone carving that had once been part of a head but was now only a mouth with thick stone lips and six enormous decurved fangs, three on each side of four large curved teeth. He set the terrifying stone mouth on the counter. He stepped back from the fangs and hungry mouth. "This is a miniature replica. The real mouth is the size of a room. The plumed serpent: Quetzalcoatl."

We each looked in our own way at the terrifying stone eating machine on the counter.

"Senseless and sublime. I guess you could say that about a lot of religions. We all try to answer the same question. Why death? The Aztec answer was maybe not so crazy. You look at the world they saw, it's a reasonable conclusion. As reasonable as the bloody religion I grew up with in Mexico. Maybe as logical as heaven, nirvana, or The Preacher believing bullets can't kill us."

He picked up the mouth and fangs of the great Aztec god, handed it to me. "A souvenir of The Preacher. There's damned little connection between the ideas and explanations of educated people, and the dark places of the imagination."

I thought of the dusty grassland and brush over in Africa, the thick rain forest and rivers. It was in land much like that the Aztecs built the Templo Mayor of Tenochtitlán. A temple to their gods. The People and The Preacher had gone to Africa for their beliefs, built their temple of beliefs.

I said, "Is that what happened over there? Imagination won over education?"

"Something like that," Medina said.

"The world stopped and they all died?" I said. "But they didn't all die, did they? The dark places of the imagination. Blood and ritual. Ritual and blood. The murders of the two survivors are ritual murders."

Medina closed his cabinet of grotesque ancient gods and masks, the glorious and sublime mosaic paintings of those gods, and walked out through the kitchen into the back yard again. He stood breathing as if he needed to know he was still alive. In my hand the hungry gray stone mouth of the great plumed serpent of Mexico felt alive. I wanted to drop it and run.

"Blood ritual," Medina said. "Because he's afraid."

"He's alive, and so are a lot more than only Crispin Brown. Maybe all the unaccounted for. You did see him and Rogers, and maybe they've both gone insane with guilt and fear."

"Just fear. That's all. Fear he was wrong and God is going to kill him."

"Crispin Brown." I said. "A relapsed addict. From Miami. And he'd do anything for The Preacher."

"Anything," Medina said.

"He would never have deserted The Preacher."

"No."

I sat on the wooden kitchen chair, put the mouth of Quetzalcoatl in the dirt. "Why?"

"I said it, Fortune. They've gone crazy. Fear."

243

"I don't think it's enough. There's planning behind the shootings, especially of you and Gabriel Sarguis. Behind Crispin Brown appearing all of a sudden. I don't believe he was hiding among those tribesmen, shooting up in some remote grass hut. He was hiding, yes, but somewhere else."

His dark eyes looked into my face. "With The Preacher? The Preacher sent him to back up Gabriel's story, discredit me, prove he was dead."

"You say there was nowhere George Rogers could have made a call from in that area after the attack. Colonel Ngane says there was nowhere. Sybil Rogers insists he did call, but the calls could have been a day after, two days, three. So he would have to have called from somewhere else. That means . . ."

I heard it. In my head. The voice of Colonel Ngane.

I had to fly to Santa Barbara first, call the colonel in Africa, be sure I was right. I called ahead to Kay, told her to pack a bag, buy me a ticket north.

When I got to Santa Barbara, I ran for my car in the airport parking lot. Ran into the wall of pain that exploded the day in a flash of green and red and thick white fog like the inside of a giant pearl.

12.

I am in my chair in the open doorway, my Sig-Sauer in my hand. Kay has brought a chair to sit with me. She is inside in the shadows of the office. She listens for the sheriff or Sergeant Chavalas. I don't listen. I know what I know.

"I remember."

Across the office the fangs of the fierce stone head shine in the moonlight. The mouth of Quetzalcoatl. Great stone teeth that curve like scimitars behind lips that grin as if the monstrous serpent sees its meal. A meal of blood and death. So it can live. The universe can live.

"When I was in Africa, Colonel Ngane said something. I remembered it before I was shot, I remember it now. Gabriel Sarguis says he saw Medina murder The Preacher and Rogers, passed out and woke up in a hospital that same day. No one knew about Medina or The Preacher and Rogers. He thought it was all an illusion, a dream. But when Medina reappeared last month, he says he knew it had all been real.

"But Colonel Ngane said Gabriel surrendered to the soldiers three or four days after the attack. That's what I knew. Where had Gabriel been? Why did he lie? If he hadn't been unconscious in a hospital, why doubt what he said he saw? When he heard that the bodies of The Preacher and Rogers and Medina hadn't been found, why not tell about Medina then?"

Kay said, "Because he knew The Preacher and George Rogers were alive."

"He'd been with them those two or three days, and maybe with some of the others who are still missing."

"What would he have to gain by not telling the truth, then or now?"

"For some reason he wants to keep The Preacher hidden." I push the chair back hard when I stand. It bangs into the wall, echoes loud in the office like something slamming against the side door that bursts open and a man hurls through, hits a chair, staggers against the desk.

The knife is bright steel.

A face outside, pale in moonlight, appears and disappears in the violent swings of the door like the flicker of an old black-and-white movie.

I watch the knife and the eyes inside the room. Eyes brighter than the steel of the knife. Mirrors in a rigid face.

I remember the Sig-Sauer in my hand, fire. Kay throws her chair, sprawls him over the couch. I fire at the face outside.

I hook my gun and hand under her arm, pull us both into the hall, feel the warm blood wet under my bandages.

In the living room, I push her down behind the couch, turn to see the tall figure that bangs against the hall walls into the living room, the knife like a sword.

I lean against the couch, fire.

The lunging figure cries out.

I fire.

The figure blocks the light, fills the whole room around me. I go in under the knife, my shoulder low into the figure that falls away and down on a shattered coffee table, the knife shining away across the living room like a falling star.

I breathe, hold to a chair back against the violent pain in my shoulder that bleeds under the bandages, look down at the eyes of the man with the knife. Eyes that no longer shine. I breathe hard through the pain and blood hot on my shoulder.

Kay sits on the dark floor. "Is he—?"

"I sure the fuck hope so. Don't go outside."

There is another. At the door into my silver office, the bullet misses me. The pale face looks at me from a small, thin, dark haired man. I don't know how close my bullets come to him. Then he's gone.

The sirens are near.

The feet run away across the back yard beyond the windows and the open door. At the door I am too late, the second man has vanished, the yard empty. Only the path of moonlight.

But I have seen the second man. Gabriel Sarguis's drug rehabilitation hope. The small man who wondered over my arm in the office of The Church of the Universal Resurrection, shivered at the imagined bite of a shark. Angel.

CRIME, PUNISHMENT AND RESURRECTION

On our couch, the broken coffee table is in front of us. The deputies have talked to us for hours, ignore us now. The body of the man I killed has been taken away by the coroner's deputies. The deputies and Sergeant Gus Chavalas shake their heads over the tall dead man who hadn't stopped coming toward me with his knife until I knocked him over with the lunge of my shoulder.

"You hit him all three shots, Fortune. At least two should have done the job. Drugged to the ears or sick in the head."

"Maybe both," I said.

It was Chavalas who kept us out of the county jail for the night. The deputies all knew me, but that wouldn't have kept them from taking us in to get our stories the official way. I'd killed a man. Chavalas had no official status in the county, but it's a small town, Santa Barbara, he had a killing in the same case, and they had to live with each other. They taped off the house and yard, left a man to watch, warned us they'd be back tomorrow, and went home.

After Kay had made us a pot of tea to calm down by, and gone up to bed, Gus Chavalas stood at the window to look out at the deputy bored in his car on the street.

"You told the deputies straight about The Preacher, George Rogers, the other killings and shootings. You don't know who the dead guy is, but you think it's all the same killers. You think Perez Medina can identify the guy. What didn't you tell them, Dan?"

He was getting to know me too well.

"I don't know who the dead man was, but I'm pretty sure what he was."

"What was he?"

"One of The People. A survivor, but not one we knew about. I think there're a lot of them alive somewhere, and wherever they are The Preacher's with them, and maybe George Rogers."

"Where would that be?"

"I don't know, but I think I know who does."

"How do you know that?"

I drank my tea. "I recognized the second man."

The San Francisco Police Department detective was named Albano. "We've had an eye on that church. Too many of their people got drug sheets longer than I've been on the force, and their drug rehabilitation program doesn't show a hell of a lot of results. They've been in business less than a year, so it was too soon to be sure, and with all the brouhaha over The Preacher and The People we had to go careful. He started right here, you know? The Preacher."

I told him I knew. He tried to get a search warrant, while Chavalas and I got restless. If it had been Gabriel Sarguis and Rafael who sent Angel and the dead man, they wouldn't wait once Angel got back with the bad news. If he did. I hoped Angel would take a beeline south from Santa Barbara and not look back. In the end the captain didn't go to a judge anyway.

"We don't have enough. Go with Fortune and Sergeant Chavalas, Albano, get us something more."

Albano and two other detectives drove us to The Church of the Universal Resurrection in two cars. We parked a block away, but there was no light in the converted building. No light and no sound. The front door was open as it always was. Inside, Gabriel's office was dark, everything gone from his desk top and drawers. The shelves were bare. The back yard was as dark as the church and office. So were his cottage, and the two outbuildings with the bars on their windows. We looked in the cottage windows first.

Angel was sprawled in a doorway inside the cottage. They didn't need a warrant now. One detective called in for the homicide team, one called for the medical examiner. Albano examined the body without touching much or moving anything until the photographer and lab people got there.

I'd hit Angel down in Summerland, a flesh wound high on his left arm that had bled on his leather jacket. That wasn't what had killed him. Where he was sprawled in the doorway between the living room and the kitchen his narrow back was a mass of blood, the dark pool thick under him. In line with the body and the kitchen, pictures on the wall were shattered.

"He was in the doorway," Albano said. "Someone opened up from the kitchen. Coming in or going out, the M.E.'ll tell us."

"Going out," Chavalas said. "He's on his face."

"Could have hit the door, been spun," Albano said.

"Going out," I said. "He was the only link between Gabriel and Rafael and the attack on me. A liability. He probably knew a lot too much about them anyway. Even where they'd hide."

They found the drugs stashed in the rehabilitation and AIDS counseling buildings. It explained the barred windows. Coke, H, the best marijuana. From the stencils on the wrappers, all from South and Central America and Mexico by way of Mexico. It wasn't the first time a drug rehab center, or even a church, had been used as a cover for a distribution center.

"Any ideas, Fortune?" Albano said. "Where they'd hide out?"

"One, but a lot depends how long they've had, how much they thought was out in the open, and how close they thought we were to being behind them."

"Let's take a look."

The house where Michael Sarguis had lived when he moved from the *barrio* the first time, where he'd had The Vision, was as dark as The Church of the Universal Resurrection. Unlike the church, it was locked up tight. The detec-

249

tives kicked the door down. They were in pursuit of fugitives with reason to suspect they could be inside.

Flowers were there in front of the picture of The Preacher, offerings of incense and food and even wine. Upstairs at the shrine of The Window That Was Never Closed, the light fell on the picture of The Preacher and nothing else. The rows of replicas of the figure in black of The Vision had gathered more dust. Nothing else was in the house. Nothing and no one, and no leads to where the Sarguises could have run.

The San Francisco police didn't need us anymore, would do all the slow work of combing the church and house for leads. Talk to anyone they could find who had known Gabriel and Rafael, send out the inquiries and calls for help and cooperation.

"We'll contact the cops down in Mexico, but won't hold our breaths for cooperation," the captain said. "Not if those two have money and contacts."

At the airport, Chavalas and I waited for our flight south.

"That's all of it?" Chavalas said. "Drugs?"

"For Rafael, probably."

"And Gabriel?"

"Something more. The myth and legend. A rock to build a safer and richer future on than drugs."

"The Preacher's alive somewhere?"

"He's alive. I don't know where."

"George Rogers?"

"He was alive after the attack. With The Preacher and Gabriel Sarguis. I'm sure of that now."

What I didn't know was if George Rogers was still alive.

13.

Perez Medina sat in our living room.

"They brought him up to identify the man you killed," Kay said. "He's got an idea about The Preacher."

Two days out of the hospital, battered and ripped up, what I wanted was a beer and a nap. I would settle for a shower and the beer. "Give him a beer, I'll be back."

"He has a beer. You want to rest, Dan?"

"I can come back," Medina said.

I must have looked even worse than I felt. "Just have a beer ready."

I took my bag up to the bedroom, washed the grime and strain of San Francisco and United Airlines off in the shower, and went back downstairs. Kay brought me a Red Tail, sat and watched me for signs that said she should whisk me away to rest.

"You look better," I said to Medina.

"I think I'll survive." He didn't smile. "I wasn't sure."

"The loss of a hope can do that."

"You have to find a different hope. Or learn how to live without hope."

"That what you wanted to tell me?"

"No. They asked me to come up and identify the man you shot. Martin Quintana. Unstable even among The People. A violent man with a lot of fear. I saw his kind many times in Mexico. Gets drunk, becomes violent, even kills someone. Wakes up the next morning so full of fear for what God would do to him that he crawls on his belly to church and cries to the priest. Death such a horror to them they kill first. Aztecs."

"He was one of the missing People?"

Medina leaned forward on the couch. "I thought a lot about

251

blood rituals after we talked the day you were shot. Remembered a lot of material I read when I was at UCLA. All the religions in the world. Primitive ones, tribal cults. From Africa and the Caribbean."

"And?"

"What you saw in Barstow and here is *palo mayombe.* A variation. An African religion."

"You mean The Preacher found another religion over there? Turned to it after the massacre."

"I think he picked up *palo mayombe,* but not from over there. It's from Central and West Africa, the Congo, came over here in the slave ships. It protects you from evil with sacrifices to the gods. Animal sacrifice, but over here they added human sacrifice like the Aztecs. Maybe we carry it in our minds from the Aztecs. Blood ritual to protect from evil and death."

Kay said, "He'd been wrong, The Word had failed. The victim of evil, the devil. He had believed in good. Now he had to believe in evil."

"Where would he be, Medina? Somewhere from the past? Maybe a place where The People were?"

"San Francisco, the *barrio?*"

"The police up there are looking into that, but it would have been hard for him to hide up there. Anyway, I think he's still got some of The People with him."

Kay said, "Fresno? The mountain camp here in Santa Barbara?"

"Fresno police say no. The sheriff found nothing up at the camp. I think it would have to be somewhere remote."

"Nicaragua?" Medina said.

"That's a long way for Gabriel and Rafael to keep close contact, arrange the murders and shootings. They were probably using him to bring the drugs into this country, would need him somewhere closer to the border."

"They're using The Preacher?" Kay said. "Not the other way around?"

"I don't know who's using who, but I know Gabriel and Rafael set up that shooting of Gabriel to make it look like the killers were after him, too. They couldn't trust Baltieri to only wing Gabriel, so Rafael probably shot him with Baltieri's gun, then killed the old man. I think the way they got to Pugo and Baltieri was by having The Preacher behind them."

"Remote, but not too far," Medina said. "Mexico?"

In my head I heard another voice. Sybil Rogers.

"George Rogers," I said. "If he's with them, he's got a brother. A priest, maybe somewhere in Mexico."

The early evening sun of the Santa Ynez Valley flashed off her binoculars as we drove up the dirt road. There was a chill in the late spring night air of the valley where the temperatures are always hotter or colder than on the coast.

"Coffee or a cocktail? I'm going to have a martini. George and I always did at this hour when he was home."

She looked at Perez Medina, and talked. I had always come out to the valley alone. Something was different. She had waited too long to think it would be good when we told her, talked to keep whatever it was away a little longer.

"Coffee," Perez Medina said.

I nodded. She went into the kitchen, talked to us over her shoulder as she went. "You're looking so much better than the last time I saw you, Mr. Medina. Are you feeling better, Dan? Kay was worried sick. I feel guilty. You were hurt on my account." She came out with cups, spoons, cream, sugar and a coffeepot on a silver tray. After she'd served us, she began to make her martini at the wet bar between the living room and the kitchen, her back to us.

"Is he dead?"

"I don't know," I said.

"Then why is Medina—?"

I said, "We're pretty sure he was alive after the attack. We don't know if he still is."

She finished stirring her martini, sat down facing both of us. "What does that mean?"

I told her what I had remembered, that Gabriel Sarguis, contrary to his story of the murders of The Preacher and George Rogers, had been missing for three or four days before he reappeared over there in Africa. "Gabriel had no reason not to tell what he'd seen right then. If it had ever happened."

"But I was missing then," Medina said. "As dead as everyone else, including the Preacher and your husband. Gabriel had no reason to think anyone would question that the missing were dead. Not until I walked out of the bush and said they were alive after the attack."

Sybil Rogers sat on the edge of her upholstered chair. "And if he were hiding them, keeping them prisoner, he had to deny your story, discredit you."

"We don't think he's holding them prisoner," I said. "At least not The Preacher." I told her what we did think. That The Preacher had sent some of The People who had survived with him to do the killings. That he was being used by Gabriel and Rafael to cover a drug operation, make money on what had happened. "What we don't know is how George fits in. If he's with them, or even still alive."

"If he isn't with The Preacher, where would he be?"

She still rejected out of hand that her husband could be dead. The hope and the belief.

"That's why we came to you, Sybil," I said. "Where could he go if he wanted to hide? With or without The Preacher?"

"Why would he want to hide? He loves his life. He loves me. He wouldn't hide."

There is a popular television game show that tells us no one knows that much about the hidden places of another person, even a husband or lover, parent or child. It's a shallow show whose contestants and viewers fail to see the implications, but they are there for anyone who wants to think about them.

I said, "Sybil, say George did convert, become a follower of The Preacher. Then came the attack, the massacre."

"I told you. He would never have joined them."

"I think he did, Sybil. A man raised as an intellectual Catholic. A man who then rejected his Church as hollow, lost his religion, especially one who lost it in anger over a personal loss, is a prime candidate to succumb to a messianic new religion. And an equally prime candidate to revert again under the stress of a disaster as shattering as what happened to The People. A reversion that would be full of trauma, neurotic."

She drank her martini. "What does any of that matter, Dan?"

"You said George had a younger brother. Very close to him. Dennis became a priest, maybe in Mexico. Do you know where Dennis is?"

"No." She finished her martini. "I think there were letters. I never read any. Handwritten letters. George didn't get many letters written by hand. Those were usually mine, women's letters."

"Do you have any of the letters?"

"I suppose George might have some in his office."

I found them in a bottom drawer of George Rogers's desk. Over twenty letters. The return address was Fr. Dennis Rogers, Abadia de Monasterio de San Miguel Arcangel, Coatitlán, Mexico.

14.

The old stone walls of the Abadia de Monasterio de San Miguel Archangel sat on an ochre hill above the brown land of olive trees and dusty orchards that looked like the land the first padres had left behind in Spain. A touch of home in the heathen New World they had come to save for God, acquire for King, Inquisition and Order—Jesuit, Franciscan or whichever it happened to be.

"Is he here, Father Rogers?"

In his robes, Dennis Rogers was a medium-sized man with a round face and glasses. He looked like a middle-aged small businessman. Except for the softness of the face, the calm eyes and manner. Even on an early spring morning, the reception room was warm with the sun. It seemed to have no effect on Rogers despite the heavy robes.

"The newspapers all say my brother died over there in Africa with the group that called itself The People."

"His wife doesn't think so," I said. "Mr. Medina, who was there, saw both The Preacher and your brother alive after the attack."

Dennis Rogers looked at Perez Medina. "How can anyone be duped by such a movement?"

"It's not hard if you hurt enough," Perez Medina said. "If you need and ask and no one else answers your questions the way you want."

"God doesn't always give us the answers we want. Only the true answers," Rogers said. "You must have been born Catholic."

"Yes." Medina had not used the word "father" once.

"So was your brother," I said. "Is he here?"

Dennis Rogers sat down, clasped his soft hands. "Why are you looking for him?"

"His wife hired me. I want to tell her he *is* alive."

"If he's alive, wanted her to know, he would tell her himself, wouldn't he?"

He had not confirmed that George Rogers was at the monastery, or that he was alive. But he had not denied it either. I didn't know how far his concept of lying went, or of his responsibility to telling the truth.

"We think The Preacher is alive too," I said. "There's another former member of The People we think is using The Preacher to commit crimes, including ritual murder."

I told him the whole thing. It took some time. He still clasped his hands where he sat in the warm room.

"We hope your brother can help us find The Preacher, stop Gabriel Sarguis and his uncle."

The silence in the room with its heavy old furniture of colonial Spain went on. Dennis Rogers seemed to be turning the problem every way he could to come up with the answer he wanted. Or didn't want but, in the end, couldn't evade.

"My brother has been ill, mentally and physically. He asked for total isolation, took a vow of silence, wants no visitors." He stood. "I will have to ask him if he will speak to you."

I said, "Tell him if he doesn't there'll be more ritual murders of innocents. Tell him that if he won't talk to us, we'll go to the Mexican and American governments, make it all public, and then he'll have to talk to a lot more people than us."

The calm eyes showed an unsaintly flash at the threat, but he turned and left the room. Medina watched him go without sympathy, went to stand at a window that overlooked the cloister of the old abbey. He had said little since we arrived, and we sat in silence in the hushed atmosphere and waited until the door finally opened again, and my search came to one of its ends.

"Mr. Rogers?"

The man who came in was George Rogers, and not George Rogers. Pale and thin in one of the monastery's dark robes, he looked little like the robust international investigative journalist and globe-trotter I had seen in the photographs in the magazines and books. The dashing clothes were gone, the alert eyes, the daring smile. In their place was a small, slow-moving man whose face was blank as he looked at me. But the biggest difference was in the eyes.

"I have all I need here. I wish to remain here. Thank you for coming."

Hot and empty eyes. I would have said feverish eyes, but the thin, quiet man in front of me didn't seem to be in physical ill-health. Remote eyes in a face without expression. Eyes in a different place and time.

"Sybil wants you to come home, George."

He sat down, folded his hands in his lap. "No, I can't go home. Not now. Not ever."

"Why not, George?"

"I have to atone, find forgiveness. Atonement and penance and mercy."

Perez Medina's voice was a snarl, "Because they died and you didn't? Because you believed The Preacher? We all believed—"

His distant eyes focused slowly on Medina. "Disciple Medina? You were spared, too. I thank God. Join with me in prayer for that mercy."

He bent his head, began to pray.

"Atone for what, George?"

George Rogers's head remained bent, his voice low and serene. "I failed God, lost myself in a false god. Denied Him and failed myself. I have to atone, find my way back. Find the path again. Return to the truth."

Medina's voice was still harsh. "I saw you leading The Preacher that day. Where did you go?"

George Rogers nodded. Up and down, up and down. His

voice became stronger, but as distant as his eyes. "They were all dead. Everyone. The soldiers killed them all. The bullets killed them." He looked up at me. What I saw in the thin face and feverish eyes was neither atonement nor penance, but horror and a bottomless fear. "I had listened to evil, to Satan. I failed God and lost myself." His head went down, his neck bent as for the axe. "Atonement, penance and resurrection."

His voice was still quiet. But I had seen the horror and the fear. He was a shell, hollow and burned out. Like a building that seems untouched after a terrible fire but everything inside is gone. The horror of that day had burned through him and left only a shell behind eyes feverish with fear that saw nothing outside.

I said, "Where did you call Sybil from?"

For a time in the warmth of the room I thought he hadn't heard, too deep inside his own mind. But he had heard. "She is better off without me. He let me call her, but I couldn't talk to her. No. I failed her, I'm sorry for that. I don't want her to look for me. I must atone, return to God."

"Who let you call her?"

"The disciple Gabriel. He had a truck. I wanted to kill Michael Sarguis. He is the anti-Christ. But that was wrong, and God sent Gabriel, and he took us to the place where the airplane was. He let me call my wife but I couldn't talk to her."

"Where did he take you, George? Where did you go?"

"Home here with God."

"Before that?"

"To the plane."

"After the plane but before you came here?"

"The ranch."

Medina said, "Your ranch, Rogers?"

"The ranch where my brother came to bring me home to God."

"Is The Preacher at the ranch?" I said.

The horror filled his eyes, the enormous fear. "Penance and

atonement and mercy." His head bent once more. "I failed the truth, embraced falsehood. They all died. Everyone died. I was blind, a blasphemer, I must atone—"

The door opened and Dennis Rogers came in. Anger almost as hot in his eyes as the fear in George's. The man with Dennis Rogers had eyes that showed neither anger nor fear nor anything else. As opaque as brown granite. A man in his seventies, with a smile as closed as his eyes, the assurance of certainty.

"The Father Superior thinks that's enough, Mr. Fortune," Dennis Rogers said. Alone, he would not have been so polite.

The older man bent his head to us. "Mr. Rogers has endured much. If Mrs. Rogers wishes to speak with him herself, now that you have found him against his will, we will receive her. But inform her that the wishes of Mr. Rogers will come first."

"I'll tell her," I said. "But it's The Preacher and Gabriel Sarguis we want. Mr. Rogers said there is a ranch where his brother came for him. Where is it?"

Dennis Rogers was bent over his brother. He spoke softly, a parent soothing a child. Roles had been reversed, and Dennis Rogers liked being the older brother, even the father. George Rogers only listened, his head bent again where he sat in the warm room with the brown Sonoran desert outside.

"I think, Father Rogers," the Father Superior said, "we can tell them that."

Dennis Rogers didn't look up. "The Miranda Ranch across the border, perhaps fifty miles from Agua Prieta."

"In the States?"

"Yes."

"Why did you go there?"

"A man called, George wanted to see me. I thought he had died in that horror. I went."

"Who called?"

"A voice on the telephone. When I got there, George was alone. He was dirty, hungry, out of his mind."

Dennis Rogers didn't like me. I was there badgering George, returning past horror. But it was more than that. I came from Sybil, from the magazine, from a world he blamed for taking his brother from him as much as George had blamed the Church for taking Dennis from him. He blamed the modern world for taking George from God, for, ultimately, sending him to the horror and heresy of The Preacher.

The Father Superior smiled. "He is well now, Father, he has come back to God. He can rest in peace."

The older man's voice had a deep satisfaction. He was happy for George Rogers who had been lost in error, and through horror and suffering had returned to renounce his error. Pleased for himself, and for his God. Perez Medina walked from the room.

I said, "That's all you can tell us about that ranch?"

"It's abandoned, but everyone in the town on the highway knows where it is."

"What town?"

"I think it was called Sunsites."

The Father Superior said, "And I think we have finished, Mr. Fortune."

Dennis Rogers took George out. In the corridor the Father Superior turned me over to the young monk he had assigned to guide and watch us, who shepherded me out to where Perez Medina sat in our rented car. His anger stared out through the windshield at the olive trees and orchards, at the barren brown hills. He said nothing until I left the dirt road and turned west on the narrow Mexican highway.

"You hear his voice? That Father Superior? He's happy! Another mind broken and returned to the path of truth."

I watched the road. Driving off the major highways in Mexico can be an adventure for orderly Americans. Even on the main highways. Medina wasn't thinking of highways.

"You know anything about Sor Juana?"

"A Spanish poet. Seventeenth or eighteenth century. Something like that."

"Sor Juana Inés de la Cruz, a seventeenth-century Mexican nun and maybe the greatest poet of colonial Mexico."

Young Juana Inés de la Cruz grows up in the household of her stepfather, a minor landowner in the colonial Mexico of the seventeenth century. She is a quick, bright, independent girl, something that is not particularly encouraged in a rigid colonial society more like fifteenth-century Spain. Perhaps because she is a stepchild in a hierarchical world.

A stubborn child, determined and sure of what she wants and does not want. She refuses to eat cheese in a world of limited diet because she thinks cheese makes one stupid. Juana Inés de la Cruz has no intention of being stupid. She becomes a constant reader, even voracious, reads her grandfather's library from cover to cover.

At fifteen, she finds a place in the entourage of the vicereine, the wife of the ruler of this part of New Spain. She is a beautiful young woman at a court where the traditions of sexually charged flirtation, *galanteo*, still hold sway, is soon noticed and admired. Her wit and poetic talent make a strong impression on the viceregal court. Written in the sophisticated high-Baroque style, her poetry is polished and worldly.

In a time and place where marriage is the only career for a woman, the only way to escape from the closed and sealed world of her family, she has little interest in a husband and not very good prospects for getting one. There is only one other source of security and independence away from the family: the Church.

A few years after her dazzling entry into the high world of the viceroy and his wife, Juana Inés de la Cruz joins the Hieronymite Order of nuns, becomes Sor Juana. The Hieronymites are a gentle, worldly order, she can continue to write her secular poetry, build a library of her own, have her servants. She can and does hold regular intellectual salons, where the talk is of the court, love and philosophy, the subjects of most of her poetry.

Feminist, rationalist, existentialist who distinguishes chaos from despair, an eighteenth-century mind born too soon, her freedom is protected for a long time by her connections to the court of the viceroy. She is an intimate friend of the vicereine Marquise of Mancera, perhaps even closer to the vicereine Countess of Paredes to whom much of her amorous poetry is dedicated. (Is this a lesbian love? History will never know for certain, not from a seventeenth-century world that was more like the fifteenth century.)

Her poems are read throughout the Spanish-speaking world, her plays performed across the Spanish empire. Her long metaphysical poem, *First Dream*, is celebrated and wondered over. Hers is the triumph of a rational, speculative mind in a backward Church-dominated society. A triumph that is not long in seventeenth-century colonial Mexico.

A new archbishop takes office in Mexico. An ascetic, fundamentalist archbishop who does not approve of an intellectual life, certainly not for a woman, and above all not for a nun. Sor Juana de la Cruz loses her protection, must abandon her writing, her library, her salon, and return to prayer. She renounces her gifts and her unorthodox beliefs, makes her apologies to God, spends the rest of her days on her knees.

The archbishop and her confessor rejoice. Through their holy efforts she has progressed from her secular folly to a true path. Through her renunciation, Sor Juana de la Cruz has found her way to true happiness, to saintliness.

❧

Perez Medina said, "The Aztecs cut out the hearts, the blood. The churches cut out the mind, the humanity. Humanity is all we have, Fortune, each other."

"Is that what you learned from it all?"

"Just us," Medina said.

In Hermosillo we caught a jet to fly us north.

15.

The sheriff's lieutenant met us at the airport outside the small town north of Agua Prieta and the border, south of Willcox. It still had a windsock that drooped in the noon sun before the winds came up.

"We found them out at the old Miranda place right enough. Ain't sure it's gonna do what you people want."

I'd called Sergeant Chavalas from Mexico, had him contact the sheriff's office in Cochise County, ask them to locate the Miranda Ranch and hold anyone who was there for an outstanding warrant from Santa Barbara. Then he flew to meet us in Tucson. From Tucson we took the small plane into the heart of Cochise County to meet the sheriff's deputies.

Now we all rode out to the remote ranch that stood on high ground in a sheltered canyon at the base of red and ochre cliffs, the pine mountains behind. The ranch had been abandoned years ago, the low whitewashed adobe buildings, wooden barns and horse corrals in ruins. A single large old jacaranda brought from New Orleans or Houston or even Brazil by some long-ago Miranda stood in front of the ruined hacienda.

"A lot of them ran off before we got here," the lieutenant

told Chavalas. "But there were six still outside in the shade of that jacaranda. They showed us the bodies."

As we walked from the cars, I saw that tin roofs had been put over the ruins, a modern electric pump installed in the well and hidden from the air. There was a portable generator under a cover that supplied the electricity for the pump and lights through wires run along the ground and all but invisible.

"That's one of them."

Gabriel Sarguis lay on his back in the dirt in front of a tin shed with an open side like a shrine, a heavy wooden table like a crude altar inside. His blood had spread and thickened on the baked brick earth under the fierce sun. A large iron cauldron stood where his feet had been. The black candles at the end of each arm where he had no hands. Women's black clothing had been laid over his body, some singed twenty-dollar bills near his head.

"We found his hands and feet up there on that table inside the shed."

"What killed him?" I asked.

"Looks like a machete blow to the back of the head. The weapon's in the shed, too."

The feet and hands were on the altar under the tin roof, with the blindfolded statue of some saint and a skull draped with beads. The machete stood bloody in a corner of the tin shack with two jagged swords. Michael Sarguis, The Preacher, sat in a tall wooden chair behind the altar table. He had been shot in the head and chest, had slumped down with his chin on his chest and his long dark hair over his eyes like a shrunken head of the Jívaro.

"A forty-five from the exit wounds. Near as we can tell, the one in the chair, they call him The Preacher or somesuch, got mad at the dead guy out front and some other guy named Rafael. He had the others grab 'em and kill the one guy and lay him out like that. Damned if I know what the feet and hands mean."

"To lose fear. Every time you cut off part of a human you lose some fear," Perez Medina said. "And an offering so the gods can travel, eat, won't take you in death."

Chavalas said, "What about Rafael?"

"They tied him up in one of the buildings," the lieutenant said. "Only they must have done a lousy job, 'cause when they went to get him, lay him out like the first one I guess, he comes out with the gun and shoots The Preacher dead."

"Where is he now?" Chavalas said.

"Gone. Had the car they came in, took off fast after he shot The Preacher guy. The rest of them were useless when The Preacher guy was finished. The ones that didn't run for the hills still are. Some of 'em are stoned, we found a shitload of Guatemalan H and good coke in a storage building. Most of 'em are scared crazy. None of 'em look like they know what to do next, or give much of a damn."

I said, "Where are they?"

The deputies had put them in the only building with a door. We went in with the lieutenant. The six silent men sat on the dirty wood floor, their backs against the adobe walls. Perez Medina nodded. They were all missing survivors of the attack in Africa.

Medina spoke to them, "What happened to The Preacher?"

Two looked up at the sound of his voice. One had that same bottomless fear I'd seen in George Rogers's eyes. He looked at Perez Medina with the terror the German villagers had when they saw the monster of Dr. Frankenstein.

Medina turned to the other, "How did it happen, Mason?"

The man, Mason, said, "Perez Medina. Hey, you're okay."

"So far. What happened here? Over there?"

Mason was a large blond man no longer that large or that blond. His clothes hung so loose he could have been a skeleton, his hair was filthy and darkened in mottled patches.

There was shock behind his pale eyes, but I didn't see the fear of the others, the terror. Burned out, but calm inside his shell like a captured guerrilla who has fought all his life but knows it is over, he will die tomorrow. A resignation, not to horror or fear, but to uncertainty. Even a kind of acceptance.

"He wasn't God, you know?" Mason said. "The bullets killed us, shot us down, and he wasn't God. We thought he was blind in the village when we found him. There was a river. We were thirsty. He wanted to drown in the river but we stopped him. Gabriel was there, I don't know when that was."

Mason considered the problem of when Gabriel was with him and The Preacher in the village by the river. The five other survivors of The People sat curled around themselves as if they could hear nothing but the hammer of their own blood in their ears. Maybe they couldn't.

I said, "Gabriel was with The Preacher?"

"He wasn't God. God was evil. The Vision was death. The Word was a lie. Death ruled. We would all die because death ruled, death was God. All the gods were death, lived on the dead. He'd been fooled, all lies, a vision of Satan."

"Gabriel brought you all here," I said. "How? They were looking for you over there."

Mason was going down his own mental journey. "We got to give God the dead. The Preacher would protect us from the evil, from Satan. Gods wanted blood, death. Gods wanted to kill us, make us die. But The Preacher had a way. We got to give dead animals, dead people, so God and Satan wouldn't take us."

I said, "You flew here on a plane. The Preacher and George Rogers and all of you. How many were there?"

"The Preacher went away. It was dark a long time. Where we waited for The Preacher, the disciple Gabriel. A long time. We waited. Then we all rode again, came here."

He knew what had happened, but not how or where or

when. Time and place meant nothing to him. They had to have been hidden somewhere over in Africa, then flown out when the search for survivors tapered off. By Gabriel and probably Rafael by then. The Contra, the drug dealer.

"Rafael would have had the connections," I said. "The planes, safe routes and cover from his Contra days."

Chavalas said to Mason, "What happened here? In Barstow and Santa Barbara?"

Mason didn't answer. None of the others even moved. Perez Medina sat down against the wall beside Mason.

"Gabriel came back," Medina said. "He wanted The Preacher to help him. Soames and the woman Ebersole knew The Preacher had returned. The Preacher had sent word when you got here."

Mason said, "He got mad, Gabriel. Disciple Medina wasn't dead, was telling lies. Satan would find The Preacher. The Preacher sent us to sacrifice the two. Gabriel got mad. The Preacher said only sacrifice would stop death. Gabriel told The Preacher we had to stay here. Don't do nothing, don't send no one nowhere. Only if he comes and gets one of us."

The loud voices were outside the dim interior where the six survivors sat against the old walls. Voices that came closer, stopped outside the door of the building. All but one voice that went on. Whining and protesting. A deputy looked in the door.

"Lieutenant? You want to come out here?"

The lieutenant went out. Mason had subsided into a brooding silence.

I said, "The Preacher, Rogers, some other survivors and the money. Gabriel had to have had some of their money. Had it, found it or taken it, whatever. And Rafael's help. He could hide them over there, but he would have needed Rafael to get The Preacher, Rogers, all the others out of Africa. The Preacher and Rogers first, the others later, a few at a time.

Maybe twenty or so, I'd guess. The other missing really died over there."

The sheriff's lieutenant came back in. "Chavalas, Fortune."

We went out behind him. Three deputies stood around a heavy man with a long face and a thick mustache. His black-and-yellow shirt, yellow pants, silver-and-turquoise bolo tie were torn and stained with dirt and debris. His was the voice protesting.

"Jesus, man, I could of died out there. I'm gonna die right here you don't get me to a hospital. I got sunstroke, man. Heat stroke at least. I don't know what the hell took a bite out of me out there. What you guys waitin' for? You gotta get me—"

The lieutenant said, "Tell it to these two, de Leon."

"Sure, sure." The heavy man turned to us. "Like I said, I works for Rafael. I'm here so the shipments go in and out right. You got to watch these nuts. We got a sweet system, the nuts moves the stuff camp-to-camp from Guatemala on up, but you got to watch 'em. Anyway, Rafael and Gabriel show up on the run. The ride's over, we got to grab the shit and make the border. Gabe tells the number one nut he blew it with his goddamn sacrifices up north, he's on his fucking own, he better split before the devil comes and gets him. That makes *numero uno* flip, he tells his nuts to grab Gabe and Rafael. I'm loading the shit in the car, they forget me, I don't wait. I got no keys for the car, take off into the hills. Finds a hole and pulls it in. I hears yellin', and screamin', and shootin'. I don't go nowhere out of them hills 'till I sees all you uniforms down here and I'm bit, and burned and passin' out."

"Where is Rafael?" Chavalas said.

"If he ain't dead, who knows?"

We talked to them for two more hours. De Leon never stopped telling us about the drug operation, the nuts who'd killed Gabriel Sarguis. Mason roamed in his memory and delusion. The others never spoke. It was all we were going to get until the police found Rafael. If they ever did.

We gave the sheriff the whole story, took a jet out of Tucson. In the window seat, I looked at the sky. The same sky that was over Africa.

"When Sybil Rogers hired me, they knew The Preacher had sent word to all the survivors he was alive. All except Medina who was still in Africa then, presumed dead. They decided to silence Soames and Ebersole before I got to them, wanted to stay clear themselves, so told The Preacher to send his men."

"But he ordered the ritual killings," Medina said. "They couldn't control him."

"They were mad and scared," I said. "But it was too late, the damage had been done, the murders were psycho and connected."

Chavalas said, "They had to try to stop you two. They could control Pugo and Baltieri, or any of the rest as long as Angel was along. They tried again for Dan. When it didn't work, they were finished."

I looked out at the clouds and the distant ground so far below. "And Gabriel used The Preacher once too often."

"He says he's sorry. He can't talk to you, he doesn't want to come home."

Sybil Rogers sat in my office.

"I paid you to bring him home."

"You wanted to believe he was alive, you paid me to make it come true. I did. If you want more, go down and talk to him."

"He's not rational, out of his mind. He needs help."

"Maybe. And maybe no more than the rest of us."

"We'll get the embassy, the Mexican police. A psychiatrist. He's sick."

I said, "It's not the embassy you want. Not the police or even a psychiatrist. It's something stronger than his guilt and fear and need."

Perez Medina sat in the sun on the bench in Venice, a book open in his hands. A history of the Aztecs.

"What else could they think, the Aztecs? They lived in a world of volcanoes, earthquakes, savage animals, diseases they knew nothing about. Death early, often, and random."

I said, "So they invented a belief to explain it. But it wasn't true."

"Is Kali true? Wotan? Isis? Baal? Ahura Mazda? The devil? Angels?" He closed the book, looked down at the bright mosaic of Quetzalcoatl on the jacket. "All our art, theory, speculation, is an attempt to make sense of life. The truth is there isn't any sense, Fortune. We're a physical, chemical phenomenon like an animal, a tree, a star, cosmic dust. The universe isn't good, bad or indifferent. It's mechanical, chemical. Within pretty rigid natural laws, it's all chance."

All along the oceanfront people walked and skated in their bizarre finery, their blue hair and shaved heads.

I still hurt, I still listen in the night. But Kay is there.

"What made him, Dan? The Preacher? What happened?"

"Fear. If you don't believe what I believe, how can I be sure that what I believe is true? I have to have the truth to accept life and death."

"There can't be multiple truths? Infinite truths?"

"Most of us find that too hard. We need to know that we're

important to something. If not a special god, then the life force, nirvana. To know it won't all end in nothing."

"What will it end in?"

"I don't know. No one does."

She listens to the surf and the traffic outside in the late spring night. "That wasn't enough for The Preacher, for The People, for George Rogers."

"No." I listen to the distant pulse of the dark surf. "Not many of us really want to know, we want to believe."